DRIVING INTO THE SUN

About the author

Marcella Polain was born in Singapore and immigrated to Australia at the age of two, with her Irish father and Armenian mother. She writes poetry, narrative fiction and lyric essays; her work has been published nationally and internationally, and in translation. Her first novel, *The Edge of the World* (2007, Fremantle Press), was shortlisted for a Commonwealth Writers' Prize. Marcella's short fiction has twice won the Patricia Hackett Prize. She has published three collections of poetry: *Dumbstruck* (1996, Five Islands Press) won the Anne Elder Poetry Prize, *Each Clear Night* (2000, Five Islands Press) was shortlisted for the WA Premier's Prize for Poetry, and *Therapy Like Fish: New and Selected Poems* (2008, John Leonard Press) was shortlisted for the Judith Wright Prize. In 2015, she was awarded the Gold Medal by the Writers' Union of Armenia, and the International Grand Prize for Poetry in Curtea des Arges, Romania. She is Senior Lecturer in the Writing program at Edith Cowan University, Perth.

DRIVING INTO THE SUN

MARCELLA POLAIN

 FREMANTLE PRESS

For my father, William Orr Kirk

'Thinking I think of you and me.
Our empty spaces where fathers should be.'

— *A Girl is a Half-formed Thing*, Eimear McBride

1

Cold and still, the moon overhead, and the track from the sheds to the farmhouse overhung by trees. It isn't far. They're walking up ahead of him, eager now that it's all over. He can hear them joking about, shoving one another, laughing. He'd smile, too, if he could. Because it's hard dirty work, this work, best done at night. And that means they've all been here, the other lads and him, for the past three nights, and he's not been getting home till dawn, falling into bed beside Henrietta, falling into a dead sleep, woken groggy and nauseous by the kids an hour later. Snatches of sleep through the past two days — they were Saturday and Sunday, weren't they? — while Henry's been at work herself. Then a nap when she gets back, a shower — leaning against the wall, the hot water pouring on him — and off to work again.

He'd smile now if he could because the job's finished. But his legs are lead, he's short of breath, queasy, more tired than he can recall ever being. He'd smile because now it's Monday, the important day, because there were moments he wasn't sure he'd — well, the ten o'clock appointment is almost here, so … He'd smile because it must be nearly dawn (though he's not sure; he left his watch in his car) and the stinking job is over and he can begin to believe that he will, he will turn up in his suit beside his Henry and sign the contract. If he could stretch out his arm he could almost touch it, and he wants to smile; he does. This important day.

From up ahead he hears one of the lads yawn extravagantly and say it's nearly three and that makes sense, and then mid-step he's pain, he clutches his, opens his, staggers; he pitches forward, makes the aarrgh sound of all breath leaving, his legs already gone from him, and he hits the ground hard.

And he hasn't been kind to his girl, his good girl, Orla; he hasn't; he hasn't been kind to her.

2

One long Sunday afternoon, the year before, when they still lived in the hills, Orla had come in from the light and heat, from the clicking forest, its bushes, its pointy leaves, its tiny plants between stones festooned with flowers; from lizards scurrying and glossy in the sun, from trails of ants; from birds calling in the big warm air. She brought her bush-ears with her, ears she used in slow walks between trees, her feet cracking twigs; ears for the rustle of snakes, the flit of a low bird's wing, its sharp beak ready.

The house, when she entered, was dim and cool and quiet. Her arms radiated heat. She walked slowly with her bush-ears listening. For an instant, a fear clutched at her — they had disappeared while she had been among other creatures; they had disappeared and left her alone. Then a sound she had heard before, mechanical; she had been curious about it then, had asked her mother. And her mother had said, in a firm voice, that her father was writing and was not to be disturbed.

Orla loved the idea of good, so she had done what she was told, had pressed her curiosity down inside her, had just listened to the busy, clanking sound, its joyous bell. And when her father had re-emerged that time, she had studied him in the first moments, studied him closely as he crossed the lounge room. He had looked like the same man — same clothes, same hair — but she saw at once he was not. His face was different. Something, she knew, had happened to him. For those first few moments, until he spoke, until he sat down for lunch, he was glowing, electric.

This time her mother was not in the kitchen to ask, and there was no need to ask anyway. This time she was radiating so much heat into the cool, dim house she felt like the sun, filled it with the hot thrill of flowers and lizards, ants and birds, bush-sounds and bush-scents and bush-colours of banksia, eucalypt. She was not just a girl and the idea of good had loosened in her. She tiptoed to her parents' room. The door was wide open, as in fairytales. Which meant only one thing. When the mesmerising mechanical sound paused so did she. When it began again, loud and ringing — taptaptataptaptaptatapding — she held her breath, crept closer.

His desk faced the window; he sat with his back to her, shoulders hunched. She could see the muscles and sinews flexing in his arms and neck. One more step and, over his shoulder, the whole metal contraption — the carriage and keys and casing — came into view. And there, the trapped white paper, the punched black letters, words appearing from the tips of his fingers, like magic. She squinted, took one last step and the phrase came into focus: *The Arab stood in the shadow of the doorway. From the fold of his robe he removed a knife. Light glinted along its blade.*

Her father's head turned sharply towards her. 'Get out.' He scowled at her. She gasped, rocked on her heels, spun away. She was good, had always been good; who was this other daughter, disobeying? She had done what she knew she shouldn't, and it was too late, too late now. His words, their tone, had lodged in her gullet — she could feel them there; she swallowed her sobs and they slipped deeper, stuck in her chest.

'Get out,' he'd growled. She had barely recognised him.

How could she have known what her father carried in him, a world like that, full of Arabs and shadows and knives.

~

Her father had been silent all day, had been silent more often lately. He sat on the divan with a book, his legs tucked up alongside him. Orla was cross-legged on the carpet in the centre of the room. Her mother called it the central carpet. Orla loved the central carpet; it was thick and soft and covered in a pattern of flowers — rose-pink, apple-green, gold, powder-blue. Like sitting in a garden.

Her book was spread open in front of her. Ahead, the big lounge room windows faced west; afternoon sun poured in. She looked at her pages but watched him. Heard him turn his pages, heard the kitchen clock tick. Sunlight edged further and further over her. All around, the carpet shone. She had to close her eyes.

~

She heard him stand. She watched him leave the room. Heard her mother come in the back door. Heard her father speak, his voice too low. Her mother said, 'How long will you be?'

Her father crossed the room. Orla stood. She said, 'Where are you going?'

He didn't answer. He reached the front door. Orla turned towards the kitchen. Her mother was already standing by the table, watching him. Orla asked, 'Where's Daddy going?'

'For a walk.'

Orla turned back to him. 'Can I go, too, please, Daddy?'

He opened the door. Orla looked at her mother. Henrietta gave a small shrug, shook her head a little.

Orla looked back to her father. 'Please, Daddy?'

He stood in the open doorway, his hand on the lock, his back to them. He was perfectly still. He was looking outside. Orla's mother said, 'Your daughter is talking to you.'

Orla looked hard at his back. He shrugged. He took a step. Orla looked at her mother again. Her mother's mouth made the shape of a smile. She nodded.

Her father stepped onto the porch; Orla followed him.

~

At first she walked by his side. She said, 'Where are we going?' He didn't look at her. He didn't speak. She dropped back a little. She couldn't see his face. He turned onto the main road. It was a long incline. From a few steps behind, she watched him. He might realise she wasn't beside him. He might wonder where she had gone, might turn to see if she was all right, slow his steps, say, 'Sorry, Tweety.'

Instead, she watched him steadily draw away. He walked with head bowed, arms swinging. He walked fast; so did she. He didn't run so she didn't either. She didn't call out. As much as possible, she stared at his back, willing him to turn, and afraid to look away. In case. She walked as fast as she could but she. She couldn't. He was far ahead of her. And this wasn't right, was it. This wasn't normal. She had known to watch him, to follow him. Someone needed to. Because this was. Something was. Wrong and now he was even further away, becoming smaller and smaller as he climbed the incline, and he wasn't going to stop for her, was he, wasn't even going to glance behind, she knew, and she wasn't going to be able to catch him, and although she couldn't see it yet she knew the crossroad up ahead, and what would happen when he reached it, she wouldn't even be close enough to see which way he went. And then he crested the top of the slope and vanished. For a minute or two she kept walking hard and then she slowed. By the time she reached the crossroad, she knew, he'd be gone. She slowed some more. And then she stopped. She stood, staring at the crest of the hill. In case. Any moment he. Remember. That she had sat near and quiet. That she had followed him.

She looked around. On both sides of the road the bush was dense and black and grey and green. She sat. The gravelly earth was hard but her body was tired. She waited. The sun dropped behind the trees and the shade was cold. No cars passed. After a while she stood up and walked home.

~

In the kitchen, her mother turned with a smile. 'Oh!' she said. She blinked. 'It's you. That didn't take long.'

Orla filled a glass with water. Out of the corner of her eye she could see her mother looking at her.

Her mother said, 'Is Daddy here?'

Orla gulped the water. She shook her head.

Her mother nodded. 'Oh.' She looked away. 'Where is he?'

Orla stared at the sink. She turned on the tap to fill the glass again. 'I don't know,' she said. Water crashed into the glass. Orla was glad it was so loud. Maybe her mother wouldn't hear the strange wobble in her voice.

Alongside her, Henrietta was silent. Then she reached over and patted Orla's arm. As if she knew.

3

From the hills it was a long drive to the beach but, if their father felt happy, he would sometimes take them. Orla's little sister would stick her head out the window, stick out her tongue like a dog. Their mother would say, 'The wind will dry your mouth and then what will you do.'

Their father would laugh. 'Sit down before you're decapitated.'

And Deebee would laugh: 'De-cab-it-at-ed!' And their father would laugh even more.

Orla would laugh, too, because laughing is like that, sometimes you can't help it, but the word made her shiver. She would laugh and put her face closer to the window for the air to blast the word, the idea, its picture, out of her head.

Their mother would scowl at their father. 'Will you give over with that talk!'

There was a public pool in the hills where they lived but their mother was allergic so they didn't go. She was allergic to other things, too. Some days she said she was allergic to children. Those days Orla and Deebee would stay outside as much as they could.

On the way to the beach they would pick up Aunt Kit, who was not their real aunt but a friend from before Orla was born. Kit's hair was pale as sunlight and curly all over her head. She had been married once but there were no kids — which puzzled Orla. At the beach, Kit would set off on long walks, come back with a handful of shells, hold them up to the Orla's ear. 'Listen,' she'd say. 'Iya.' And Orla would hear the iya, the water, of her first-ever home, the place in the jungle where her parents and Kit had lived, and where she had lived with them, too, they told her, where the inlet water swished calmly onto shore, in that sheltered place they talked and talked and talked about, that place which, no matter how hard she pressed the shell to her ear, Orla couldn't remember. Still she smiled at Kit's smile, and replied, 'Iya.'

It was always afternoon by the time they arrived at the beach. Families would be leaving, the water ruffled and dark. Orla knew — didn't everybody know? — morning was best for swimming. But she never said it; better the ocean in the afternoon than never the ocean at all.

Deebee would climb their father's legs and their father would say, 'Come here, my monkey,' and sit her on his hip, carry her though the white water while their mother would watch, her lips pressed together, her hand shading her face. Orla would stand at the water's edge and suppose their father used to do that with her before Deebee but she couldn't remember that either. She'd push her toes into the wet sand, watch the water well up between. Sunlight flashed; shadows rippled over the sandy sea-floor; other kids laughed and chased each other; sea-foam hissed and popped and vanished.

Kit wore a one-piece bathing suit and a rubber cap on her head with rubber flowers all over it. She looked like a bouquet. She breaststroked in circles close to shore, her head up. When she stood, her suit clung. Orla would look at her shape, long and lean, so different to her mother's short, curvy body. When Kit bent to pick up her towel, she kept her back very straight, pointed her toe like a ballerina, and Orla would look at her mother then, but her mother's face was always stern and looking straight ahead, watching her husband slip his hands under Deebee's arms, raise her up and lower her, dipping her gently into the cup of the sea as if she were a ginger snap. Deebee kicked her legs and squealed. Their father's slicked-back hair fell across his eyes and nose, so that all Orla could see of his face when he turned her way was his grin. He lifted Deebee high, onto his shoulders — 'Climb up, little monkey'. And Deebee would squirm and giggle, her father holding her knees with his big hands, striding away from the solid world. Like this, he would swim the two of them a long way out; it seemed to Orla they would surely disappear, and she would stand frozen, watching them move further and further away from her until they were out in the deep where she knew even adult legs could no longer stand, where, she had read in encyclopaedias, the sea floor plummeted and strange creatures lived: sharks, whales, giant squid that upturned ships. All her insides would clench.

And then he would turn and come back to her, swimming hard with his arms, his head up, and she would watch till she was sure they were safe, until she could see clearly her father's hands on her sister's knees, until she could see clearly her sister's open, laughing mouth, until he climbed them up the slope of the shore, streaming wet and smiling, his hair in his eyes. It was only then she'd feel her stiffened limbs, tight chest, her heart banging, and would open her mouth and gasp, gasp, the sea air pouring in. Sometimes, watching them swim back, Orla would stare at her sister's hands, her fingers that clung to the sides of their father's face and, once they were very near, Deebee would sometimes let go of him. She'd grin and wave and flap her arms. When she did that, she looked as if she were skimming across the surface of the sea, holding their father's head like a ball retrieved, holding it above water to bring it back, so he could live, breathe, gripped in the bony lock of her knees, and for a moment Deebee was not a little sister at all but an ocean creature from a storybook, strong and winged and flying.

And then they were on shore, their father reaching up, swinging her down so her legs inscribed two quick arcs in the air before he set her on the sand, and Deebee was herself again, jumping, jumping, shivering, shrieking: 'Do it again, Daddy! Do it again!' And Orla would squint at her sister, at her bony knees and elbows, her legs wet and goosebumped, jumping, her hands open and beseeching, her face scowling and turning away as their father settled himself on his towel. As if, Orla mused, she had no idea what she had done.

But Orla was glad, too, that he sat beside their mother, pushed his wet hair from his eyes, his chest still heaving with the effort of going so far, among sharks and whales. She knew the sea was not a true friend. On the calmest days, she would walk in up to her hips, duck-dive, flip onto her back, spread her arms and legs, feel her hair tug lightly at her scalp. Her ears would fill, the sound of the world turned thick. The sun would beat her face; the inside of her eyelids glowed. She would feel her body begin to drift. Or, disconcertingly, she wouldn't feel it at all. She'd stand, and be shocked at how far she'd gone, turn to shore, blink the salty water away, glance once, twice over her shoulder in case of a fin, a surfboard, a tsunami. Kids she didn't know would splash water onto her and she'd run, up the sand, everywhere dazzling.

If she could, she'd lie facedown beside her father, turn her head from side to side, feel the sun heat her back, water trickle warmly from her ears, listen to the rise and fall of voices, closer, distant, the shouts and crying, the loud crunch of passing feet. She'd burrow deeper into her towel, the sand squeaking under her. 'Hello, little mouse,' she'd whisper to it, smiling.

Once they left it all too late: an hour's drive from the hills, sitting on their scratchy towels, peeling their sweaty backs from the green vinyl. They arrived at the deserted shore, flung open the doors, tumbled out, Orla and her sister, already running. The southerly gale snatched Orla's hat, spun it through the air. She took off after it, sand whipping the backs of her legs, her hair mad in her eyes, the roar of the wind and the sea and her sister's voice wailing. The hat flew and rolled and she chased and chased, then at last in a lull she pounced and had it, ran back as fast as she could into wind and sand, shielding her face with the crook of one arm, the brim of that hat gripped tightly in her other fist, and she reached her, her Deebee, hunched with her back to the wind. There was sand in her ears and neck and hair, her eyes screwed shut and wet with tears, her mouth open and sand in her teeth — Orla could see into her sister's mouth — and her howl came out like a cloud, all disappointment. In the distance Orla heard their parents' voices, looked up, saw them by the car, Kit too, beckoning. Deebee clung to her, and Orla hauled her up, arms clasped underneath her like a sling. She kept her mouth shut tight, trudged through sand, overbalancing, falling onto one knee, putting Deebee down, righting, pushing herself up, lifting her sister, sand blasting their skin, her own feet disappearing, swallowed up by the hungry mouths of the dune, up to her knees there was so much of it, a whole world of it around them, a desert, the Sahara, and Deebee was little and sad, and Orla the one who saved her.

4

All night Orla dreamed of horses. If anyone had asked her, she might have said it was because Kit gave her *Thunderhead* and because she had kept it under her pillow so that, when she slept, the words would rise up from the page, the way they did when she read them, and slip into her head. If she woke in the dark, she slid her hand into the soft place between her mattress and pillow to touch it, her new and deepest conviction, slowly building her love and courage. But no-one asked. And anyway, she knew that answer wasn't quite right. It was not just that book, not just that grey stallion. Before Deebee was born, there had been Fury on TV, black, mane and tail streaming as he galloped into frame, pawed the ground, took away her breath. And before that there had been a bright rocking horse beneath a Christmas tree. She couldn't remember a time she hadn't loved a horse.

On the morning she went to work with her father, she wore her good tartan skirt, her red jumper, believed she had never been so happy, alone in her father's calmness, the wind blowing through the car window and hard into her hair, going somewhere with him she had never been. She climbed out onto white sand and limestone, stood looking at a huddle of oddly shaped buildings, low scrub all around, a few banksias with their flowers like lamps, the land beyond them stretching flat in every direction, huge blue sky. She followed her father; dust rose in small white puffs at his heels. They passed through a gate: on one side, a squat wooden office with a sliding glass door; on the other, a very long shed with big metal doors. Between the two, a tower, circular corrugated iron. Orla had to tip back her head to see the top of it, and she looked for Rapunzel and her long, long hair. But there were no windows in this tower, no air and light and no escape. Her father stood beside her and called it a silo. It flashed and glinted in the sun.

At the long shed, he opened a padlock, pulled back the doors. It was dim inside; there was a strong sweet smell. Sun poured in, dust spun in air alive with cheeping. She squinted. Dead ahead, a very wide container full of lights and tiny yellow things. She peered at them. Against a thin gap she pressed her fingertip. Chicks scattered. She could feel how warm it was in there. Edging around to a bigger gap, she cornered one, touched it with the side of her little finger, stroked. Beneath its yellow down, softer even than Deebee's baby-head, its body was bone, fragile as twig.

Her father reappeared, stood beside her, looking down. 'This is an incubator. They hatch in here. It's the same temperature as their mother,' he said.

Orla frowned, nodded. She had heard the word incubator before, when Deebee was born. But Deebee had a mother, their mother, who had been in a bed in a room nearby. If the chicks had a mother, where was she? Orla looked around. Incubator after incubator. Each one with more chicks then she could count. She thought about orphanages, had thought about that before, about being an orphan, about her sister and herself and what would happen, that maybe they'd live with Kit. She knew, secretly, which parent she would rather lose, if one had to die, and she also knew that this was a thing she could never speak. She looked down at the chicks huddling, their tiny eyes closed. 'What happened to their mother?' They were so small, so many.

Her father laughed a little, put his hand on her shoulder. 'Let's go.'

She took a deep breath, inhaling the warm grainy smell of their food. 'Daddy,' she said, turning to him. And then she asked him. If she could have a horse. Just like that. She watched his face, thought he might frown or laugh again but he didn't. He just looked back at her steadily, without speaking, and nodded, as if what she had asked was an ordinary thing, as if he had been thinking about it, too.

'We'll see,' he said.

5

There's something you should know about that house in the hills. Orla didn't know about it when she and Deebee shared a room at the front of the house, and the room at the back was where they played and where, in the mornings, light poured through the window while they dressed up or spread Mousetrap on the floor in a golden slab of sun. How could she? If she had known, she wouldn't have asked for a room of her own.

But she did ask, and her parents gave her that play room, positioned her bed so that when she sat up in it she could see through the window into the bush, and she placed her doll and her teddy bear side by side on her pillow so they could take in the view all day. She slipped her fipel, a square of fabric, pale and worn as skin, under her pillow with *Thunderhead*. The rest of her books filled her small white bookshelf. Her white wardrobe stood behind the door. During the day, she loved her new room: its window was filled with sky and light, the broad valley with wildflowers and tuart trees, birds flitting. The first night, the easterly breeze picked up and moaned at the pane till she imagined a face. At dawn, the rising sun shone straight into her eyes and woke her, blinded and blinking.

The second night, even her fipel couldn't help. The green glow of the TV poured up the hall. She lay rigid, her back to the wall, staring hard at the door, imagining the place where the light came from, imagining her parents there, side by side. She heard snatches of TV she didn't understand, music that frightened. There was something — a mass of it, she knew; she could feel it — shifting in the wall at her back, and it was very, very important she didn't turn around. If she did, it would open its mouth and swallow her.

Eventually she slept. When the sun woke her, the wall glowed softly pink with light. She touched her finger gingerly to its surface, cool and flat and gently breathing, and wondered. So, it's nocturnal, she thought, remembering the word, and lifted her finger quickly from it, not wanting to wake it, knowing how hard it can be to sleep well in the light of that sun.

~

It was a weekend afternoon, warm. She went into her new room just to slip her hand beneath her pillow for the fipel's edge because then everything would be all right. But there was just the book sheet pillow case and she lifted her pillow and it was book and sheet and it must be her sister who and she shouted and looked around but couldn't see — 'Mummy!' she screamed into the hall but nothing she ran to the kitchen laundry back door 'Mummy!' but no-one at the washing line the loud sky the bush gawked a sound above her head through the little bathroom window 'Mummy!' ran and skidded in the bathroom doorway and froze hand gripping the door jamb.

The light was on and the room. At first Orla wasn't sure what. The bathroom had been pink and grey, now was pink and black and was it really the? Her mother on the floor on her hands and knees, looking at the floor, not looking up, and 'Mummy! Did you hear me?' The bath at the back of the room curved pink, the tiles on the wall pink and shiny. They winked. She saw the yellow overhead light in them. Her mother on her hands and knees, still not looking. A tin beside. Open. Its inside shiny black. Her mother rubbing black over the floor, slowly spreading. Her mother's hair black, too, one side tucked behind an ear, the other swinging shining under the light glinting as she moved rubbing the floor black, only looking at the floor, her mouth a line. Because — because, Orla thought, because, I'm not really here, not really seeing, because this can't.

Her mother's lips pressed. Her hair swung and shone. Her hand moved the cloth and the cloth moved the paint. The floor turning black. Was her mother really here? 'Mummy?' she said. She needed to make; she needed. 'Mummy?' She looked hard at her mother's, followed her mother's: down to the hand and the cloth that was black but one edge.

Orla opened her mouth. She looked up. The side of her mother's face. The shadows on her cheek. Her lips a line. Light winked from her mother's hair. Winked from the bath and tiles. She looked down at her mother's hand, at the cloth. Its edge. Its fipel-pink.

~

She crawled into bed, curled up tight, her face to the wall, sobbed till she retched. After a while, Deebee appeared. 'You all right, Orly?'

She didn't move. 'Go away,' she gasped at last. Then it was dinnertime.

That night, her mother leaned in and kissed her cheek, brushed hair from her face. 'You're a big girl. You asked for your own room. You don't need that dirty thing anymore.'

Orla watched her mother leave the door open, as always, listened to her receding footfalls. She lay very still. The TV light came in. Beneath her head, new emptiness. Everything else came in, too.

6

He hears one of the lads up ahead yawn, exclaim it's nearly
three a.m., the relief in his voice, and he feels it too. It's been
three days and three nights since he slept properly, and he is
more tired than he can remember being, but thank the Lord
this job is over at last. These three nights from dark till just
before dawn, walking silently to the poultry sheds, whispering,
taking turns to hold the torches, lunge at roosting pullets, grab
hundreds and hundreds by their legs, the squawking, flapping,
the counting them into crates, the not letting go of them. He
knows he's covered — feathers, manure, fear; bits in his hair, on
his boots, hands, overalls. But now, along the tree-lined track
back to the farmhouse, a different feeling. The other men are
joking about up ahead, pushing each other around like kids,
happy. He can't see them well — he's lagging behind — but he
can tell. His listens and he wants to join in but he's not sure he'd
be able to even if he were with them, even if they waited for
him. His feet are lead; it takes all concentration to put one in
front of the other, and still he drops back, and they don't seem
to notice but it doesn't matter because they're good men and
it's Monday and thank the Lord. He feels like smiling, thinking
of it — only seven hours left till they sign the builder's contract
for their house. At last. Henry happy. Orla back to her friends.
Even though. Even though he was unkind to her yesterday, and
shouldn't have been. Today he can tell her they are building
their house and that will make her happy. Enough time now
to go home for a shower, a kip, his suit and tie. He would smile

if he could because of all the years, the struggle, new country, young kids, the no longer being young themselves. He would smile because he wasn't sure he'd make it to Monday the way he's feeling, and now, at last, he can almost touch the ten o'clock, and he'd smile because he knows the builder has insurance and, once that paper's signed, Henry will get the house no matter what. Because no-one can take a home from a man in this country, not like where they came from, a place they thought would be British forever, leaving everything — a house he built with his own hands, a farm, all their furniture — arriving here with just a few tea chests, because in this country at least there's fairness, he knows at least there's that.

One cold, clear winter night she was woken by a magpie's singing. From her bed she stared through the window and into the moonlit sky. On and on it went. She imagined it in one of the trees just there, its feathers fluffed up the way chickens do, its head tilted back a little, its sharp beak just opening enough, its throat moving. On and on and on. She drifted back to sleep on the rise and fall of it.

In the morning she told her father. He frowned. 'Impossible,' he said. 'Magpies sleep all night. Like people. You must have been dreaming.'

~

Weeks passed after she had asked her father in the poultry shed, weeks after he had said, 'We'll see.' And then it was one endless school day when she couldn't eat, couldn't tell her friends — because she couldn't believe it, and what if it didn't, if it wasn't. A perfect, cloudless day, stretched long and thin before her father was to pick her up at half-past three. Which he never did, never, and would he really? It was pressing her hands together when she was outside to stop them flapping, to stop her winging her way into the blue just as Deebee had that day over the sea, to stop her gliding up, over the school yard, its red brick buildings, the surrounding forest and all the roads, soaring till she saw the silo where he worked and came down to land, in case he forgot the half-past-three, her feet stumbling, raising limestone dust, her father's face amazed and grinning, turning to the other men: 'That's my daughter!' It was trying not to look at the clock, her hands over her ears so she couldn't hear it tick, tick, her voice shouting at her in her head, staring at pages until letters made words and the words made sense. It was the home-time bell and watching her legs as she walked to the gate because legs weren't to run after school, even if they were going to buy a horse; and it was seeing her father in his car across the road, his grey slicked-back hair, his brown-stained fingers, his cigarette smoke out the window that made her know it was really him. And running, flat out running onto the road and lifting off and flying, amazed, and falling through the air of the long, thin, cloudless afternoon, the air so fine it couldn't hold her. And hitting the gravel, sliding, and for a while it didn't even hurt.

And because she ran — without looking, onto the road, in front of a car — her father and another man lifted her onto the back seat and her father folded his jacket under her head, so all the way the scent of him — cigarettes, hair oil — was close, and then the car door opened and other men lifted her, and there were lights and when she woke again she was in a white bed, white room, and when she moved she hurt. A doctor peered at her and said she had been foolish, a very foolish little girl, and was lucky that hurt was all she was.

When he left, she turned to the wall. The doctor was right. She was foolish. And she knew what foolish meant. Anyone stupid enough to run out in front of a car can't be trusted to look after herself, let alone a horse. No-one gets a second chance at owning a horse; no, not at that.

~

A week later she went back to school. For a while she limped and the scabs itched and the bruises faded. She did as she was told, and she waited. She knew it was the only way to show them that foolish was not all she was, not always, that she could be sensible.

Then her father came home one afternoon and everything changed.

It was a suburb close to the beach, on the other side of the city, her parents said. There was nothing they could do. The landlord wanted his house back. Orla wept. Because of the bush, her school, her friends, and would there ever be a horse now. They promised: just one year, long enough to build a house on a block they owned in the hills, the one they had visited, the one covered with scrub that they had walked through, saying: 'This is the front door … Here is your room.' And after that there'd be a horse. Until then, riding lessons, and it wasn't their fault, of course it wasn't, that they had to move so far away, that there were so few houses to rent nowadays that took young children. And anyway, her father said, 'You have to learn there's no use crying over split milk. Look at your sister. She's much younger than you and she's not crying.'

Orla sniffed and looked at Deebee looking up at the three of them, her serious eyes, two fingers in her mouth.

It had rickety stairs from the back door and neighbours close on every side, but if Orla stood on tiptoes at the kitchen sink she could see, on the horizon, the blue line of the sea.

The first thing she would think of when she woke every Friday in that house — and then, as the months passed and her father complained, every second Friday — was that it was only one more sleep till she pulled on her jodhpurs, boots and hat, and sat beside him as he drove all the way to the riding school by the river; only one more sleep till she stroked the pony the instructor had matched her with, the one called Nugget.

'Like the shoe polish?' she had asked after the first lesson.

'Like a piece of gold,' her father had smiled.

Only one more sleep, she'd remember, till she checked Nugget's saddle and stirrups, stroked her warm neck, cooed in her ear, breathed the thick horse scent of her.

When she woke in the morning in the new house, there were spots of golden light like coins on her bedroom ceiling. She could reach for the cord and open the blinds and see a bit of eastern sky. She knew this was the house nearer the sea, the not-in-the-hills house, the just-for-a-year-house, but the pink walls her father had painted glowed in the morning, just like in the old house. And, as much as she missed the forest, the wildflowers, at night there was no monster in this room. And sometimes, like this morning, there were kookaburras outside, just two of them, even though there was no bush nearby, and they shouted at her, their overlapping laughter making her smile. She closed her eyes and listened, knowing they told her something special, a secret, if only she could work out what it was.

She sat up. It was a second Saturday. And what was this, this tingling skin, this happiness? This anticipation of a horse's body, her own body remembering it. This was past and future pushed together as she sat in her father's car, looking out the window at all the familiar landmarks passing so that she was sure they were flying along in the right direction, getting closer, closer. This was being in exactly the right place and time, that there was nowhere else in the world for her nor ever would be.

It was the sight of quiet Nugget in the sun, utterly still at the hitching rail, eyes closed, empty saddle on her back, her rider-lessness, the space made just for Orla for one enchanted hour. It was her tingling second Saturday morning skin that made her think of all of this.

They had just left home, were still in their street when it happened. Orla gasped, jerked forward, shouted. Her father swung the steering wheel, swerved across the road and back again. It was just a flash of reddish brown, dog's legs, dog's head, dog's body, dog running. Orla swivelled around to look behind. No yelp, no bump beneath the wheels. No dog lying in the road. No dog at all.

Her father said, 'You shouldn't have done that.'

She said, 'But there was a dog —'

'It doesn't matter. It's dangerous. Understand? We could have crashed. It's just a dog. Don't ever do that again.'

She looked at the air in front of her face and blinked. He had swung the wheel. They had missed the dog. She had thought he would be pleased, too. She looked down at her hands. 'Sorry, Daddy.'

~

When they lived in the house in the hills, her father would make a scarf disappear. Their mother would stand by the divan and watch, and he would tell Orla and Deebee to close their eyes and then to open them, and the scarf he had been holding would be gone. On his instructions, they would rush to their parents' room, to a wardrobe or dressing table drawer and find it tucked in there, just as he had said it would be. Once Orla had asked him to do it while she watched to make sure he had not gone anywhere but he said, 'Magic doesn't work unless you do what you're told.'

And anyway, Orla listened very closely; she knew he hadn't left the room; every time he had stayed right there on the divan in front of her and had made the scarf fly through the air and pass through the wood of the door or drawer, and fold itself neatly and hide, waiting there for her and her sister.

~

Soon after they had moved to the only-for-a-year house, there was a noise in the street, louder than anything Orla had ever heard. She and Deebee stared at one another. A truck, huge and gleaming, turned into next door's driveway, not twenty feet from their faces agape at the lounge room window. Its engine shut off and a man climbed down from the cab, all arms and legs, and leapt to the ground. Two little kids ran across the lawn to him, followed by a fat woman holding a tiny baby in a pink shawl. The little boy flung his arms around the man's legs, looked up at him. The man picked up the toddling girl. He kissed the woman on her lips, touched the baby's face.

Every week or so, the truck left in morning dark, the noise waking everyone, and returned several days later in the afternoon. If she was home, Orla would join Deebee on the divan to watch the man climb down, his skin nut-brown, wrinkled, his blue shorts and singlet faded, his walk like a cowboy in the Westerns their father watched on TV. Their mother called it bandy-legged. Deebee giggled. Once, their father had laughed as he told Orla she would walk like that if she spent too much time on horses. Orla had stared at him, her eyes filling. Later, when she asked her mother if it were true, Henry had glared at her husband: 'Why must you keep on so?'

The bandy-legged man had a lank, grey ponytail. One afternoon, Orla had wandered outside, leaned against the carport, watched him as he worked beneath his truck, his legs sticking out of his shorts, the hairs on them glinting gold in the sun. Eventually he had slid out, stood, brushed off the dust, looked her in the eye and smiled, smoothing his hair with one hand. Some of his teeth were missing. Orla had smiled back quickly, shy, and turned away.

If her mother was nearby when the truck pulled in, she'd look at Orla, 'You stay away from that man. He's no good.' And she'd flap her tea towel at Orla's head and Orla would see the set of her mouth, the fierce, perplexing look in her eye.

Then one day, when her father was out and her sister asleep, there was a different noise, sudden and loud. In her room, Orla's body turned icy, froze. When she could, she moved her limbs towards it — into the passageway, across the lounge room until she stood before the fireplace, staring at the chimney's clean, wide-open mouth. Shouting and weeping poured from it and swirled into her, the room, the house. Her mother appeared, a tea towel in her fist. They looked at one another then back at the shadowy and wailing grate.

They had heard the kids next door crying before but this was not their furious screaming or indignant tears. This was a woman crying, her voice so distressed it chilled. This was children frightened, ear-piercing. Then suddenly her mother was pushing at Orla. 'Go to your room. Go.'

Orla walked the perimeter of her room, the empty spaces between door, wardrobe, dressing table. She perched on the edge of her bed, her feet pressed flat on carpet, fingers gripping the mattress edge. She stared at her shoes. She straightened her spine, swivelled, looked out her window; her head felt unsteady on her neck. There were no clues out there, just lawn, verge tree, street. No worried neighbours stood about. And still the noise filled every. It clogged. She could barely. She slid her hand beneath her pillow for her book, but her book wasn't; it was in the lounge room. She had carried it there, put it down, and she wasn't going back for it.

Car doors slammed. She peered. A car on the verge. More shouting, crying. Her body ached from rigidness. She put her hands over her ears. The truck started up. It drove away. Car doors slammed again. The car left, too.

After a long quiet she opened the front door slowly. Still no-one in the street. She stepped out. Hadn't they heard? She stared over the low fence at the house next door, now dumb and still. A toy truck on the porch, tangle of garden hose on the lawn, orange sprinkler attached. Above the sky was frighteningly blue. No dogs barked; no kids pedalled their bikes in slow circles, gawking. No cars passed. She went back inside, closed the door behind her.

A few days later the next door kids were playing in their yard again, their voices just as they had always been and, in the following days and weeks, except for the truck not coming back, everything sounded as it always had, as if the whole thing — the truck, the noise, the chimney, the man — had never even happened.

9

On Sunday morning at breakfast in the house near the sea, the sky through the window was a big blue bowl someone held up over them, and Orla's mother had looked at her father over her cup and said, 'Such a lovely day. Too lovely to be stuck inside.' Orla had looked at him, too. Even Deebee had looked at him. But he had just sipped his coffee.

That night her mother opened the front door and Orla saw rain shining in circles of street light. Her father sat on the divan, watching a man talking on TV. He was very still, her father, so still that Orla wasn't sure: was he breathing? She stared. Something painful shot through her. She looked from him to the talking man and back. Her mother was holding the front door open. Her mother said, 'Well, we're going. Are you coming with us?'

But her father couldn't hear her. He didn't move or speak. Orla looked up at her mother. She looked at one of her mother's hands on the door, the other on Deebee's shoulder. Deebee was staring up at their mother, too. Suddenly Orla didn't want to go anywhere. She wanted to stay home. She looked at her father who wasn't her father but a statue of her father, stared hard at the side of his face to make him move, to make him turn his head and look at her, to pat the seat beside him and say, 'Come here, Tweety.'

'All right,' her mother said. She opened the door wider. Orla felt her mother turn towards it; she felt her sister turn towards it, too. Orla didn't need to turn. She already knew it was cold and wet and dark outside and her mother couldn't drive and in the moment thinking stopped she looked away from her father and her mother and her sister, turned to look back into the house, towards where she knew was kitchen, stove, sink, table; she wished she could magic herself there or into bed or into the toilet and close the door or into the cramped space at the bottom of her parents' wardrobes, the hems of her mother's dresses all around her head. She told her legs to move, move — even if it was just to curl themselves, curl her up at her mother's feet, her body curling tighter and tighter until she was just a pebble someone could pick up and put safely in their pocket. She told her legs to move, move, lift her up and fly her out of the room, light as a scarf, or just walk her, all of her, head and heart and hands, just as she was, an ordinary girl, onto her father's knee, into his arms, the warm smoky smell of him. If this was what she thought it was, it was all back to front. It should be him at the door with Orla and Deebee, his car keys in his hand. It should be her mother in the middle of the room, shouting, 'Go! Get out! Get out, all of you!' the way she did.

Just a few minutes earlier, Orla had been in her new room of their new house, on her bed, reading *My Friend Flicka*, and her mother had called, 'Get ready, we're going out.' And she and Deebee had raced to put on their good shoes and coats, and her mother had sat Deebee on her bed and stooped to tie her laces. And everything had been normal until they were here, at the open door, with the rain shining prettily outside, and their father not moving, and their mother had said, 'Are you coming with us?' And then somehow Orla was by the door with her mother and Deebee, and their father was too far over there on the divan and she could hear herself start the way she did, and her feet wouldn't move, she could only move her hands which couldn't become wings and she covered her face with them and bowed her head so no-one could see her weep.

Her mother never cried. She always said, 'For pity's sake, will you give over,' or 'Get out of my sight if you're going to do that.' But once it had started Orla couldn't give over. So she. And then there was. Just her and. The too loud voice of the TV man because. Daddy was going to let her. Take them away he. Must have forgotten he had. Forgotten the plan Orla had made: what he was supposed to, what he must have thought about, too, surely, when she shouted. He hadn't even. Looked at her. Didn't he know it was Mummy who needed to go, that. She and Deebee would stay with him, that they'd. All be happier then, that. She could cook dinner and wash dishes, that. Maybe Kit could live with them. That then there'd be no more shouting.

She felt her mother's soft belly against her cheek, her mother's arm around her; she heard her mother's voice that didn't sound like her mother. 'It's all right.' And the door clicking shut against the dark, cold rain.

~

Next morning there were pancakes. Deebee looked at the stack of them in the centre of the table and then up at their mother, 'Is it your birthday?' and their mother made a laughing sound, set down a plate of chopped banana, a jar of honey.

Orla watched her sister squash holes in her pancake with her finger. Their father said, 'Don't play with your food,' and Deebee stuck her finger in her mouth and looked up at him. Their mother glanced sideways at her, backhanded her. Deebee's hand flew from her startled face and hit the table's edge. 'And don't lick your fingers,' their mother said, picking up her knife and fork.

Orla looked down at her plate so she didn't have to see her sister, but still her eyes stung at the sound Deebee made and the pancake thickened in her mouth. She took a gulp of milk, swallowed, glanced at her parents. Their mouths were tight. They stared at the table and chewed.

She pushed her pancake with her fork. Her mother looked at Orla's plate and then at her, said, 'I hope you're not taking ill again.'

Deebee wiped her face with her sleeve and their father took out his handkerchief, put it over her nose. 'Blow.'

Their mother stacked the plates and took them to the kitchen. Their father went out the front door. Orla knelt on the divan and watched him through the lounge room window. He crossed the lawn, picked up the rolled-up newspaper from the verge, sauntered back towards the house, sliding the rubber band onto his wrist. He slowed, stopped, read the front page in the sun. He opened the paper and his mouth fell softly open, too, and his face and shirt were as grey as his hair. The wind fluttered the newspaper in his hands; his hair flopped into his eyes. She liked the windy mess of him, the way he looked for a moment like someone else, someone younger, happier. He smoothed his hair back over his head, pressed it into place with his palm, came back through the door.

She tried to read but words slid around. She sat on her bed, stared at the carpet, went looking for her father again. Now he was at the table with his back to her, the paper spread out in front of him. He licked his finger and turned the page. It made a sound like a little wave rushing up the shore. Orla settled into a corner of the divan with her legs tucked in beside her, just the way he did when he sat there. From that place, if she flicked her gaze up from her book she could easily see him. The light from the window beside him made part of his head disappear. He flicked the pages, closed the paper, passed her on his way out to the garden. Her mother said, 'It's spring out there. The two of you go and play.'

Orla said, 'We don't have spring here, we have djilba.'

'What? Who told you that?'

'My teacher.'

Her mother stared at her. 'Don't be ridiculous.'

In the garden, their father was on his knees. Deebee swept up a handful of weeds and tossed them in the air. They landed on her head and shoulders. She said, 'Orly says there's no such thing as spring.'

Their father's fingers worked fast, snatching at the soft green stems. 'Oh, yes? I wish someone would tell the weeds.'

Deebee giggled. 'Weeds don't have ears, Daddy!' Their father sat back on his haunches, lifted a weed close to his face and said, 'Now you listen to me, you weed, I've just about had enough of you!' Deebee's mouth burst open with a laugh like a shout.

Orla took her book into the treehouse. Now and then, when the words slid, she looked down at her father scraping weeds with the rake or digging them out with the spade or tipping them into the old forty-four gallon drum behind the Hills hoist. She watched her sister trail after him, in her tee-shirt and shorts and her boy's haircut, watched her throw in weedy fistfuls too, the wind catching them. Even from where she was, Orla could see the soil on her little sister's face; her father brushed dirt from his hands, his shirt. She heard more laughter, the wind shifting leaves in the branches of trees, her father's low voice, bits of his speech, the funny sound he made when Deebee chased him, the roaring sound he made when he chased her. She heard her sister's happy squeals, and later the crackle of flame. She caught the thin smell of burning, looked down. The two of them stood, side by side, a little away from the smoking drum, one of her father's hands on Deebee's shoulder, the other holding the garden hose. Silver water arced from it, shifted and re-became itself. It disappeared in the shaggy grass. The smoke coloured, thickened, wind blew it over her. She closed her eyes, held her breath and her book to her face like a shield.

She ran to the back stairs as fast as she could and just kept going, up, up, her heart pounding. At the top she gripped the railing, did not look down. She heard water in the laundry, pushed open the back door to the scent of laundry powder and her mother shoving a bundle of clothes into the tub. She looked at Orla, surprised. Then she frowned, pressed a hand to her daughter's forehead. 'Are you sure you're not ill?' Orla squirmed away, held up her book by way of an answer, went to her room.

~

From her bed, she gazed out her window to the tops of the poplars alongside the driveway. They shook. Between the house and trees, the afternoon's lengthening shadow. Each time she looked up from her reading, it had grown; she listened: her father and sister coming in the back door; her family's voices in the kitchen, lounge room; the toilet's flush. Day faded, the air darkened. She turned on her bedside lamp. If she was patient, she told herself, someone would come to her and say something, something that would explain everything about the night before.

10

There weren't as many kids as she'd thought there'd be, and from her class only Derek. He turned to look as she entered. His eyes were clear and blue. She met his gaze then looked away.

Mrs Dodd peered over her glasses, crooked her finger at someone. 'Come here, dear. What's your name?' So it was public, not like her hills school. Here, everyone had to sing the C major scale from middle to top C, once with the teacher playing the notes and once without. Mrs Dodd smiled a lot, and let some kids finish; she stopped others halfway: 'Thank you, dear. That's lovely'. And wrote something in an exercise book.

Orla watched each of them making for the door, their cheeks aflame. Outside, she saw them leap down the steps or from the veranda's edge and run. A few were kept longer, asked to sing the first two lines of the school song. Orla waited. When it was Derek's turn, he stood with his back to her, his voice pleasant but far away. Her gaze followed him as he left. He didn't look at anyone. By the time it was her turn, a lot of kids had sounded pretty good. Her stomach fluttered.

Mrs Dodd smiled at her: red lipstick; large, straight, white teeth. The scales and arpeggios were easy. 'How long have you been at this school?' Mrs Dodd asked.

'Since the beginning of the year.' She heard her voice tremble. Was there some rule? No-one else had been asked that.

Mrs Dodd nodded. 'Maybe you can sing something else for me.'

Orla watched the teacher's fingers work through her sheet music. 'It's a lot easier to sing something you've been listening to for a while, isn't it.' Orla nodded. Mrs Dodd's hands were as sinewy as trees.

'Do you know "O Come, All Ye Faithful"?' That big smile again.

So Orla sang it, all the way through, watching Mrs Dodd's tree-hands strong at the keys. And, by the time she had finished, she knew she wanted to grow up to be like her.

At the first choir practice, Orla stood behind the piano so she could look over its top, directly into Mrs Dodd's singing face, her smiling eyes, straight into her mouth as she opened it wide to let her big voice out. From there, she could see the way she lengthened her neck, pushed her voice up into her head. Sometimes she lifted one hand from the keys and, with one finger, lightly touched her forehead. Sometimes strings of saliva glistened between her teeth, or between her teeth and tongue, or stretched and snapped between her lips. Orla looked away, as if she had seen something she shouldn't. And Mrs Dodd looked around at her choir as she sang, or looked straight ahead, at the music or at Orla, and sometimes smiled at her, too. She clapped her hands when they got a phrase right, or mouthed, 'Forte' or 'Bravo' or 'Pianissimo' as they sang it without her. This new and private language.

The music was loud behind the piano; the chords shook her insides. Her teeth buzzed; floorboards hummed beneath her feet. Once she touched her finger to the piano frame; the vibrations shocked her skin. And she thought about that feeling all week until the next time, until she could shuffle forward, bit by bit, until her hip touched, made her recoil then step again, lean her pubic bone against it, feel the buzz that made her want to pee. She pressed her thighs together. When she went back to class, the soft place between her legs throbbed and she clamped her hands to the sides of her head and frowned at the page.

~

That night in bed she thought about the piano and the soft place. She thought about Nugget and how that part of her never tingled when she rode; and she felt cross and muddled up. She could hear the T.V. She knew just where her parents were sitting, that the lamp was on. She thought of all her friends at her old school, wondered what she would tell them about the in-between house and the in-between school when she saw them again next year. She wondered if they remembered her, what they said, and how long it would be until she had her own pony, one like Nugget, and where would it live. She slid her hand down to the soft place, and closed her eyes, pretended it was Friday night, and when she woke everything would be all right because it would be a second Saturday.

~

Nugget's head was short, her nose straight in the way of Arab horses Orla had seen in books. Nugget's body was small and sturdy. Learning the rising trot was surprising at first — all that bumping around — but the key to Orla keeping her seat was straightforward and immediately clear, all in the timing. On TV, cantering had always looked easy, as if all a cowboy had to do was relax. Orla leaned back, pushed her weight deep into the saddle, gripped tightly with her knees but still she felt her hold precarious, her strength never enough, her legs puny against the power of the pony's loping run. At any moment — in this stride or this — the balance of the forces would shift and she would be tossed up and arc again through the thin blue air. And it would hurt to land, as it had that day after school, even more than it did when Nugget occasionally refused or shied, and much less momentum sent Orla hurtling over the pony's head or slipping sideways from the saddle into the sawdust of the round yard. And her instructor would call, 'You all right?' And Orla would be up, brushing herself off, saying, 'I'm fine,' not looking at her, not looking at anyone, not limping if she could help it, looking only at Nugget, keeping her voice soft, her hand running over Nugget's coat, catching the reins, left foot up and into the stirrup, hands gripping the saddle, right leg lifted over, and back on, no question.

After her lessons, Orla would unsaddle Nugget and take to her coat with a currycomb, murmuring as she brushed her quivering flanks and withers, chest, hindquarters. Nugget would stand quietly, close her eyes. Between lessons, Orla dreamed of bringing her dull bay coat up to gleaming so that everyone would look at how pretty she was, notice how kind and obedient her nature, see just how much she was loved; but, no matter how hard Orla worked, she could never get all the dust out before her father would sidle up, before she would see his shuffling feet in the corner of her eye, before he'd say, 'Time to go.'

She'd replace the combs and brushes in the tack shed, stand at Nugget's dozing head and press her own face against the pony's, breathe her in, stroke her muscular neck and whisper sounds that were words she didn't know the meaning of, could never have explained, hold her open hand under Nugget's muzzle to feel her breath, to feel her lips lightly searching. Nothing else had ever smelled as good and warm, nothing had ever felt as soft, as living. All the way home she would breathe Nugget's scent from her palms, marvel at the dirt in the fine network of lines, good stuck dirt that made her own hands strange to her.

11

A few minutes ago, he had swung the last trailer gate shut, slid the bolts to, given the all clear. The truck had rumbled out of the yard, and he had listened to it — good riddance! — to its lumbering, squealing, its gear shifts as it had turned onto the tarred road, accelerated away, grown faint. Up ahead of him now, he hears one of the lads yawn exuberantly and exclaim it's nearly three a.m., the relief in his voice. He can't catch them up. His legs. He's nauseous; he sweats; isn't sure he'll make it to his suit and tie, to Henry in her good frock, the builder, the contract, the ten o'clock signing. At last, at last. And then something takes him: his chest, his legs and all his breath, a sound like he's been punched, and he's on his side in the dirt. He groans. *Ah, Christ.*

12

Since they had moved to the house near the sea and their mother had taken a weekend job, Saturdays and Sundays were quiet. But this Sunday morning was quieter still: muffled, hot; the sky low, grey; no wind; no birds. Orla stepped off the front porch to look. Uneasy, she said, 'Let's go back inside. I'll play with you there.' And Deebee followed her.

The house was cold as a pool. They drank water from the fridge. Deebee lined up her cars on the carpet and the two of them pushed them around, crashed them into one another. Deebee laughed so hard that Orla couldn't help but laugh, and they were on their backs, roaring, with their legs in the air when their father brought out the chessboard and started setting it up.

Orla looked at her sister. Deebee said, 'But you said you'd play with me.' And Orla looked at her father, at the methodical placing of the pieces. She said, 'I'll play with you again after we finish.'

Deebee's eyes filled. She said, 'But it takes too long.'

'You play with your cars. Leave your sister alone.'

So Orla watched her push a car round and round; Deebee was right: even when you're playing it, chess takes much too long.

When their mother had told her daughters that, from now on, she'd be at work on the weekends, so it would just be them and their father at home during the day and they had to be sure they looked after him, something inside Orla, something she felt as small and winged, had lifted off. Her father carried hush with him. He spoke softly and smiled when he saw her, and it was like this from the time they awoke on weekends until the late afternoon when someone else's car would pull up on the street and Deebee would rush out the front door and fling her arms around her mother's legs, and their father would take the baking dish from their mother's hands, and everyone would be smiling. The lady in the passenger seat would turn and wave as a man in the driver's seat put the car in gear and the indicator on, and took them away.

In the kitchen, the food their mother had cooked where she worked smelled delicious and, although Orla could see her mother was tired, that her lipstick was just two spots in the corners of her mouth, that her hair needed combing, she also saw that her mother smiled a lot, and would set the table so they could eat before the food grew cold, and make sure the girls were in their baths and pyjamas before the sun went down.

As their father set the pieces on the board and Deebee inscribed circles with her car, Orla stared through the lounge room window at that low sky. Her father was always white, so she waited for him to begin, moved her pawn, glanced out the window again. Nothing out there had changed but she couldn't help looking, took her turn and went to the front door, opened it. She shifted her gaze between the sky and trees; she glanced back at the board. Her black knights gleamed, just like Fury had done. A teacher had once told her that black was every colour and she liked that idea of being everything but when Orla had mixed her paints together all she got was a kind of brown. She put her fingertip on one of her knights. She liked their L-shaped moves; if you traced where they had been, they made a chain, each move linking into the one before. She was sure her father chose white because he liked cowboy movies where the goodie wore a white hat and the baddie wore a black. Her father sat on the edge of the chair with his elbows on his knees and Orla loved to be black because it gleamed, and because of Fury and because of everything, so she would rest her finger lightly on a black knight's head and imagine her own horse one day. Her father leaned towards the board as if he were really interested. He moved a bishop. She went back to the board, moved another pawn. She ran her finger along the edge of the side-table her parents had brought with them from the iya place. When her parents and Kit talked about that place, they would start out sounding happy and end up sounding sad.

'It's so quiet,' Orla said, as she watched her father take his turn. 'Isn't it very quiet, Daddy?'

'Hm,' he replied, not looking up. 'Close the door. It's too warm out there.'

A low rumble. Could have been thunder. Chess pieces shivered, then jumped, and then it was on them, fast and loud. The floor moved. Chess pieces fell. The kitchen clattered. Orla struggled to her feet, bent over from the waist to keep her balance. Cupboard doors rattled hard, hard, hard. Pawns skipped across the floor. Orla leaned on the wall. It heaved against her. She gasped, 'Daddy?' and looked at him. 'Daddy?'

He was trying to stand, holding onto the back of his chair. His eyes were round, his mouth open. She shouted, 'What is it, Daddy?' because she was sure he would know, he knew everything. He stared back at her. She heard Deebee crying, saw her trying to stand, toppling, and in the space between them, the floor rose and fell and rose. Their father stretched out his arms, one in front and one behind, his feet apart, body leaning forward as if surfing. Then it slowed and something else came for them, a galloping, a stampede. Underground hooves. She heard it arrive from across the street, pass directly under them, moving flat out as a spooked horse, swerving suddenly right, beneath the kitchen, shooting away from the back door, under the sandpit, under the fence, under the next door neighbour's yard, and gone.

The world was silent and still. Then their father said, 'Out, quickly, out,' scooped up Deebee and was at the front door with Orla right behind him, watching her father's hand turn the door knob, her sister's hands at the back of his neck. They sat on prickly grass in the shade of their verge tree. It was still hot, the sky dull. No birds. No dogs. Orla looked up and down the street but, as usual, there was no-one. After a long time, a black taxi arrived and their mother got out, and then everyone talked at once. Their father trod on a pawn inside the door and hopped about. Orla gathered all the pieces: under the divan, the chairs, the coffee table, on the hearth, along the passageway. The kitchen sparkled with broken glass. Their mother cooked scrambled eggs for dinner. Orla ate bread because egg made her sick. Her father didn't mind.

At school the next day kids bobbed up and down in their seats: they were swimming, in a car, kicking a ball, up a tree; their grandma or uncle had been on the toilet. The road had slithered from side to side. Everyone wading up to their knees had fallen sideways into the sea. They could see daylight between the bricks of a wall. Orla raised her hand but the teacher was looking everywhere else, and after a while she put it down again. She turned in her seat to look at all the kids who spoke. Their faces shone and they shouted over one another and laughed, and that day the teacher laughed too and didn't care. At first Orla laughed, as well, but the more she listened the quieter she became. They were at picnics, the beach, with grandparents, cousins. She waited for someone to mention the absence of birds, the underground hooves. Then suddenly the teacher looked at her and asked what she had been doing. Her cheeks flushed. 'Playing chess.' The teacher stared at her.

Someone said, 'My next door neighbours were playing Twister,' and everyone laughed at the thought of that, and Orla was glad she hadn't had to talk about the birds and the hooves.

~

The following week they began to learn Christmas carols in choir: 'Good King Wenceslas', which was easy, and 'Gloria in Excelsis Deo', which wasn't. Mrs Dodd would smile with her big white teeth: 'More runs than a stocking!'

~

October days were warm, the finish of the year at the in-between house drew closer. Soon, she knew, she would see her friends again and she worried for a moment that they may not be her friends. Because things change, because she hadn't heard from them. She imagined their surprise when they saw her again, and that the year had filled them with stories, too, so she wouldn't have to tell them about the vanishing dog, that rainy night, her father a statue, having to play chess, the hooves, the birds, lunchtimes watching other girls play. Sometimes, walking to and from school, she would try out sentences that could make it sound all right, sentences that would start well but then fail, when all the words she thought she knew — words that could rescue her, change it from what it was into what she wanted it to be — just vanished.

13

Since their mother had started weekend work, Orla hadn't seen Nugget; instead she had woken to the Saturday hush of her father moving in the kitchen. She'd follow it, lean on the bench, watch him. 'Hello, Daddy.'

He would turn his head and smile. 'Hello, Tweety,' as he put the kettle on. No-one had mentioned horseriding. She knew she had to be patient, quiet, good.

But this Sunday morning the kitchen was empty. From the dining room, she could see through the half-open door of her parents' room that their curtains were closed, the room dark. Everything in there quiet.

'Daddy?' she called.

'Yes.'

She peered in. He was lying on his bed. He half sat up, leaned on one elbow. 'I'll be there in a minute.'

He had washed the breakfast dishes and said, 'I'm just going to lie down.' And later, Orla had stood outside her parents' bedroom door again, listening. She wanted to call him just to hear him answer, but she didn't because. Because he. Because he might. She walked away. She returned. She watched the clock's loud ticking face. She walked up and down. She went to his door. She sat on the divan to wait.

He didn't speak as he made cheese on toast for lunch. When they'd finished, he told Deebee to have a nap. Orla watched her sister's face fall. She put her finger in her mouth and left the table, her soft footfalls receding along the passageway. Her father turned to Orla. 'And you clean your room.'

She glanced beyond him, out the window, at the sunny day, thought about the treehouse, the wind and sky. But she went to the laundry, took a clean rag from under the sink. She always cleaned the same way: dolls, jewellery box, knick-knacks and books went in separate sections on her bed while she cleaned the chest of drawers, bookshelf, bedside table. Then she sat on the edge of her bed and, one by one, cleaned each small thing and returned it to its place. Sometimes she changed where things were kept. Sometimes she polished other furniture in the house: coffee table, side tables, sideboard. If the chessboard was out she cleaned that, too, and each little piece. But not today. Today, it seemed, her father was the one allergic to children.

But it was so sunny, her room full of light. She put the Mr Sheen and the cloth on the floor by her bed, took her knick-knacks, one by one, and put them by her pillow. Then she sat cross-legged in the middle of her bed and studied them, these things she loved: the small porcelain Black Beauty; a tiny white Pekinese dog with a pink bow in her hair; a painted floral thimble; a curvy cat, black for luck, with white whiskers and a red bow tie; a pink and blue plastic bubble pipe and a small plastic bottle of bubble liquid; an inch-high white porcelain vase, a minute pink and green garden painted on its front and gleaming gold paint on its tiny curved handles, its rim.

She stood in front of her chest of drawers and opened her jewellery box. The ballerina in her pink tutu turned and turned to 'Lavender Green'. She sang along, put on her charm bracelet, her crystal necklace, the white clip-on earrings she had won at the Royal Show, her silver hair slide. She looked at herself in the wardrobe mirror.

A sound at the door made her turn. Her father glared at her, then glanced around her room. 'Have you finished yet?'

She pushed her fingers together in front of her, dropped her gaze. She felt the slide in her hair, the necklace and bracelet against her hot skin. He had always told her to tell the truth. She said, 'I'm sorry, Daddy. I got distracted.' She forced herself to look up at him. She said, 'I'll do it now.' He held her gaze and nodded. She turned away.

It was a single sound, like a rifle shot in one of his TV Westerns. She gasped, grabbed her leg. The force of it. He had always told her to tell the truth. He must have swung with all his might. She staggered forward, turned her head to look over her shoulder but he wasn't there. She could hear his footsteps growing faint. She reached the bed, propelled, grasped its edge, climbed on, curled up beside her things, curled as tightly as she could.

She couldn't stop. Her mother hit Deebee and shouted at all of them. She'd say, 'Get away with you!' or 'Why must you follow me like a bad smell?' Her father never shouted. When her mother hit her sister, Orla would cry, too, and then, scared she'd be hit, as well, for crying, she'd hide. When her father hit Deebee it was because her mother would ask and ask and ask him to. He'd go into the Deebee's room and close the door, and Orla would stand outside, her fingers gripping the door handle, listening to her sister's screams, to the hissing sound of her father slipping the belt from his pants, the sound of it hitting, hitting. She'd put her hand on the door knob, rehearsing in her head the words she'd need: 'Please stop, Daddy!' Imagining the surprise on his face, his arm high and frozen. But instead her whole body would shake until everything stopped on the other side of the still-closed door — the hissing, the hitting, the screams — and she'd move jerkily back to her room and Deebee's door would open and her father would leave, and she'd hear her sister crying, and would stay in her room for a long time.

And now she couldn't stop. Even when her leg stopped stinging, the middle of her chest ached, and the sobs rose up, up her throat from some hurting place. He had never hit her, never. She had told the truth. Then suddenly he was there again, beside her, touching her shoulder. He sat on the edge of her bed, put his arm around her. She shuffled close to him. He hugged her for a long time, and she was filled with sorrow and with love. 'I'm sorry,' he whispered. 'I'm sorry.'

~

At dinner the previous evening, her father had stared at his plate. Her mother had said, 'How did it go last night?'

He had shrugged a little. 'All right.'

Deebee had asked, 'What do you do with the chickens?'

Their father had pushed his food around with his fork. 'We put them in crates.'

'Why?'

Their father had sighed.

Their mother had said, 'The crates go on a truck and the truck driver takes them to their new home.'

Deebee had said, 'But why do you have to do it at night?'

Their mother had smiled at her. 'Because when it gets dark, the chickens go to sleep, so then you can creep in and grab them by their feet.' She'd made a swipe at an imaginary bird.

'But why?'

'So they can't fly away. Chickens have wings and if you're not careful, they'll get frightened and flap their wings and fly away and then they'll get lost. If you hold them by their feet, like an umbrella, you can carry them upside down and they can't get away.'

Orla had thought about crates and umbrellas and what it was to be turned upside down. Before Deebee was born, her father had grabbed her ankles in one of his big hands, turned her upside down so her skirt hung down around her ears. He had banged his fist on her back. The humbug in her throat had clattered across the floor and she had breathed.

~

But the next night, Sunday night, it was dusk by the time they sat down for dinner. When it pressed against the chair, the back of Orla's leg still ached. Their mother looked at their father and scowled. 'Tell them you can't do it tonight. Tell them your wife worked during the day.'

Orla looked from her mother to her father but he just shrugged.

Her mother pressed. 'For pity's sake, look at you. You've already done two nights. Tell them you're ailing.'

When he answered, his voice was quiet. 'I have to do it.'

Her mother didn't say anything, just looked back to her plate, cut her food. After a while, her father put his knife and fork together, rose from his chair. Orla looked at him. She had never seen him leave the table mid-meal before. She looked down at his plate. Most of his food was still on it. She had never seen that before, either. He said, 'Sorry. It's delicious. I'm just not hungry.' He went to the kitchen. Orla heard the clink of his keys.

She looked to her mother, who gave a little smile. 'Daddy has to work again tonight.'

Orla felt her throat constrict. 'Why?'

Her father reappeared, his keys in his hand. Orla looked at him. Her mother said, 'Just like the last two. He has to help a farmer catch his chickens.'

She looked back to her mother. Her stomach flipped over. She remembered the incubator, the yellow chicks, the feel of the bones beneath the feathers. She turned to her father, panic in her voice. 'When will you be back?'

Her mother said, 'Don't worry, he'll be home before you go to school.'

Her father reached out and stroked her mother's hair; her mother smiled up at him, surprised. Orla wondered if her mother knew what had happened — that she hadn't done what she was told and she'd told the truth, that he'd hit her anyway then said sorry. If her mother knew, she gave no sign of it. And if she didn't, Orla knew as sure as her heart knew how to beat that she would never tell her mother, either. She heard her father's car start, watched his headlights sweep once across the front of the house as he backed up onto the road and drove away.

14

'Ah, Christ,' he groans. 'Ah, bastard.' He tries to see up ahead, he tries to call them, to turn his head but nothing except the night overhead, stars between trees, all that space which, he remembers, men are flying through, reaching for the moon — and then, and then who knows? Far beyond this track, this farmhouse, its veranda light, far from the dark roads and lumbering trucks, crates jostling with dozing pullets going off to die, far beyond this range of hills and everywhere he has ever lived; beyond Henry turning in her sleep, her outstretched hand feeling he is not yet home, beyond his sleeping girls, little Deebee, with her fingers in her mouth, wiry and nimble as a son, beyond Orla's eyes on him always, beyond her books beneath her pillow beneath her head; beyond the oceans he had crossed, hopeful; the banks of boyhood streams, listening for frogs in the deepening afternoon, his blue-white fingers cupping their slippery bodies out of mud; the fields where he kicked a football to his brothers, where he chased them, angry when they took it from him, where he thumped and wrestled as they laughed and swatted him away; beyond the thick green Belfast River, its spillway where he'd lean to watch the sticks and leaves he'd drop spin, plunge, be overwhelmed; beyond his schools, prizes, masters telling him he could be anything he put his mind to; beyond his mother's kitchen, his sister's smile, the rustle of his father's evening newspaper. Beyond the face now leaning over him, a strong brown farmer's face, the face of a man he has known for years, who is lifting his shoulders, cradling his head as he would a child, saying, 'You all right?' Who is shouting now, 'Call an ambulance!' And beyond the sound of feet thumping away down the track, of other feet shuffling close, of voices, 'What's happened?' Beyond all that.

He looks up. Way. Into the space. He used to know what he is looking at. He has already forgotten all his science. Stars. Light. Fire. There is a fire flashing through him. Long ago. Could have been anything. His fine mind. Light years away.

15

The voice was foreign and loud and she didn't understand it.

Everything in her room was in its place: her body, her bed, window, bookshelf, chest of drawers, wardrobe, her door half-open to the rest of the house, the fat yellow light coming through. Her skin prickled; her limbs rigid. Another voice murmuring. She listened but. Didn't know how long. It felt long long but she didn't.

He was at work. He was working. It was his last night of. In the morning. Everything would be. And then. She squeezed her eyes shut because. Her voice in her head spoke to her very calmly, 'When you open your eyes it will just be a dream. When you open your eyes it —.' But the wailing and. She opened them and she knew she knew and she lay cold and frozen with the knowing.

She had to get up. Because she could be. She could be wrong. She had to breathe and breathe. Her heart. She could be wrong. She had to. She was so often wrong. Wrong legs. Wrong face. Wrong crying. Wrong idea. She had to. Get up. And. Push blankets, push legs. Stand. Press fingers. Together. Walk to the door. Stand. Listen. Breathe. Her body shaking hard and deep. Shaking from her belly. Something very. Walk the passage. Slow. Stop. Press fingers. Look. Look. Breathe. Face it.

Face into the room. That used to be. That used to be the lounge room.

Breathe.

Porch light seeped in around the edges of the blinds and through the glass of the front door, made pale grey shapes on dark grey furniture, carpet. In the furthest corner, her mother sat, on the edge of the divan in a pool of yellow lamplight. She was such a long way away, and bent as a comma, her back curved, her arms on her knees, head in her hands. Her hair stuck up, black and fine as burnt twig.

Orla heard her own voice in her own head. Mummy!

It was a terrible voice her mother had.

In the circle of light was everything. Outside it was the everything else. The fireplace stared straight back at Orla, its face shadowed, its shocked mouth wide. Above it, barely visible, the little face of her father's radio. To one side, the TV watched with its empty, dark green eye.

Mummy! She was so far away. Between Orla and the lamplight, the long stretch of carpet, miles of it, all charcoal grey. And she shouldn't have sat there. Why did she sit there? She never sat there. Everyone knew that was where he sat. His legs curled up beside him like a leaf. Mummy! She was in the wrong place, had the wrong voice. And he didn't sit there last night, and not the night before. No, and. Everything was. Mummy!

In the corner of her eye, Deebee. Clown faces on her pyjamas. Deebee, who looked straight ahead. Right into the deep cave of the room, right down its throat to the golden circle of light, of fire. Orla watched Deebee's eyes. Two black holes seeing. Blink. What were they seeing? Light glinted on her little forehead, her cheek, a spike of her hair. Orla felt her push past. No, Deebee, if you go in, you. You won't come out, you. Wait. Deebee, stay here with me with your fingers in your mouth. Put your whole hand in. Better that way, to swallow yourself.

And then a shape, a movement. Between Deebee and the front door. Shadows, tall and. Two. Two men. But not. Not. Neither. Two men in front of the closed door, guarding the way in, out. They didn't speak. Didn't look. They watched their hands. Their hands held hats. They turned their white hats round and round. Their pale hats spun, glowing like planets, like twin moons circling, and they stared at them, their hats, their hands.

Behind them, against the frosted front door glass, a moth, its wings frantic, trying to bash its way out.

Deebee pushed past, made a sound in her throat. And Orla watched their mother, across the room, all those miles away, lift her head, settle it back onto her shoulders as if it really belonged to her, and look at her daughters with a face like a drawing of itself. It opened its mouth and arms, and said, 'Come here.' Deebee ran. In her head, Orla took a step after her, stretched out her elastic arm, snatched her sister by a fistful of her hair, said don't don't don't you see — the lounge room's a cave, the lamp is fire. See how her hair is burned black twig. See the pair of white moons spinning. It's all wrong. She's in the wrong place and look, Deebee, look, she has someone else's idea of her face.

But Deebee ran. Ahead and into her mother's arms, and for a moment there was only Orla stranded, alone and looking, and she took another step and hoped she was stupid, wrong, didn't know a thing, and she took another step and another but she knew she knew she knew she knew, and she couldn't help it, she was already crying, and as she crossed the room step step step one man turned his face to look at her and what else, what else could she do but just keep going.

It took a long time to reach them, her mother, her sister. They were so far away, it took years. And then, at last, arms holding, holding, and her mother said, she said she said he, he had, but

Orla knew she knew she already knew shut up shut up and the man the police who was not her father, who was the wrong, swivelled his face away like a chair and didn't do a single thing to help them.

16

A morning. But how does morning come. And then come.

Orla lay on her back, fully dressed, under her blanket. Stared at the ceiling. Arms at her sides. Then there was sound. As if underwater. She blinked, broke through to the surface. The sound arrived again. Sharpening as if tuning radio. Voices. At the front door. Her mother. A man. The door clicking shut. And there was no thought, just Orla rising from her bed, standing tense in the centre of her room, her heart thumping. Though she could hear the voice and the voice was the wrong. But still. But still.

Deebee in her doorway. 'Mummy wants you.'

When Orla saw him she slowed, hesitated. The man in a long black dress sat on the divan. His hands rested on his knees. That white thing she had heard adults call a dog collar. She knew him. Clasped her hands together, approached. He turned to her, gave a small smile, looked away, as if he'd never seen her before. She perched in the nearest armchair. Glanced at the side of his face.

She knew his name. Sometimes he appeared in scripture class in his black clothes. When he was there, the usual scripture teacher, an old lady in hat and gloves, sat by the windows and watched him. One day he had asked how many of them owned a pet. Lots of kids had raised their hands. He had looked around the room then, told them he had a cat called Sin. There had been a silence. He had asked, 'What colour do you think my cat is?'

From behind, Orla had heard a small voice: 'Black?'

He had grinned then. 'Yes.' He had been so pleased. After that he had opened *The Children's Bible*, talked about something Orla could no longer remember. She hadn't been able to listen, had only been able to stare at him. Wondered if he had any children. If he was kind to them. Kind to the cat. Imagined him calling it for dinner: 'Sin! Sin!'

Now he was here. In their lounge room. On their divan. Instead of their. She glanced again at the side of his face: brown curly hair, light freckles. Looked down at the wide gold wedding ring. Why was he here? Deebee stared at him from the other chair, swung her legs. Henry's voice reached them from the kitchen. He lifted his chin, spoke loudly in reply, gazed at the carpet again until she appeared, carrying a tray. He took a mug from it, held it carefully between his small, clean hands. The ring clinked against the cup. The coffee steamed. Biscuits appeared on a plate. Deebee took a Milk Arrowroot and sucked it, still staring.

Henrietta sat on the divan beside him. Orla looked at them, watched her mother's fingers hook stray strands of her hair behind her ears, wrap around her cup and lift it, fidget with the handle. Henry stared at the carpet, too. Sometimes she nodded. As if she understood. Orla looked down at the carpet, as well. But nothing there made sense.

The reverend leaned forward into a long silence. 'All of us wonder why God takes some people too soon.'

Orla's chest hurt. It was hard to breathe. Still, she looked at him, hopeful. Behind his head the day was so pretty, the window filled with it.

Into the continuing silence, he said, 'God only takes the best first.'

Orla looked down. When she looked up again the adults were still staring at the floor. What was down there? Orla watched her mother. 'Yes,' she heard Henry say at last, her voice sad. 'Thank you.'

At the door he shook Henry's hand. 'Again, my condolences.' He nodded at Orla. He turned away; his clothes swished. She watched him walk to his car, open the door with one hand, gather his gown about him. He did not look back. Orla shut the front door quietly. She thought of his cat. How pleased he had been. Behind her, Henry gathered the dirty dishes onto the tray. The clattering of cups so loud.

~

On Friday morning, their mother said, 'You go with this lady.'

Orla opened the car's rear door for Deebee. The lady said to Orla, 'You sit next to me,' and she was glad she didn't have to explain about strange cars and sickness. The lady turned in the driver's seat and looked at Deebee. 'Will you be all right all on your own?' Orla turned to look, too. Deebee sucked her fingers, nodded, turned her face to the window.

The lady drove; she moved her arms and legs and didn't speak. Sometimes Orla watched her from the corner of her eye. She did all the things their father did behind the wheel. She had dark curly hair. Once she glanced at Orla and smiled with her pretty teeth. Orla made the shape of a smile then stared out the passenger window. She didn't know the lady's name. She looked off into the distance, tried not to think about where they were going, about what had happened, about; she leaned hard into the door so she could feel her bones and muscles. She wondered if it would fly open, if she would fall out onto the road, fall under the wheels, vanish like that brown dog. She imagined it, leaned harder.

She wore her best red dress, her black patent shoes, white socks. All the windows were down, the wind loud, the sky all blue and stupid.

~

They stood in front of the sign: Penguin Pool. The pool was made of grey cement someone had smoothed with a trowel, left long even ripples. Orla stared at them. Her father had a trowel. Deebee had called it a towel; everyone had laughed.

Its water was thick, green, dark as forests in fairytales, forests that swallow children, forests they should stay out of but never did.

She looked down at the bitumen. Her shoes gleamed blacker. She looked up, around. A stand of trees, earth beneath raked into the same long parallel of ridges and furrows, the soft black, newly turned soil. Her father had a rake. She had used it, knew it was tricky to make a pattern like that. At her feet shadows moved. She looked up, way up. Clouds scuttled, slid. It must be windy up there. She looked again at the stand of trees. Paperbarks. Her father had told her. Their spotted trunks, peeling. Strips hung from them like skin.

How long had she been standing here? She looked around. She shouldn't still be here. Her sister stood in front of her. From behind she could see Deebee's hand was at her mouth. What did she know about time or anything. The lady stood to one side, a gold watch on her wrist. From here she couldn't read it. The sun was hot. She was confused. She needed to work. Things. Out. Why were they staring at the penguin pool?

She had been here before. With her parents, Deebee, Kit. Her father had sat Orla on the merry-go-round; she had waved to them all as she spun by; they had all waved back. There was a kiosk near that merry-go-round, on top of it a big clock. She turned. It was there. Twenty-three minutes past ten. Was it right? Was it? The lady had made a terrible mistake, taken them to the wrong. Twenty-three minutes past hard to. Breathe. The lady had forgotten. Or she had got lost. Or misunderstood.

She looked up. The sky, sun, clouds rushing. Was that right? Her mother had said, 'You go with this lady.' She always did what she was told; she had been as quiet as, as. She hadn't made a fuss in front of anyone. After the first night and the white hats. If she had needed to make a fuss she had gone away because no-one should have to put up with that. When people had knocked on the front door she had opened it. She had listened to the adults who had come and gone and come again. Sometimes they had touched her hair or cheek or shoulder. She had said hello and goodbye, made the shapes of smiles; they had made the same shapes back and their bags and coats, the floor, their shoes. She had put on her good shoes, too. 'You go with this lady.' Twenty-four minutes past. Late, late. White rabbit late. Her shoes were shiny. The car was shiny. Children listen. They get into the car, stand where they're told, watch small fat shiny penguins slip into thick green water.

Her hands hung off the ends of her arms. Lace circled the top of each sock. Legs disappeared into socks and shoes. How could she be sure her feet were there? That they were her feet? Twenty-five minutes. Past. She had to open her mouth. To speak. To breathe. Nothing came out. No words. No air. Her heart thumped in her head.

The night before, she had dreamt he had given her a day-old chick, yellow and fluffy as the ones in the incubator, and when she closed her hand around it she could feel again its tiny bones. In her dream she put the chick in an empty matchbox, closed the lid so it could sleep, and when she opened it the chick was dead.

Before Deebee, there had been a yellow canary that sang and sang and sang in a cage. One morning it was lying on its scattered seeds and droppings. Someone had wrapped it in a handkerchief, laid it in a shoebox. Someone had dug a hole and put the shoebox in it. Someone had said a prayer and filled in the hole. It didn't take long. She had picked a flower from the garden and put it on the grave. Then they had all walked back to the house, and she had seen her parents smile at one another when they thought she wasn't looking, and she hadn't minded much.

She had listened Monday, Tuesday, Wednesday, Thursday. She knew about funerals and coffins and graves. People have bodies, just like birds.

She closed her mouth and opened it, pressed her fingers together. Presspress. Presspress. She flapped one hand at her side and then the other. She closed her mouth. She opened it. No sound except the wind pushing clouds far above, her hand flapping. The tick of the watch on the lady's wrist. The peeling of the trees' skins. Their soft, pink underneaths. She closed her mouth. She flapped her hand. There were five paperbarks. Leaning in together. Skins coming off. Twenty-six minutes. She flapped her hands. She opened her mouth. Someone was putting her father in a hole, had already put him in a box; someone was going to cover him up; it was hard to breathe they were leaning together a shadow between them cool and dark she stepped towards, one foot, another, her black shoes shining. Above her clouds passed squirrels chattered in the distance monkeys howled.

A hand on her shoulder and she turned. She turned to the lady and smiled, smiled. The lady had realised, remembered, would take them there. She felt her eyes fill. The lady had already turned away, was walking ahead, towards the kiosk, holding Deebee's hand. Orla followed. The lady stopped at an outdoor table.

'Wait here,' she said. Orla watched the lady walk to the kiosk. Above the lady's head, the big clock. Twenty-eight minutes. She watched the lady speak to a man. Orla squeezed her fingers hard soft hard soft. She watched the lady. She didn't blink. If she blinked, something bad would. Yes, the lady would disappear, like in a story, and they would be left here with the animals, with no way to get to where they should have been. The lady turned and walked towards to them. She held three ice creams in front of her like a bunch of flowers. She gave one to Deebee, held one out to Orla. Orla watched her own hand take it. 'Thank you,' she whispered. The lady took a handkerchief from her sleeve, wrapped it around her own cone. Orla watched the lady's pink tongue flick out, scoop, disappear. She watched Deebee push ice cream between her lips, sucking. She watched ants running across the table. Her ice cream melted in her fist.

Deebee said, 'It's good, Orly. Don't you want to eat it?' Her eyes shining. So she pushed her tongue into the ice cream and swallowed it, swallowed.

17

He opens his mouth, pitches forward. Dirt on his tongue, he smells coffees, sees Henry in her good frock, pouring two cups. He looks at her. She glances at him, smiles. She is younger than he remembers, happier. The coffee pours thick and dark, the way he likes. He shakes his head a little. Ah, mavourneen, where has time gone? Surely it can't be morning already?

18

The car turned into their driveway. The wheels crunched. Orla said, 'Thank you,' and got out, closed her door, opened the rear door again. It shut with a shout. She held her sister's hand; they walked, her shoes slipped on the gravel. Behind them, the wheels crunched again, the whiny sound of reverse.

The handle of the flyscreen door squeaked. Her teeth hurt. There were murmurings in the kitchen. Her heart thumped. A man, soft. She held her breath. She knew. This time. She knew it. She wanted to run, squeezed Deebee's hand to make herself, to just breathe, walk.

She turned the corner and stopped. Her mother's navy clutch bag on the yellow kitchen bench. Her mother at the dining table in her good navy dress. Orla let go of Deebee. Deebee ran to their mother. Orla squeezed her fingers together. There was a man she didn't know. Sitting in her father's. Nothing like her father. Her mother wasn't wearing her pearls; she hadn't put on a face. Her hair was pushed back by a navy blue band, her cheeks sunken, as pale as her father's had been; specks of lipstick at the corners of her mouth. As if she'd come home from work. Her hands were tight around a coffee cup and her fingernails, as always, short and bare. Her wedding ring shone. She didn't look up.

And next to her was Mrs West, their neighbour from the hills. Her own husband had died while Orla and her family had been living there. Another man across the road had died, too, and a third in the house on the corner. She had heard adults talk, heard her mother tell her father the street was cursed and she for one was glad to be leaving it.

Mrs West smiled — pink lipstick, tall orange hair, sparkly blue eyes, white skin in folds. The man was not as old as Mrs West. He stared at Orla, at her face, chest, hem. Orla looked from his face to his large belly. Mrs West tipped her head a little to one side. 'Hello, dears.' Orla looked at the floor and said hello; Deebee hid her face against her mother.

~

Later, their mother said, 'Mrs West and Mr McIntyre are leaving,' and when Orla didn't speak, looked hard at her. So Orla made a smile, said goodbye. Mrs West kissed Orla's cheek. Her skin was smooth and dry as talc.

Mr McIntyre took Orla's hand and shook it. When Orla looked at him, he was staring at her with shining eyes. His fingers were hard. He held her hand. He looked from her face to her mother. 'Perhaps we could take the children to the beach some time?'

Deebee said, 'Can we go to the beach, Mummy, can we, can we?'

Their mother said, 'That's very kind; they'd enjoy that.'

Orla watched them walk to their car. It was big and beige and parked on the verge. Mr McIntyre opened the door for Mrs West. Then he squeezed himself into the driver's seat. Deebee giggled. 'He's fat.'

Henry's arms dangled at her sides. She didn't say anything. She stared at the car as it moved away. Mrs West turned her head to look back. She gave a little smile. For a moment Henry lifted an open palm.

In the kitchen the girls watched their mother take a casserole dish from the fridge and set it on the bench. Orla stared at the dish — milky white with small blue flowers. She had never seen it before. Her mother lifted the lid and looked inside. Orla squeezed her fingers. Her mother set the lid on the bench with a loud clatter. She still stared at what was in the dish, and she opened her arms and said, 'Come here,' and the two of them rushed in hard and put their arms around her. Orla felt her mother tilt and lean against the edge of the bench. She heard the sound of her mother's linen dress in her ear like a scrape, the sounds of the three of them breathing against one another. Then their mother stepped away and pushed them a little, said, 'You must be hungry.' Orla looked at the floor.

She wanted to say penguin pool, paperbarks, ice cream. She wanted her mother to say she was sorry, that it had been a mistake. Instead she watched as her mother's hands smoothed the creases they had made in her dress and then opened the crockery cupboard.

The spoon scraped the inside of the saucepan. Orla took four placemats to the table and then remembered and took one off but her mother said, 'Leave it.' She set out four glasses, four knives, four forks. She stood behind her father's chair and straightened everything again. Her mother spooned chicken and potatoes and thick orange gravy onto each of the plates and put one plate on each of the placemats. Orla looked at the plates and squeezed her fingers. Her mother said, 'Could you fetch water?' Then the salt and pepper shakers.

If she only watched her own plate, Orla couldn't see the empty chair, the plate of cooling food. Couldn't see Deebee push chicken around her plate with her finger that made her chest tighten but their mother didn't say anything. Orla broke a potato with her fork, lifted a fragment to her mouth, squashed it between her tongue and her palette, sat perfectly still until it dissolved. She could see her mother's hands resting on the table's edge, one on each side of her plate. Deebee made slurping sounds sucking gravy from her fingers. Her mother's fingers twitched. Orla placed her fork in the middle of her plate, very straight, and said, 'May I please leave the table?' Her mother said, 'Yes,' without looking up.

She sat on her bed and stared at the shoes on the ends of her legs, pushed them hard into her purple carpet, rubbed them back and forth till the soles felt warm. Beneath the carpet the floorboards were hard. Fourth plate, fourth glass, fourth knife, fork, spoon. The clatter of dishes, running water. She should go help dry them the way her father did, put them away. But, if she did that, it would mean she knew he wouldn't be coming home, and she didn't know that, how could she?

She lay on her side on her bedspread, her feet still on the floor because that was the rule: shoes on the floor. Imagined herself in the kitchen, watching her mother's hand move the dishmop round and round and round. Plates, glasses. Her father there, beside them. Just her and her father, standing on the sideline, waving, her mother laughing, waving the dishmop at them as she passed on the merry-go-round.

Something pulled at her foot. She opened her eyes. Her mother unbuckling her shoes, peeling off her socks. She took Orla's elbow, said, 'Sit up,' unbuttoned Orla's dress, wiggled it over her head, said, 'Don't worry about pyjamas,' and tugged back the covers, pulled them up to Orla's chin.

The sheets were cool. She watched her mother move about. Dusk was greying the sky through the venetian blinds, their shadow a ladder of stripes across her mother's face. Then, in a still moment, her mother looked Orla in the eye, and her mother's eyes, almost hidden in the gathering dark, were so sad Orla had to close her own. 'I'm tired,' Orla breathed, and heard her mother inhale as if to speak. Then Orla felt her lean in and kiss her forehead, heard her walk away, and she opened her eyes to catch a glimpse of her dress as she disappeared. She had forgotten to close the venetian blinds. The room was still striped, dark grey on lighter, growing darker as she watched. The dressing table mirror deep and hazy. An ache welled in her, violent, unstoppable, and she pushed her knuckles into her mouth, the blanket over her head.

~

Towards morning, he came home. She was waiting for him on the driveway and she watched him get out of his car, and they stood together outside that house in the hills in the late afternoon light, looking around, smiling, and she recognised it all: the bushes a dugite had once slid into as she approached; the timbered gully out of which a herd of brumbies had once galloped, among them a grey, as if Thunderhead himself had fled the pages of her book; the open, sunny stretch of stony ground where, every year, small, dull, prickly plants she didn't know the names of burst into tiny, vivid, complicated flowers.

Her father had crouched by the garden bed nearest the road, the one he had dug himself, and he had turned the clay with a hand-fork, tossing aside all the clay-coloured stones. It was very cold. She pulled the sleeves of her jumper over her fingers, tucked her hands under her arms, crouched beside him to watch. Nearby, a green hose trickled, turning the orange clay to mud. Beside her father, a brown paper bag, its top folded over, held down by a pebble. He took her cold hand; she opened her fingers. Against them his own were icy. He upended the paper bag into her palm: a small mound of seeds. She peered: oval-shaped black, yellow crescent moons, tiny green spheres, larger brown ones, purple twists like pieces of thread.

A bird called. Her eyes opened. Where was she? One arm was flung back over her pillow, the backs of her fingers curved against the cold wall. She lay very still. For a long time she could feel the mound of seeds in that half-closed fist. She stared at the ceiling, seeing her father's smile, the low sky, the rivulets of mud, the trees moving in the sharp wind, feeling her woollen jumper rough against her skin. She closed her fist tight, drew it slowly down over her shoulder to rest beneath her chin. She could still smell damp earth. Then she sat up, cradling that fist in her lap. Morning light sparkled gold through the gaps in the venetians. Spots of light on the carpet, bedspread, walls. Someone had closed the blinds in the night. She opened her hand a little but she already knew, had already felt the dream slip from her, her palm hollow, the bright tiny things gone.

From the kitchen, Henry's voice, Deebee's. Her heart lurched with loss and wishing. She folded forward from the hinge of her hips, closed herself, her chest and face against her legs, one arm pressed between like a flower in a book. She lay with eyes closed, trying hard to return to the dream, heard the clatter of kitchen: cups, bowls, spoons. She thought about how she must look, folded up like that, her empty hand, the only thing inside, a disappointment.

Later, she realised it must have been because she had been crying in the night that she hadn't heard the key in the lock. If she had, she would have thrown off her covers and run to the lounge room to greet Kit. And when she had been sent back to bed, she would have lain awake, and heard everything.

~

It was dark when Kit had turned the key, the house lit but silent. Henry stood facing the door, her arms limp, face shadowed. Behind her, the lamp burned in its corner.

Kit said, 'Sorry, Hen, it took — have you been waiting?' and set her overnight by the wall. She rested her hands on Henry's shoulders, kissed her cheek.

Henry said, 'Coffee?', turned to the kitchen.

To her back, Kit said, 'Lovely,' and sounded just like him, and neither woman spoke for a while. Kit listened to the water running, looked at the clean ashtrays, the TV's closed-off face. Even though she had just watched his coffin lowered, she had to catch her breath. So, she thought loudly, it's true.

Under the kitchen's fluorescent light, Henry's hair was awry, her skin pale, lips dry, cheeks hollow. She gazed back at Kit from beneath half-closed lids. Her fingers fidgeted on the bench. The electric jug rumbled; all around, the surfaces were empty and clean.

Henry asked, 'Have you eaten?'

Kit nodded, clicked open her handbag. 'Cigarette?'

Henry watched her friend slip two from the pack, hold them between her lips, press open her chrome lighter, bring its flame close, snap it shut and drop it into her bag with a thud. The handbag's catch snapped shut.

Kit glanced up, squinting against the smoke, to see Henry look at her in a way that made her shiver. She took the cigarettes from her mouth, held one out, and looked again. The expression was gone: had she imagined it? She said, 'Remember how he would do this for us?'

Henry said, 'I've given up.'

Kit waved the cigarette about. 'I know,' she said. 'I just thought.'

Henry looked at the cigarette's dark tip, its thin blue smoke. He would leave his lighter anywhere, she remembered, even near the children. At least I won't do that, she thought as she took it.

The jug boiled. Henry handed Kit her cup. They sipped. There was wind in the trees. Kit sighed. 'I'm sorry I missed the children.'

Henry stared ahead. 'They were tired. The zoo.'

Kit drew back deeply, lifted her chin, blew out a long stream of grey. 'Can I see them?'

Orla's door, straight ahead, ajar, beyond it dim. Closer on the right, Deebee's was wide with a weak yellow light. Poor little thing: would she remember her father at all? Kit paused, listened. She peered around at her. 'You still awake, darling?' She was sitting on the lino in singlet and underpants, her back against her iron bed frame, a toy truck in her hand. Her bedclothes were kicked back. She looked up with her father's serious eyes. Kit's own eyes smarted.

'I don't want pyjamas.'

'That's all right.' Kit sat on the edge of the bed. 'I just came to say hello.'

Deebee leaned her head against Kit's knee. Kit slipped her hand under the little girl's arm, and she climbed onto her lap. Easy as that. Kit's arms around her and her chin on the top of Deebee's head.

'Daddy says I'm too old for cuddles.'

When she could, she said, 'Oh, well,' and squeezed her tight.

19

There's grit and blood on teeth and tongue and the farmer his friend wipes at it with a shirt sleeve, lies him gently, flat on his back, puts a hand then an ear to his mouth, gropes for something in his neck — where? where should it be? — presses his ear hard against his chest. 'Oh, Jesus,' he whispers. 'Jesus, Jesus.' He takes a deep breath, seals his dead friend's mouth with his own, breathes out hard — 'Jesus, Jesus' — to make, to undead, to make him live, recalling Lazarus, miracles, resurrection.

These two migrant men who met through business, who have known one another now for years; who, each to their respective wives in their respective beds or kitchens, has referred to the other as friend; who, together and alone, has felt the wonder of this, the beginning of new friendship in a new country in middle age when it is no longer easy. Each has wanted to say, 'Bring the family over,' but there were always tight budgets, upset wives, sick kids, too few chairs.

Breathe. Jesus, I. Breathe. Will make. Breathe. Him.

20

It was loud, close; Henry bolt upright before her eyes opened.
She knew what it was, the only one thing it —. The curtains were
open — the room so high no-one could look in, so they left them
wide to see the stars — and the room now full of moonlight.
She knew she should spring up, get there while there was still a
chance. But her legs wouldn't. Beside her, Kit whispered, 'What
was that?' And those three words threw some switch. Henry felt
herself leap to the window in one fluid movement, as if she were
a girl again. She gripped the sill, looked down, saw only blocks
and lines of shadow, some silvery, some grey, some velvet black.
The moon-licked arms of the Hills hoist. The kids' makeshift
cubby against the base of the sheoaks all textured and luminous.
The squat, thick dark of that ramshackle shed behind, horrid
thing, nine sheets of corrugated iron, three walls and a roof, all
rusted and holed, sunlight piercing it in the day like tiny crazed
searchlights. Half a front to it, and no door. Just a black opening
at night. She stared.

'Henny?'

'It's … the window,' she whispered.

'What?'

'Sshh. The window. The latch is broken.'

'What? Turn on the light.'

'No.' She heard Kit fumble behind her. 'Don't! He'll see.' Then the click, and the room bright.

'Jesus!' Henry tugged the curtains closed, spun to face her. 'Why did you do that? I told you not to do that!'

Kit's face was flushed, her hair dishevelled. 'What the hell is going on?'

Henry put her face in her hands. 'Oh, God, God. It was the window. The broken latch.'

'What do you mean? What latch?'

'For pity's sake, are you deaf? What do you think I mean?'

Kit flung back the covers, swung her feet to the floor. 'I don't know! Why did it bang?'

Henry held out her arm. 'Stay there! Turn off the light. He'll see!'

Kit stared at her friend. Everything frightened Henry: driving in cars, a plant growing too close to a door, insects, swimming pools, the sea; she thought the worst would happen wherever she was. But Kit couldn't deny she had heard it. 'Henny, darling,' she said gently, 'why would anyone trying to get in a window bang the window shut?'

Henry gasped. 'The children!' And she was at the bedroom door, saying over her shoulder, 'Wait here, just in case.' And then she was only the quick, muffled thud of bare feet running.

Kit looked at the closed curtains. It made no sense. She parted them and slipped in behind, unclipped the flywire, felt for the window's handle. There was something flat and ridged, about half an inch wide. She ran her fingers along it. It was tied between the stub of the broken window handle and the hook on the window frame. She pushed at the glass and the window opened under the pressure of her hand, snapped back onto her finger. Ow. Christ. Elastic. The kind you put in a waistband. Who ties a broken window with that? She tucked her smarting finger under her arm, re-clipped the screen awkwardly with her clumsy other.

She looked out and up but the light in the room made the sky indistinct. She replayed her own question: 'Why would anyone trying to get in a window bang the window shut?' She looked down into the yard: from what she could see, the wind had died; nothing moved in the big rectangle of light on the grass directly below, her own silhouette looming hugely in it. She felt suddenly cold. How did he even get up here? Christ, Dan, she thought. Couldn't you have fixed the bloody window?

~

As she had run from one end of the house to the other, Henry had tried to think: she couldn't remember opening their windows. But she couldn't remember closing them either. She remembered tucking them in and she was usually careful — but that night — that day — maybe she had not been as careful, not a good mother, not herself.

There was the shadowy doorway to the laundry, the darker space of the toilet and bathroom beyond. She was the swish of her nightdress, a sound like breathing, the creak of the floor beneath her.

She pushed open the door. Their Danielle, Danny, Deebee — tomboy consolation when they had prayed so hard for a son, who they dressed in blue because she liked it and who's to say girls can't, who could pass as a boy. For now. Two single beds, a chest of drawers between, wide window above. A spare bed for when she made friends. Window closed, venetians open. Still she checked, poked her fingers through the slats, unclipped the screens, pushed the window latches down hard into their places. Had she really left the blinds open? She snapped them shut and turned. No-one stood behind the door. The wardrobe right where it belonged. Just in case, she opened it. Deebee stirred, turned over.

Orla's bed was beneath the window, along the wall and hard up against. She had insisted and they had thought what did it matter? But now. These blinds open, too. Surely she was old enough to close them herself?

Henry looked through them to the street but there was lawn and verge tree and the neighbouring houses, all moon-blue, a couple of yellow pools of street-light. She listened, heard her own breath and heart and the girl's deep sleep-breathing.

He wouldn't stand out there, would he, as bold as brass. He'd be gone. Or in a shadow like that shed, watching. She squinted into the dark of the shrubbery, beneath trees. He could be staring back at her now. Her skin prickled. She peered at the window latches. They were both closed firm. She reached across her daughter for the cord by the head of the bed, eased the blinds shut.

She didn't even stir, this strange daughter. After so many disappointments Henry had barely believed she was pregnant. Hadn't bought a thing. She wasn't as pretty as Henry had wished. Not vivacious, not funny. But at least she was clever. Did what she was told, not like the other, and they had always been thankful for that. But she howled over the smallest thing. She lacked — guts, she supposed it was. That word Australians used — vulgar, she disliked it — but useful in this case, accurate. Howled when she first laid eyes on the world and has barely stopped. Born missing something, Henry had long ago decided. Still, she'd learn; she'd have to. And bless her, no-one wanted any harm. She wasn't bad. Now there was no-one else to raise her. Now she was mother and father both, and suddenly she hated the very thought of it. How could you, Dan. How could you leave me alone like this.

Back in her own room, Henry smiled a little. 'They're fine.'

Kit jerked her chin towards the window behind her. 'And what about that?'

'I'll use something. Tie it firmly.'

'And the police?'

'Should I?'

'And shouldn't the owner fix it?'

'We meant to call but — you know. We've been so busy. The house and now —.' Henry looked at the floor. 'I'll get some rope.'

She clicked on the light. The laundry felt like a box: white ceiling, white walls, cold black cement floor. When they'd moved in, he had painted it black with the rest of the paint she had used in the other house. For a moment she saw it: the cloth in her hand, the blackening floor, Orla's feet; heard her frantic call: 'Mummy!' She felt a flush of heat. She hadn't been able to look at her. It wasn't supposed to have happened that way. The thing was just supposed to disappear: they were supposed to tell Orla she must have lost it, that no, no-one knew where it was but it would turn up again, not to worry. She hadn't ever imagined she'd be caught like that, be made to feel ashamed by her own child. How dare she stand there, looking at her that way. Everyone had agreed it had to be done: it was ruining her teeth and they didn't have money for orthodontists; besides, the girl was too old to be sucking her thumb. Why couldn't she just stay away, standing there like that, as if she had a right.

When Dan had put his feet up on the divan after painting the laundry floor, his soles were smeared and speckled black, and she had brought a rag and some spirit, spread newspaper, tried to rub them clean. He had laughed at her, pulled his feet away: 'If you're

Mary Magdalene, who does that make me?' And here was the cloth and the bottle of spirit in the cupboard under the laundry sink where she had left them. And kerosene for the heater, an open bottle of Reckitt's Blue, a plunger, an open packet of washing powder, a jar of nails, a hammer, an old pair of shorts, a piece of white sheet, a worn-out white business shirt. She picked it up. He should be doing this for her. She held the shirt to her face. This was not what she was supposed to do. The shirt didn't smell of him. It smelled of kerosene, Omo. Where was he now? Where had he gone, really? She pressed the shirt to her eyes. And where was rope? Damn it, don't men keep rope?

In the kitchen she rummaged through drawers: a paint chart; three old screwdrivers, varying sizes; a rusting adjustable spanner; an open tube of wood glue; some used sandpaper; a small block of wood. No rope, no string. In the laundry she took out his old shirt again, used her teeth to tear it into strips.

Kit listened — the kitchen drawer, the fabric ripping. She understood what that meant. But truly, who doesn't even have a ball of string? She had put on her dressing-gown and slippers, sat on the edge of the bed to think, rested her palms flat against the bottom sheet. It was warm. She pressed until she felt the springs. This was where he slept, where he had been every night she had thought of him. And she was here, at last, as she had always dreamed — but not with him. Everything was wrong. And then Henry was back with a fist full of cloth and a quivering chin. 'I had to rip up his old shirt.'

~

They sat up with the remains of his Johnny Walker Red. Henry's with soda water; Kit's neat. Just as he drinks it. Drank. At the cocktail party where Kit had first met him, she had seen him do a double take, heard him say she was the only woman he knew to drink it that way. She had wondered if there were admiration in his voice but, when she glanced at him again, he was already turning away.

Henry poured hefty slugs, topped hers with soda, gulped. Sometimes she put her head in her hands and wept; sometimes she fell silent. Kit sipped steadily, tried not to think again of where she was. Her stomach hurt. She wanted him back here. She had always wanted him. To herself. As it once had been, a long time ago, before. But she would have settled, happily, for him just to be back in his bed with his wife. And it wasn't that she resented being here — it was what people did — but she felt dizzy, wanted her single bed, her single thoughts. The way things had been for years.

She had changed the pillowslip — but still he was everywhere in here. A book — could it really be his? — open and facedown on his bedside table: *Live and Let Die*. His slippers on the floor by her feet. She could see their inner soles, worn away. And when she had put her head down to sleep she could still smell him.

~

Towards morning, Kit made coffee and they laughed, remembered the way, years ago, before Deebee, he had driven them all home from a work barbecue — Henry in front, Kit and Orla behind — the car weaving across the road, and the way he had patted Henry's hand when she grabbed at the wheel. How he had said, his accent thicker, "'Tis all right. 'Tis all right, darlin." Because he was a happy drunk, happier drunk than sober, because he never came home half-cut and shouted, never shouted at Henry, even when she was ashamed and scared, her hand dangerously on the wheel, glaring at him. They laughed and then cried at how lucky they were — to get home, to know him.

'What am I going to do?' Henry wailed. 'I'm all alone.'

Kit took a breath. 'You have the children.'

'Them?' Henry waved her cup about. Kit watched the coffee swing. 'They're no company.'

'But you have them.'

'It'd be better if I didn't.'

'For Christ's sake, Hen. They're your children. And his.'

'I'd be free.'

Kit looked into her drink. 'You don't know how lucky you are.'

'Lucky! Did you say lucky?'

'Oh, Henny, you know I didn't mean it like that.'

Henry looked hard at her friend. Her voice, when it came, was ice. 'Don't you dare. I chose marriage. You didn't.'

Kit stared into her cup. Her eyes stung. She swallowed. 'That's unfair, Hen. I've told you what it was like.'

Henry sipped, nodded slowly. 'Hm. So you say.'

Kit stared. 'What do you mean?'

Henry shrugged, swirled the coffee cautiously in her cup.

'I've told you what he did to me — remember?'

'I remember, but it doesn't change the truth of what I said: you chose not to be married. I didn't.' Henry held her cup to her lips.

'Don't you believe me?'

'Oh, Kit! What does it matter, believe or not believe? All I know is every marriage has its ups and downs.'

'It matters to me, Hen. Do you think I've lied to you, all this time?'

Henry placed her cup carefully on her bedside table. 'Of course.' And turned to look at her friend. Her heart beat in her throat.

Kit scanned Henry's face, her flushed cheeks, red-rimmed eyes. She looked away. 'I, I don't know how you can say that.

Henry held her trembling hands tightly in her lap. 'Really? Oh, come on, Kit, I think you do. I have eyes. And ears. I've seen the way you look at him, the way you speak to him. Spoke. To him.'

Kit shook her head. 'Hen, I —'

'Please. Don't. And don't "Hen" me.'

In the long silence, Kit opened her pack, slid out a cigarette, pushed the open pack across the bedspread to Henry. She clicked open her lighter, lit her cigarette, held it out for her friend. The flame shook.

Eventually, Henry spoke. 'You know, don't you,' she said, quietly, 'that whatever you had with my husband was of no importance at all.' She tapped her cigarette against the rim of the ashtray.

Kit's voice was steady. 'He wouldn't have said that.'

Henry smiled. 'Oh, Kit. Of course he did. How else would I know? Surely you realised, in all the years since, that you meant absolutely nothing?'

'No. He wouldn't have —'

'Oh, don't be pathetic! Do you think my husband — *my husband* — thought about you once when he was in bed with me?'

Kit smiled thinly. 'You don't know what he thought.'

'I think I know a hell of a lot more about my husband than you do.'

'No-one really knows what anyone else thinks.'

'Oh, bravo! Bravo! You're not just Kit the divorcee and adulterer; now you're Kit the philosopher, the psychoanalyst!'

Kit looked away, ground out her cigarette. 'It's late. I have to get up for work.' She rose unsteadily, turned off the light, stumbled back. In the bed she lay on her side for a long time, staring into the dark. Soon she could make out the closed and gleaming wardrobe doors like two strict faces glowering back at her.

~

Henry opened her eyes to the morning, her head pounding, and knew all over again that her husband was dead, that the day before she had buried him. As she rolled over, turned her back to her bedroom door, she wondered for a moment how the prowler knew. But she put her hands over her ears, let the memory of yesterday overtake her. 'Oh, God,' she said, 'Oh God, oh God, oh God, oh God, oh God.'

In the lounge room, Kit said, 'I have to go to work. Let's get you some cereal. You need to let your mother sleep. How about we put on the telly?'

~

When Henry opened her eyes again the curtains were softly aglow, the room filled with golden light. She thought this might be what heaven is like. She hoped so, that heaven took good people even if they were nonbelievers, that maybe she had died in the night and would turn over to find him in bed beside her, though she knew he would hate her thinking like that because there is no God and what about the children. Through the gap between the curtain and the wall she could see the brilliant day.

There were television sounds. She sat up carefully, pulled on her dressing-gown, shuffled out. Saturday morning. Cartoons with stupid voices. Orla on the divan, her legs pulled up alongside her just like her father. Henry stared. Deebee on the floor at her sister's feet. Both of them gazing at the screen, their mouths fixed open like doors. Then the older girl shifted her gaze, locked eyes with her mother, flicked her attention back to the screen, her expression unchanged, as if she'd looked at furniture. Henry turned away.

She filled the electric jug, plugged it in, listened to it buzz and growl. Its black plastic lid belched. She stared at it, muttered to herself: 'Of course. Of course. The funeral notice gave his address.' She switched the jug off at the wall, saw — for the first time? — fine cracks in the jug's green glaze. She couldn't take her eyes off them. So many, like a network of veins you catch sight of in a mirror. When things begin to wear out like that, when they begin to slowly die, what is that called? she wondered. Is there a name for that? She would ask Dan, she thought. He'd know. Before she remembered.

Ah, Henry. Soon you'll know. You'll ring the life insurance, I suppose, and they will tell you. I couldn't afford it anymore, you see, what with the horseriding, thought I'd just miss a payment or two, just till I could find a way, then catch it up but it didn't work out. Maybe I should have told you, true, but what could you have done about it? You were already working weekends, we were already tired every day. So, tell me, what would you have had me do? Tell her she couldn't go anymore, tell her to be brave, break her heart? She's a good girl, despite everything, never asked for much from us. And yes, I know the childhood longing at the sight and smell of horses. My father said no to me, so I had to say yes. But now I know why he said no; it was so expensive. How could we keep doing it? Then I thought: well, here's something we don't need, so that's what I did. Then thank the Lord, it was Monday morning at last and I was still alive and the contract has insurance, so … Ah, Henry-girl, I know you're angry, calling me all manner of names. Go ahead. I deserve it. I left you nothing. But I had a plan — we always have plans, don't we, mavourneen — it just didn't work out, again. Are we cursed, my love? In my coin pocket, there are twenty-one cents. In the car, my watch. On my desk, my typewriter to sell. The silver cigarette case you gave me. My cufflinks in the dressing table drawer.

She knew it was better to watch the TV; the way things are in cartoons was meant to be strange — funny, even — a bit like real life and not at all like it at the same time. But there's only so long you can feel someone stare at you before your eyes just move to look back, as if they're not really your eyes at all, as if they have their own mind or are someone else's, someone who has taken your face, who walks around on your legs and says things in your voice while you keep still and silent.

She heard the jug boil and her mother's slippers scuffing along the floor and the bathroom door close, which used to be against the rules, and she got up and walked straight to the door of her parents' room. The curtains were still closed, the room pale morning light. Her father's pillow was dented as if he had just got up. His slippers; his book, a thick paperback, open and facedown. From the doorway, she couldn't read its title. Cigarettes, full ashtray, two glasses, a bottle almost empty. No keys on the dressing table, no wallet, no lighter, no pile of coins, no watch. Where were his things? The room smelled different. Smoke but not his, and other smells she wasn't sure of.

She turned away, back past the table, through the kitchen, into the laundry. The shirt was still there, as she remembered. On a hanger. On a hook on the wall. Washed and ironed where her mother had left it for him. The way she did every night. Waiting for him. She leaned in and looked closely at its weave, remembered his body living in it, his arms moving, chest rising and falling as he breathed. She touched her finger to a cuff. It was stiff and cold.

At the bathroom door, she pressed up her ear. The running shower. She'd wait. When her mother opened the door. Before she had time to think. She would just blurt it out: why is Daddy's shirt there? She wouldn't ask about anything else: his missing things, the trip to the zoo. She had to be careful not to say too much. If she said too much her mother might guess what she was thinking. And then she might — no, she would — phone him to tell him, later, when she and Deebee were asleep, and they would change the plan. He would stay away longer, teach her a lesson for being nosey, a nosey parker.

And then, from behind the bathroom door, a sound she didn't recognise — and then did. She stepped back, staring: should she open it? The sounds of water went on and on. She stepped back and back until she was in the laundry again, beside the twin-tub and there was his starched shirt, white as a ghost, and there were doors every side — toilet and bathroom ahead, kitchen door behind, back door on her left, door to the passageway on her right and, beyond that, the two bedroom doors. All the doors waiting for her to. Do something. And outside the back door: the little landing, stairs twisting down. She opened it; outdoors came in: breeze, sun. She stepped onto the landing, closed it quietly behind her, stood holding the wobbly railing, not looking down, not listening, not.

Right in front of her eyes the garden was blooming, flowers like cups, bees blundering in, birds flitting. Beyond the jacaranda, the Chinese apple, its slim smooth trunk. No rough bark of marri and tuart in the hills. She knew she could climb the Chinese apple tree easily, sit on a limb and eat the dark pink fruits with their crisp white flesh, their juice, they way she had done when they first arrived here last summer, and now summer would be returning and nothing could stop it. She could smell it, the air dry, warmer than the last time she had stood here, a week ago, before. How fast things change, the light turning summer-white, the top of her head already feeling hot from the sun but she couldn't go back in and she couldn't go down the stairs, she could only hold the railing and listen to the sound coming clearly through the little bathroom window, leaping into the jacaranda and into the bees and into the limbs of the Chinese apple tree, slipping down the twisty stairs and over the shaded grass and into the sun again, winding up the Hills hoist and the lemon tree, and the rusty forty-four gallon drum, and all over the messy creeper, the back fence, squeezing in through all the tiny holes in the old tin shed and into the cubby, up the skinny trunks of sheoaks and between the slats of the treehouse, down over the grey pickets and into the yard where a man had once lived with his family and his truck, and among the tall pale eucalypts and among shaggy green grass, and on and on.

Close to her face, a bee, hovering, looked like the helicopters she'd seen on TV that lower themselves like whirlwinds, land bumpily, that soldiers run out of with guns. She didn't move. It buzzed away, descended, gripped the edge of a flower, climbed in. In the hills, she had walked over a carpet of jacaranda flowers when she got off the school bus. Sometimes there had been bees there too, fat and staggering, and now they had one of those trees in their yard and her father wasn't there, was he, to talk to, to ask, 'Can we plant one of these?' And him saying, 'When we build our own house.'

She squeezed the railing with her fingers. She just. She just wants. She just wants everything. To stop. Just. Stop. If she squeezes hard enough. When he comes home she will show him the tree and the tree will make him smile, say yes. Outside the back door. It will carpet their November ground each year. She will help him dig the hole, a big one, big enough for everything.

Kit will bring cuttings wrapped in wet newspaper, the way she had done wherever they had lived. Orla's father will remind her of their names: hibiscus, frangipani, gardenia, carnation. She will repeat the words to herself, bit by bit, their syllables. She will watch for his car in their driveway at five o'clock. Run outside. Follow him around to see what had grown. Just as they had always done.

Behind her the back door opened, and Deebee's voice: 'Where's Mummy?' Orla pushed her back inside, followed her in, shut the door, and Deebee yelled and Orla dragged her into the kitchen by the wrist. Deebee punched her. 'I want to go outside!'

Orla said, 'Let's go out the front.' And Deebee leaned into her, bounced against her belly as Orla shunted her along. Deebee giggled. Then Orla stepped aside suddenly and Deebee fell, as Orla knew she would, fell to the floor and cried. And Orla pulled her to her feet, roughly, said, 'Do you want to go outside or what?'

Deebee twisted away. 'Leave me alone!'

The sound of the door an instant before the 'I'm fed up!' Her mother clutching her robe to her chest, her nose and eyes red from tears. Wet hair stuck to her cheeks. She glared at Orla. 'I'm sick of you!'

'Sorry, I —'

'Can't I even have a shower in peace?'

Deebee wailed. 'She hurt me!'

Their mother lurched. Orla grabbed Deebee's arm, stumbled back, her mother yelling: 'Get out!' Orla dragged her sister across the lounge room, Deebee's feet slipping. Their mother slammed the front door behind them.

They stood, staring at the closed door, arms limp. Orla reached for Deebee's hand again but her sister pulled away, wailed, ' I said leave me alone!' as Orla turned to look at her.

Later, when she thought about it, Orla couldn't remember a sound: no squeak of the door, no shuffle of feet. Just the suddenness of being grabbed by her hair, hauled back through the front door, shaken. Her mother's voice close to her ear, high-pitched. Her mother's fist yanking her hair on: 'How — many — times — do — I — have — to — tell — you! Leave — her — alone!' Her mother's hand releasing. 'Now get out of my sight!' Her mother's hands in her back, shoving her along the passageway, her stumble-running, glancing back, into her room, slamming the door, leaning hard against it. In case.

~

Banksias twisted long, serrated leaves above; their orange-red lantern-flowers peered down at her. Which, she knew, was wrong. A noise, and she opened her eyes, was looking into the expanse of her shag pile carpet, which stretched out in front of her like a miniature purple forest.

She sat up, wiped at her face with her sleeves. That noise again, her window, and there was her sister's hand waving on the other side of the glass. Orla unlatched it, opened it wide; the air smelled warm and good and she stretched her lips into a smile, touched the back of her head. Even her hair hurt. 'Where's Mum?'

Deebee shrugged. Orla stared: for someone so little she could make a very serious face.

'Does it hurt?' Deebee asked.

She shook her head — 'Nup' — grinned, folded back the flyscreen and climbed through. Behind her, the screen flipped back into its ordinary shape. It didn't really matter; her mother wouldn't come looking. She touched her hair again. Dark strands came away in her fingers. She shook them off. 'Where do you want to go, then?'

Deebee grinned widely. 'Follow me, Orly!' and broke into a run. Orla grinned and ran, too. The air smelled like happiness.

Out of sight of home, they paused, caught their breath. Orla studied the houses as they strolled on, hearing people — voices, laughter — but seeing no-one. Her eyes were hot in their sockets. She cooled them with her fingertips, felt them aching and tight in the bone of her skull.

At the edge of the oval, she sat in shade while Deebee raced to the slide; Orla looked back the way they'd come. Although she couldn't see them, she could picture, beyond their house, the three hills that rose from the end of their street. One was just a long easy slope, rising south; she'd never had reason to go that way. The second, to the east, was short and steep. Boys rode their go-carts down it for dares. The third was a dead end to the north, one that began gently but became suddenly sharp before it reached the old church at the top. She often walked to and from school that way. It was longer but the other way — this way, across the oval where they were now — was direct and wide-open and there was something about its wide-openness she didn't like. She preferred to stand a moment at the church and look west, over the adjacent vacant block, over the wide green of this oval, over the stretch of red rooves, all the way to the sea-blue horizon. The vacant block was nothing but pale sand and weeds, some tall as a man. Nevertheless she would stand perfectly still and stare down into it, waiting for a glimpse of a scurrying, foraging creature. Something wild. Something. That never came.

Now, sitting in the shade at the oval's edge, she thought her mother was right to be sick of her. It was all her fault. The terms had always been firm: if God took one parent, it had to be her. Orla had watched long enough to see that mostly it was their father who stood between them and their mother, long enough to know very clearly how things would be if he wasn't there. It was wrong, she knew, even to think of it. But that had never stopped her and didn't mean it wasn't true. Keeping it silent, though, had made no difference; she had got what she deserved — because she was bad, because He sees everything, knows everyone's hearts. And so he had died instead, because of her. To punish her for what had been in hers. Punish them all. And Deebee — what was in her heart?

She stood, brushed off twigs and leaves and bits of grass: 'Let's go.'

Deebee climbed the slide again. 'I don't want to.'

Orla climbed up after her. Deebee slid away, turning back to look up at Orla peering down. Deebee looked even smaller way down there. Orla pulled her mouth into the shape of a smile. 'I'll make you a jam sandwich.'

They walked the long way home, past houses they didn't know, the noon light turning white and hot between the shade of the verge trees. Orla lifted her sister onto her back, glancing sideways at cars and porches, the whirr of fans, talk from TVs. Dogs barked and rushed at them. Deebee clung tight. Orla's heart banged. Male voices growled the dogs back. From dim interiors, men's arms appeared, their hands large and edged with dirt, opening latches of flyscreen doors to let their slinking pets back in.

A carport door shuddered up and a man in overalls, a cigarette tight between his lips, wiped his hands with a rag. Orla met his gaze. He narrowed his eyes, took a long drag and watched her. Orla flushed. She slid her sister from her back, took her hand, tugged her along, tried not to hear her complaints, looked straight ahead. Two houses along, she glanced back but the man was gone. The next corner came into view, the last street they needed to take them home.

A sudden voice behind: 'Hi, Orla!'

Derek was waving from a front lawn; he was smiling. She raised her arm quickly, turned her back on him, kept walking.

'Who's that?' Deebee asked.

'No-one. Come on.'

Deebee looked over her shoulder at the still-smiling Derek. 'I'm thirsty,' she whined.

'Come on,' Orla hissed.

Quietly, they crossed their front porch. The TV was off. Orla opened the wire door. It creaked. She peered in, ushered Deebee into the kitchen. They tiptoed back to the divan with bread and jam, and water, and sat together. She stared at the blank TV screen with all its reflections: the bright window, its venetian blinds, the face of the house across the street, the shimmering poplars. She supposed they were in the picture, too, but she reasoned that, if she kept as still as she could, she wouldn't catch sight of herself. Near its edges, in its corners, in all its dimmest places, the blank screen was the deep green of fairytale forests, of penguin pools.

~

After midnight Henry woke, suddenly alert. The porch light was on, just as she had left it for him that last night and every night since, just as she had done every night he was out. 'So you'll return, like a moth,' she used to tease. It poured yellow through the front door glass, filled the house sufficient for her to make her way.

She stepped close to the children to be sure. They breathed and murmured. She smoothed their blankets, was returning to her room when she saw it. How could she not, the silhouette clear in the front door. Her heart leapt, thudded. For a moment she thought — and yet at the same time she knew it wasn't. Not his hair, his build. But he stood so close, closer than if he were about to knock. He raised his hands to the sides of his face, rested their edges on the glass, cupped his eyes to peer through the glass. She froze, held her breath.

She backed up to the phone, picked up the receiver. The click and whirr of connection, so loud she worried he would hear it. She picked up its body with her other hand, held it to her, crept further back, still watching him. The telephone cord snaked black across the floor. She dialled. Her finger shook. The sound of the dial rattling its way back crashed about the room.

'Police,' she whispered. Then, 'Please send someone, there's a prowler outside.'

'Your name, please, madam. And your address.'

She spelled the name of her street for him. 'Please send someone quickly.'

'What makes you think you have a prowler, madam?' He sounded bored.

The silhouette, hands to either side of its face, pushed itself up against the glass. 'I c-can see him,' she whispered.

'You can see him.' A pause. 'And what does he look like, please, madam?'

'I — I don't know. He's, he's about six feet; his hair is dark. I can't see his face. The glass is frosted. But he's here; he's looking in.'

'You can see him but you can't. The glass is frosted.' She thought she heard laughter.

'I'm looking at him. Please! I'm here alone with my children.'

'Is your husband not at home, madam?'

'He —' She pressed her lips together. She would not sob; she wouldn't. 'I'm a — no, he isn't.'

'Ah.' A silence. 'I see, madam.'

What? What did he see? 'Please send someone now.'

Gently, she replaced the receiver, sat on the floor, her legs drawn up against her chest, the telephone beside her, and watched until her body cooled in her thin night gown. She shivered. She watched him move away, heard his footsteps on the porch, under the windows. Then she stood, shivering, listened to him circle the house. She turned her head this way and that to follow him, waiting, waiting for the police car.

When it was light enough, she went from room to room, peered out through the blinds. The morning was pale and delicate, empty.

23

Mid-step, pain grabs him and he's surprised by its strength, though he knows he shouldn't be, the way he has been feeling. After that it's quite straightforward.

He opens his mouth. He hears his own gasp, and then his breath leaving. It's like being a boy. Like being at school. Like being punched. Right in the midriff. His legs go and he pitches, twists, hits the ground hip and shoulder and left cheek first. In his head, stars flash; dirt and pebbles in his face; the tang of blood.

It hurts. More, much more than he had imagined. He gasps, can't get. For a moment, part of him relieved: at last it has, this old familiar, the one he had dodged too many times, seen take others, faces, torsos, limbs he had never stopped seeing: men he knew and men he didn't. Bombs, machine guns, hand grenades, knives. But not him. Not him because he had been somewhere else, been on leave, been early, been late. So he had had years more. Twenty years. A wife, children, one migration, another. Each further from a past he had heard other Irish call home. Not him, though. Never. He was never sure what they meant.

He is looking up. At trees. Beyond them. Night sky bends, twinkles. Oh God, Ma. It's lovely, can you see it? For a moment more he knows his science. So many suns. So far away.

He could have been. He could have been anything. All those worlds out there.

24

It wasn't that she didn't expect it. Because she couldn't drive, because it was sitting in the carport, gleaming, still with its new car smell. But when the phone rang she wasn't sure what to say.

They came in another company car, shiny and new, the two of them: the boss and his secretary. They knocked. She let them in, offered them coffee. They were polite, declined. She understood. The funeral was over. This was work. They referred to it as a company asset. They had to replace him, they said, and so would need it. She looked back at them. She wanted to say how could they. How could they replace him. She wanted to ask are men just their jobs. She wanted to say she had no home of her own, no money, no insurance policy. She wanted to say she could learn to drive.

She gave them the key, closed the front door, went to her room, closed that door, too.

She heard it anyway. Its motor. Its wheels on the gravel. That used to mean something.

~

When Deebee was playing in her room it almost always meant noise but, for a while, there had been silence. Orla had lifted her head from reading once or twice, listened into the space of it, wondered. Then — had she imagined it? There it was again, murmured words, a laugh, her sister's, through the bedroom wall. Orla closed her book, stood.

On *Get Smart*, people listen at walls and hear all kinds of things. But all she heard when she pressed up her ear was the rumble of her blood, her body.

Deebee's door ajar. She leaned quietly against the jamb. There was a long pause, then: 'But they smell.' Orla leaned closer. Then came giggling: 'I know.'

She tapped gently on the door. 'Deebee?' Her voice light, sweet. Again, silence. She pushed it open a little more. Her sister was sitting on her bed, scowling.

Orla looked around. 'Who were you talking to?' She smiled.

Deebee frowned harder.

Orla shrugged. 'I heard you talking.'

'No, you didn't,' Deebee replied, eyes fierce.

'I heard you.' In the long silence, her heart pounded. She crossed her arms over her chest to keep it in. She made a smile again. 'Tell me. Please,' she said.

Deebee turned her back. 'Go away.'

~

Orla came to a halt in the laundry, where everything was still. She stared at the washing machine, silent, motionless. At its wringer, its thick rollers where you feed everything to get it squeezed flat. Above the sink, the louvres were closed, their glass fleshy — opaque, dimpled. A line of light flared from the gap around the closed door. In a swift movement, she reached for her father's shirt, flicking the top buttons back through their holes. It slipped off the hanger and into her hand with a sound like paper. It was so loud as she put it on. The cold of the collar at her nape made her shudder.

She stood inside it while it warmed on her. In her room she looked for a while at herself in her mirror. It covered her knees. Her hands had been swallowed. She couldn't imagine ever being big enough.

25

Mr Featherstone peered at the woman and child approaching him, stepped back from his office door to allow them to enter. Henry smiled brightly, thought this man was younger than she had expected, pleasing dark suit, jacket buttoned, smooth white business shirt like the one in her laundry, a thin, dark tie. She saw at once his solicitor's face — not unkind, intelligent, accustomed to listening and concentration. When she had settled Deebee in a chair beside her, she looked up. He met her gaze across his desk.

She began by reiterating what she had already told his secretary over the phone, the simple story: her husband had recently gone to work and died. He interrupted her with a quiet condolence. She nodded, glanced down her hands. Such a small thing to be thrown by, a single, well-practised sentence, murmured.

He looked at the little girl whose solemn face stared back at him. 'Tell me everything that happened,' he said to the woman. So she began again.

'... And I could see how ill he was. Anyone could have. I told him not to go. But —.' She looked at the solicitor imploringly. 'He said he had to. He was in charge of it.'

'It was his duty.'

'Yes,' she answered. 'Yes, he has a — had a — strong sense ... He served. In the Middle East. We met there.'

Mr Featherstone nodded. 'You say the night work began on the Friday night. Did his company give him that Friday off, during the day? In order to rest?'

She looked at him. 'No.'

'Did his company know of his domestic circumstances?'

She frowned.

'What I mean is,' he continued, 'did they know he was married with young children? Did they know you worked weekends?'

'Oh, yes.'

'How do you know they knew?'

'Because I told them. At a work do. We all know one another, from Christmas parties and things.'

'You accompanied your husband to these parties?'

'Of course. Wives were always included.'

'You spoke to the other wives?'

Her brow creased. 'Of course. And to their husbands. I don't mind who I talk to. I like to chatter, Mr Featherstone.' She smiled.

He straightened his papers. He thought he knew this kind of woman. 'Did you speak to your husband's boss? What about to the owner of the firm?'

'Oh, yes. Many times. To them all, and to their wives. Our children all played together.'

'Your children played together?'

'Of course. At the Christmas parties I mentioned. The company throws one every year. A big picnic or barbecue. Their children are a bit older than ours but you know what I mean. Our children were —'

Deebee's voice, light and clear. 'Santa came.'

Henry turned her face to the office window where light shimmered, to the wide Swan River and the cloudless sky. Finally she spoke, to the view, her voice small, flat: 'Yes. Santa gave them presents.'

On the bus home, she sat with her bag on her lap and gazed out the window past Deebee: clouds, trees, buildings, snatches of horizon. She had never sat in a lawyer's office before and she wondered if any of the passengers around her now could guess where she had been — that spacious office, grand desk, beautiful view. She thought about what she had told him: their last meal, his grey face, the way he had stroked her hair. That she had looked up at him when he did that, surprised, and smiled a little, despite herself, despite her irritation: he never listened to her, always did just what he wanted to do. She thought of the last Christmas party. It had been very hot, there had been so little time till Christmas Day and she still had so much she needed to do. At first she had tried to get out of attending — but she couldn't bear the disappointment on the children's faces. So she had gone with bad grace.

In Mr Featherstone's office she had realised there would be no more Christmas parties, no more Santa with his belly and his bulging sack of toys, no more calling out the children's names one by one. Now she wondered, fleetingly — but doubted — might they still be invited. Certainly not if, as Mr Featherstone had advised, she went ahead with this. She remembered how quickly they had come to take the car, how politely they had shaken her hand at the graveside, told her how sorry they were for her loss, how sorry they were that they couldn't stay for a drink, how they knew she would understand that they must return to the business, their gazes sliding past her.

Somehow she had crossed a boundary she had never known existed, her children with her, and all three now found themselves somewhere that looked the same but wasn't. There were others like them — the woman next door and her brood, for one — but, although no-one ever said it, everyone knew that a family wasn't a proper family if it didn't have a man. She knew this feeling only too well from her own childhood, and here it had come round again: all the world's widows and deserted wives and their fatherless children pressing their faces up against the glass, looking in at the picnics and barbecues, the games of cricket, country drives, beachside holidays.

She glanced around. Other passengers, mostly women like her, middle-aged, alone, stared ahead. Younger ones with babies asleep or fretting in their arms, toddlers who knelt on the seats and stared, open-mouthed, at one another. A few men reading newspapers. No-one looked back at her.

No, she thought, they won't be invited to the Christmas parties. Although it would be the kind and decent thing to do — and, as far as she had been able to tell all these years, the company was full of kind and decent men and their kind and decent wives — having her and her children there among them without a man, even only once a year, would be a reminder, impossible. They knew she worked weekends. They knew there were children at home. They hadn't even given him the Friday off. She hadn't really thought of it before Mr Featherstone asked. Not really. Not like that, a whole thought, all at once. She felt very tired. Her children's names would disappear from the Christmas present list. She knew that. As if they had never been there. Court case or no court case.

26

If someone had asked Orla, she might have been able to say it was not school she was scared of. Not exactly. It was more the not-school, the cracks she hadn't before known existed, gaps that rose up suddenly from — from where? Beneath? Roaring as if about to swallow her, coming when she was thinking about something else, numbers or spelling, drawing, reading. The ground tilting and opening, her body teetering with memory, everything turning white and breathless. It was not like being slapped. That sharp pain he'd given her in her leg and heart. His arm around her. This was everywhere like electricity, like the coyote sticking his finger in a socket in a cartoon, a jolt, every electrified part of her hurting: arms, legs, belly, eyes. Her mouth, chest, feet. She'd think, pleaseGodpleaseohpleaseGodpleaseoh.

All night she would doze and stir, sometimes waking with the image of a figure up ahead, walking away from her, and she calling out, trying to catch up to him. But what was she calling? Waking to the silence of the night house breathing. Or waking in the morning with memory of shadow shapes in her room, with a moment of puzzlement and calm before remembering slammed through, slammed through her so hard she'd clutch her belly, turn on her side, draw up her knees, wait till she could breathe again. And when she could she'd get up, walk the long way, through the lounge room to the kitchen, looking — for his cigarettes, his bunch of keys, his work shoes — sniffing for the scent of his hair oil.

Things she knew, familiar, reliable things — sleep, food, the ground beneath — had changed. At breakfast she stared at her boiled white-shelled egg in its cup, at the shell's faint fissures, and she feared the day ahead, feared that, in front of everyone, the world would yaw, that she'd forget where she was, what she was doing, and that everyone would see her teeter, fall, see her head crack open the way she cracked open her egg, see her brains run out thin and yellow, see that they weren't really much at all and neither was she, that in truth she was back at home, silent, motionless, standing against a wall or in a wall or maybe she was a wall, and her mother was walking past her, not seeing her, her mother was walking past to answer a knock, her mother holding a red tea towel, wiping her hands on a red tea towel, her mother walking by with a red tea towel in her fist. And looking from the wall through the dimply glass of their front door, she'd see him. And she'd see her mother see him. And she'd run, stumble, her mother, herself; and her hands and her mother's would tremble at the lock because because because he didn't have his keys, of course of course he didn't. And her chest would squeeze till she couldn't breathe and she'd close her eyes, pleaseGodpleaseoh, and when she'd open them she would be back in her seat, at her desk, looking at the teacher or the blackboard or out the window at the sports shed and the oval, the tall trees, the sky.

~

She had gone back to school on the Monday. In the first hour, everything continued as it always had, and then the teacher paused the class before the recess bell, handed Orla a white envelope. She opened it to a card with a blue flower on its front and blue writing: 'Thinking of you at this sad time.' Everyone had written their names inside it in two long neat columns down the left side, even the visiting teacher she hadn't even known had been there. On the right: 'To Orla Blest'. She stared at the three words, at the small, cramped handwriting and felt a sudden flush of anger at the girl at the next desk, the one whose face she could see in her peripheral vision, watching closely. All in a rush, Orla knew just how it had been: her teacher telling the class the news, the sounds they'd have made, looking at one another, the same sounds the adults who had come to their house had made, the card passed around for everyone to sign. And then the question: 'Who is Orla's friend?' And it would have been Heather, only Heather, who put up her hand, proud this was at last a question she could answer. Everyone would have turned to look. How could they know about the hills, about Orla's real friends, about her going back next year to the smell of eucalypts, to the logs she had climbed with those other girls, the songs they had sung, standing in a row up there as on a stage. How could they know that this school, this classroom, this close-to-the-sea place, was a distraction, a fill-in. All they knew was that Heather, with her wrong answers and watery eyes, was her friend, her only friend, the only one who could raise her hand when the teacher asked.

'Thank you,' she whispered and closed the card, slipped it into her desk. The squeak and rustle of chairs and paper, and she was glad no-one said anymore. She didn't look up.

At the bell, she wandered outside alone. The same girls played the same games in the same places: elastics, skippy, chasey, knucklebones. She watched them. They didn't notice her. She looked at the hands that grabbed and pushed, hair that bounced and flicked and shone, the faces that turned, shouted, laughed; at boys who ran everywhere, their thin arms and legs, who kicked footballs, the deep, loud thud of them. Who wrestled. Before, she and Heather had sometimes walked to the far side of the oval, lain on their backs under the karri trees, peered up through the branches at slow-moving clouds, the shade and sun moving over them, all the schoolyard noise far away, the wind lively in the highest, shimmering leaves. Now, even the thought of lying under those trees was impossible because it wasn't possible, was it, that everything continued: leaves, sky, wind, sun. That kids went home to fathers. That the sky was only sky. That everything she knew was a lie. And where was God and the bargain she'd struck. She wanted to see God's face, and for Him to see hers, far below on Earth, looking up, looking. Now that she knew how small she was, and how bad.

But still, her mother had been right. It was better to be at school than at home. There was order, tasks, people. Even though it was the wrong school, wrong home. At her desk she held her head in her hands, concentrated, didn't listen to kids who whispered and nudged each other. She worked as much as she could, and when those electric shocks of memory, those cracks, came she held herself rigid, waited for her heart to quieten, for the world to right itself. At the home-time bell, she packed away her things, picked up rubbish, cleaned the board, the dusters. Because it was better to be there with her teacher, Mr Woodland, who seemed to like her, who smiled and said: 'Thank you, Orla. See you tomorrow.' Better to be there than at home, just as her mother had said it would be.

And then outside and everyone gone. Just the sun and breeze, the bag over her shoulder, the walk. Past the locked-up church, watching the toes of her shoes, step and step, avoiding cracks in the pavement and road because everyone knows they break your mother's back and then what would happen to them.

~

The first hint of summer came with its even brighter light. Her legs stuck to her chair, her hair to her neck. Mr Woodland plugged in the standard fan. It turned its big face this way and that, and it felt lovely for the moments it looked at her. And on Thursday afternoon he walked between the rows, handing out strips of lined paper for mental arithmetic, stood at the front and called out the twenty questions. Sometimes Orla saw Heather looking and she covered her work with her hand the way teachers had always told them.

She wrote the nineteenth answer. Sweat pooled and trickled. She pressed her body against the inside of her clothes, jiggled her sweating feet inside her sandals, waited for the final question. Mr Woodland turned to the class. 'Write seven in Roman numerals.' So she wrote the question number, the answer, her name at the top, gave Heather a glancing smile as they swapped papers. She knew she had answered everything correctly, and when she did this her mother was happy, and when she was happy, she was kind. And when she was kind, Orla knew her mother loved her.

Mr Woodland called out the answers. Each time Orla marked an answer on Heather's paper, she remembered what she had written on her own. At question nineteen, she glanced across the narrow aisle at her paper, smiled at its column of ticks. Out of the corner of her eye she saw Heather glance her way, pencil poised. Mr Woodland called out the last answer: vii. Orla drew another cross on Heather's paper, counted the ticks and wrote the score, held the paper out for Heather to take, quickly took her own from between Heather's fingers. She saw the look on Heather's face, the not-quite-smiling, as she turned back to her desk and her answers. In a glance she took in the column of ticks and the cross at the bottom. She blinked. She knew what she had written. She looked hard at the answer: viii.

Her mouth fell open. She stared at the four small marks in HB pencil, at the last wobbly 'i' on a different slant. She turned to Heather, who was holding up the lid of her desk with one hand, rummaging beneath it with the other and smiling. Smiling, it seemed, at something in her desk.

The teacher walked along the rows, collecting the tests. Orla looked again at the viii. Mr Woodland stopped in front of her desk, held out his hand. A sentence formed on Orla's tongue. The siren went. She looked up at him, her chest hurting, heard her own voice speak the words in her mind, the way they would sound. She lifted her paper. How could anyone believe her, that someone would do this? The paper felt so light in her waiting hand. She would have to point at the tiny 'i', the way it wavers, its angle. He took the test paper from her fingers, smiling. When she looked around again, Heather had gone.

Orla had to concentrate to keep to the path. Her legs dangled and jerked and were too far apart. She watched the ground in front of her, concentrated on each step, kept seeing the viii and the cross beside it and 19/20 and Heather's fingers around the edge of the lid of her desk as she held it up. Heather's smile.

The lounge room was dim and cool. Her mother was at the kitchen bench, stringing beans. Their curls piled on a sheet of newspaper like bits of sewing thread. Henry's eyes watched what her hands were doing. She had long fingers, large nails, the kind of hands Orla wanted. Henry said, 'Hello, darling,' without looking up, offered a cheek for Orla to kiss. The girl filled a glass at the sink, looked out the kitchen window, past the loud, purple jacaranda and the Chinese apple tree. It was such a pretty day. She realised she no longer had to raise herself onto her toes to see the ocean.

When she lay on her bed, she lifted her legs into place one at a time as if they were new and strange, as if she didn't know what might happen to them. Her bones, suddenly longer, older, might start to break and never stop breaking, and all of her might turn to dust.

27

One day, Henry said, 'Just popping across the road. You stay here. Won't be long.'

Deebee stood behind the closed front door and shouted, banged her fist on the glass. Orla swooped, picked her up, heaved her onto the divan. The two of them knelt, watching through the window.

'Why is she going there?' Deebee whined, but Orla said nothing, just shrugged, frowned — because she thought she knew, had overheard her mother say something to Kit about work, about someone to take care of Deebee during the day. Orla had imagined it would be Kit because Kit didn't work weekends when Henry worked. But now, watching her mother cross the road, that didn't make sense.

Henry walked fast; she didn't look back. She heard her daughter's shouts, her banging on the door. She just looked down at her feet, her white trouser-legs flashing bright as scissors, swishswishswishswish. She climbed the front steps and knocked. The door opened; she smiled, spoke; she stepped in, disappeared.

'Mummy, come back!' Deebee wailed.

'It's all right,' Orla said, wiping her sister's face. 'She'll be back in a minute.' She smiled, sang the first few notes of her school song.

Deebee shouted louder: 'Mummy!'

Orla gathered her up, carried her around the house, singing louder and louder, through the kitchen, laundry, into the bedrooms and out again. Deebee shouted, arched her back; Orla leaned against the walls, doorframes for support: 'Deebee! What's wrong with you? Stop it!'

Deebee twisted, stretched her arms towards the front door, the street. 'Mummy,' she sobbed. 'Mummy.'

~

It was always cool in the sandpit. Sometimes leaves fluttered down, small and glossy, from the shady trees. Shadow shifted over the sand with the breeze. From where she sat, Deebee could see gaps of brilliant light between the fence palings, slashes of the deep green lawn next door. She buried her toy car, pressed the cool sand over it, patted it flat then dug it up, ran it up pickets, let it fall, watched it twist in the air and bounce. There was a sound like the flap of a bird's wing that made her press up her eye to one of those gaps.

She had seen the old lady before, folding clothes at the washing line next door and she was there again, her back turned, this time pegging up a shirt. She bent slowly, took another from the basket, held it along its bottom edge and flicked it, one, two, three times, that wing-billow sound, then pegged it up beside the other. Shirts hung upside down like kids on monkey bars, but quiet, still. Deebee stared at them, their long dripping arms.

The lady's hair was a white bun on her head. When she reached down, bits of it hung down, too. When she reached up again, they stuck out around her neck and ears, more and more of them each time, all like little wings, till her head was puffy as a dandelion.

The lady tipped the basket upside down, took a small step towards her house, then stopped. She turned to the fence, frowning a little. Deebee watched her, blinked, kept very still, and the lady stood still, too, looking at the fence with her fluffy head. Then she smiled right at Deebee. 'Why, hello, there.'

Deebee blinked. The lady's face was even wrinklier when she smiled.

'What's your name?'

'Deebee.'

The lady moved to the fence, bent down so her face was close. Below it, Deebee saw her slippers, her thick stockings, the edge of her petticoat under her skirt. 'Well, Deebee,' she whispered, 'have you been watching me?'

'No.'

She laughed. Her eyes were shiny blue. 'Do you like cake?'

'Yes.'

'Come around to the front and I'll fetch you some.'

And so there was running, running because the gate on that side of the house was all tied up with creepers, and though she pushed as hard as she could it wouldn't budge so she ran around to the other side, running under her parents' bedroom window, not looking up, not wanting to see if her mother was up there looking down because if she was she would say no, and there won't be cake. Running up the shadowed side of the house, through the dark, smelly carport where the car should be, fast past the veranda, fast across the front lawn, as fast as the roadrunner because Orly stared out windows and she might tell Mummy or she might want the cake.

In the middle of the old lady's front yard, Deebee stopped. The lawn was neat and thick and green. The house bricks were red, the awnings striped. A shiny red path led to shiny red steps and a shiny red porch. The white front door opened. The old lady stepped out. There were roses on her apron. She smiled. Deebee climbed the steps one at a time, and the lady closed the door behind them both.

In the kitchen Deebee blinked. The floor shone like a green apple. The table shone, too. The lady carried a chair to the kitchen bench and lifted Deebee onto it. She stood so close, Deebee could smell her talcum powder. She set out three plates and a glass, two saucers with cups, and told Deebee how she had made the cake. There were things Deebee knew — eggs, milk, butter, a wooden spoon — and things she didn't — flour, vanilla, baking powder. Deebee watched her pull a yellow tin along the bench towards them as she spoke. It made a big sound. The lady's fingers gripped the edge of the lid and tugged. The rings on her fingers glinted yellow, white. There were lumps on her knuckles; one finger, fatter than the others and on a strange angle. When the lid came off, the cake smell went up Deebee's nose and into her belly. The lady took a knife from a drawer and pointed it at the cake's middle. She pushed it in. She did that three more times, lifted each piece onto a plate. Yellow crumbs fell.

There was cold white milk. The lady put the kettle on the stove. Her teapot was covered in flowers. She told Deebee to sit in front of a plate at the table. She said, 'Do you need a fork?' Deebee shook her head, didn't look up from the crumbly delicious.

There was a noise behind. An old man came in. He was bent over. He looked at Deebee and smiled, took off his hat, put it on the bench. He smelled like the warm outside. He said: 'And who do we have here?' and sat at the table with them.

The lady said, 'This is Deebee, Dad, from next door.'

Deebee looked at Dad. Dad said, 'She makes a good cake, doesn't she, little mate?' and ruffled her hair.

The lady wiped Deebee's mouth and fingers with a cloth. 'I suppose you should go home. Your mummy might be worried.'

She wrapped three more pieces of cake in paper and gave it to Deebee. Deebee climbed slowly down the front steps. From the porch, the lady said, 'I hope you'll come to visit again.'

Deebee looked up at her. She was rubbing the edge of her apron with her thumb. She had a nice smile. Deebee said, 'Do any children live in your house?'

The lady just looked at her for a moment, then: 'Maybe you could bring your sister next time.'

Deebee looked down, at the lady's slippers, furry brown with pink and yellow flowers and a little brown bow; she looked at her thick brown stockings and at the thick green edge of the lawn, the bright row of flowers alongside, the white paper parcel sweating and crackling in her hands. There was a thing she knew she shouldn't say: that she didn't want to bring anyone else. She looked up at the lady who was smiling again, one hand smoothing her hair into place. Her eyes were sad.

28

When Henry slapped her hand down on the kitchen bench, Orla flinched, a hot jolt running through. But when she looked she saw her mother was smiling, lifting her hand to reveal a newly minted key. She said: 'I found a job.' Orla blinked. She thought her mother already had a job. On weekends. That she would go back to it, that Kit would —

Now, there was a list:

Morning —

Zip the key into the pocket of school bag.

Afternoon —

Walk straight home, no stopping.

Go across the road to Mrs Thompson's house.

Knock on Mrs Thompson's door; thank her politely.

Hold Deebee's hand and cross the road carefully.

Close the front door behind you.

Don't open it to anyone, no matter what.

Make a snack but never:

    cook

    use the kettle or

    hot water or

    a sharp knife

and never turn on

the heater

the iron

the washing machine.

And the most important thing:

Don't go outside.

~

The first afternoon Mrs Thompson opened her door, Orla was surprised at how young she was and how pretty. Deebee peeped out from behind her and, in the kitchen beyond, Orla could see the two Thompson kids staring, mouths open. Orla gave her sister a little wave and smile, and Mrs Thompson smiled too, turned to get her but Deebee was pushing through the gap, gripping Orla's hand, pulling her down the steps.

'Thank you,' Orla said over her shoulder and heard the door close behind them. She shook her hand loose from Deebee's, said, 'Mum told me to be polite to her. It's on my list. How can I when you're pulling me?'

Deebee didn't look at her. 'I want to go home.'

'Where else do you think we're going, stupid?'

She took the key from her bag, jiggled it in the lock. She took it out, put it back in, tried again. Deebee watched her. Orla's insides squeezed. She took the key out again, examined it.

'Is it the wrong one?' Deebee asked.

Orla shook her head. Sometimes it was better not to say anything. She slid it back in slowly, tried to turn it one way, then the other. She held it in her hand, stared at it. Deebee said, 'Are you sure it's the right one, Orly?'

She didn't look at her sister. Still she could see her worried face. She turned away, studied the key's sharp, shiny edge. Her heart pounded.

'Are you sure, Orly?'

'Yes,' she said, between her teeth.

'Then why can't you open it?'

'Shut up, all right?' She pushed the key in and twisted hard. Her eyes stung. She heard Deebee sniffle and glanced at her. 'Sorry,' she croaked.

'I'm going to tell Mummy you said that.'

Orla looked around. The list. This wasn't supposed. There was nothing about. Her mother hadn't said.

She stared across the street. 'I think we should tell Mrs Thompson.' Deebee backed away. Orla grabbed at her. 'Come on. Just till Mum gets home. I'll be there, too.'

Deebee wailed.

Orla tugged at her. 'Come on.'

'You all right, love?'

Orla spun around. The fat next-door neighbour with the pretty face, even prettier than Mrs Thompson's, stood in her driveway on the other side of the low dividing fence. For a moment Orla remembered the man, the truck, the chimney. She blinked. The woman carried a pale, chubby baby on her hip. A little girl with golden hair stood close by, staring at Deebee. A few steps away, a boy in shorts, no shirt, no shoes, was holding a stick and watching steadily.

'I — the — the key won't work.' Orla heard her voice wobble.

In three strides the woman was over the fence. She held out her hand for the key. Orla and Deebee stepped back. The boy with the stick and the golden-haired girl tried to climb the low fence, too, then ran down their driveway and up the other side. Suddenly the porch was crowded. The boy whacked his stick against one of the metal veranda poles, over and over. Ping! Ping! 'Aw!' he grinned. 'Hear that!'

Orla looked at Deebee. She was looking at the boy. Orla turned to the neighbour still struggling with the door. There was a gold bracelet on the neighbour's wrist and it jerked about as she tried the lock. The baby on her hip had twisted her head around to stare at Orla in a way that reminded Orla of an owl. She widened her eyes at the baby and grinned.

'Come on, you bugger,' the woman said, jiggling the key again. Orla's skin stung: you bugger. She studied the side of the woman's face. She didn't dare look at Deebee.

'Well,' the woman said, handing back the key, 'youse two'll have to come to my place till your mum gets home. Come on.' She strode back over the fence. The little golden-haired girl hung back, still staring. Orla hesitated. She gave the girl a thin smile and shot her sister a look but Deebee was already following the boy with the stick down the driveway and up the other side. At her front porch, the woman turned her head a little, spoke loudly over her shoulder as she opened the screen door. 'I'm Cora, by the way. What are youse two called?' And, grinning, she held the door open and stood back to let them all in.

～

Orla sniffed. Cora's house was tidy. It shone. But it had a funny smell. Cora told Steele to leave that bloody stick out in the yard, and when she put baby Whitney in the high chair, Whitney cried. Orla took her school bag with her to the toilet. She eyed the pile of wet nappies on the laundry floor. She locked the toilet door and sat longer than she needed, elbows on knees, chin resting in the cup of her hands. On her way back to the kitchen, she saw Deebee follow Steele into a room along the passageway. The little golden-haired girl, Bettie, went in there, too, but soon was back, crying. Orla couldn't understand a word Bettie said but Cora leaned out the kitchen doorway: 'You little bugger, Steele! You leave her alone!'

From the space between the fridge and the kitchen door, Orla watched Cora open a packet of biscuits. Cora smiled and winked, gave one to Whit, saying, 'This'll shut her up', then put the open packet on the edge of the bench. Bettie reached for it. Cora said, 'One at a time,' but Bettie grabbed a fistful and ran. Cora said, 'Oi! Come back here, you!' Then, quietly, 'Little bugger,' as she filled the jug, flicked it on. She took a teapot from a cupboard. 'Get the milk out, will ya, please, love?' she said, so Orla opened the fridge door. There were eggs, butter, a block of Kraft cheese, bottles of milk, red cordial, tomato sauce, and a bloody parcel in butcher's paper. Something orange in the crisper.

Steele ran in, Deebee behind, her face shining. Steele put his hands on his hips and said, 'Where are my biscuits?' Cora held out the packet to him. He took three. She said, 'One at a bloody time,' but he was already gone. Deebee took one and looked at Cora. She shook the packet at her and smiled, so she took two more and ran after Steele.

Cora swirled hot water in the pot, tipped it into the sink, then made the tea, covered it with a knitted cosy. She took out four plastic cups and half-filled them with milk. 'Drinks!' she shouted, and Steele and Bettie and Deebee came running, stood in the kitchen, gulping, took more biscuits, ran out again. Cora poured two big cups of tea with lots of milk and two heaped sugars.

'Sit down. You make the place look untidy,' she said, nodding at the table under the window. Orla sat in the nearest chair. Beside her, Whit spat out biscuit in a thick, brown stream. Orla looked away, through the window and over the fence. There was the side of her house. She had never seen it from here. There was the window above their telephone table; and there, behind the pickets, she knew, was the strip of long, cold grass that ran from the back of the carport to the sheoaks, that bit of yard that was always shaded.

Cora pulled up a chair alongside Whit and sat. 'Phew', she said, smiling.

Orla looked at her quickly and smiled, too, and then looked down at her tea. She wondered if Cora could tell how much she wanted to be home. She looked up again. 'Nice tea,' she said, just like a grown-up would. 'Thanks.'

Cora swiped at Whit's mouth with a wet, grey cloth. Whit screwed up her face, turned away. 'Keep still,' Cora said, gripping Whit's cheeks in one hand and swiping again. Whit cried some more. Cora dropped the cloth on the table. 'Dirty little buggers, aren't they, kids?'

Orla grinned and nodded, took a sip, glanced at Whit, her cheeks shiny, her open, wailing mouth, mashed-up biscuit on her tongue and teeth, her glistening eyes looking from her mother to Orla. Cora took a sip of tea. She lifted a cup of milk to Whit's mouth. 'Here,' she said. While Whit drank, Cora looked at Orla and said, 'That's all right, love. Glad you like it.'

~

Henry was cross and then she was something else and then cross again. There was no note, and how was she to know something terrible hadn't happened? She had bashed on Cora's front door and Cora had said, 'Who the bloody hell's this?' as she got up to answer. Orla heard her mother's voice and stood as Henry came into the kitchen, eyes wide, looking at Orla, saying what happened, why aren't you, and Deebee running, throwing her arms around her mother's legs and hugging for a long time, everyone speaking. Whit crying, waving her arms. Steele tearing up and down the passageway, Bettie following him, getting knocked down, shrieking. At the front door, Orla turned back to wave, felt her mother hook her tightly around her shoulders and squeeze till it hurt. Then the front door closed and their mother walked them, wobbling, down Cora's drive, one child squeezed tight against each side of her, and they were almost falling over, saying, 'What are you doing, Mum? Stop it,' and she wouldn't let go until they were standing outside their own door and she had to so she could get her key, and she just kept saying don't you ever, ever do that to me again, do you hear me? Don't ever, her voice all weird.

The next morning, their mother came into the kitchen all dressed up, and Deebee started to cry. Henry wiped her face and kissed her but nothing could stop it. Orla said, 'Can we go to Cora's after school?' and glanced at her sister.

Henry said, 'Oh. I don't know. I don't think so. Do you really want to?'

Deebee nodded.

'Oh. All right. I'll ask her,' Henry shrugged. 'And I'll get another key cut at lunchtime so tomorrow everything will be the way we planned.'

Orla knew Deebee would start to cry again when she was taken back to Mrs Thompson's. At first she could think about nothing else, stepping carefully along the footpath to avoid all those cracks that would break her mother.

~

So, days later, after school started to feel normal: Mrs Thompson's door, crossing the road with Deebee, holding her breath as she turned the new key that worked — because surely God had heard her by now, looked down at her face, because surely her parents had punished her enough and her dad would come home, just come home — and there was jam sandwiches, milk, turning on the TV. Then, one afternoon when she knew Deebee was settled with cartoons, there was going to her father's desk, sliding open the drawer.

Typing paper; carbon paper; pencil; eraser. Her fingers scrabbling. Because it must be there, hidden, scrunched up. Where else would it? She had seen it, over his shoulder and it was important — like his James Bond book, his ironed shirt. She read books, too: whatever happens to them, people leave clues. They turn their head and growl 'Get out'; they hit you from behind; they let policemen into the house in the night, then wail; they change your answer; they smile under the lid of their desk. They go to work and they don't come back. Everywhere there are cracks in the world that other people can't see.

And now there was nothing but the bottom of the drawer, its smooth timber, nothing but more space ahead of her hand, and then more. She pushed her wrist in further, her forearm, elbow, till her shoulder was jammed against the frame. She sweated, frowned, pulled herself out again, rubbed the red marks on her arm, stepped back, staring at it. It looked so normal, but everything did so what. She tried her other hand, its different magic, its awkwardness. Only smooth wood and space as far as she could reach. No end to it.

So both arms in, head turned, cheek pressed hard against paper that stuck and slipped, creased, loud in her ear. Dust in her throat. A cough. Fingers deep into emptiness. On the balls of her feet because maybe she could get an extra inch and the desk rocked, groaned, teetered. She pushed. It was impossible, of course, all of this. And then it fell. And she fell with it, her arms trapped. Her shoulder wrenched. Heavy on her chest and her feet slid and she was on her side, her back, her head thudded and and and it was all was all and how how could how could she breathe with this this this.

White ceiling, light fitting dead centre, two bulbs deep inside and staring, her sister beside her with her own round eyes and her mouth opening, saying, 'What are you doing to Daddy's desk?' And she understood but she couldn't speak and what could she say anyway when she didn't know where the writing had gone or what kind of thing this desk really was. So she frowned at her sister's inverted face, opened and closed her mouth like a fish, squirmed herself free, over onto her hands and knees, stood slowly, straightened. She stood in the empty space beside her sister, gaped at the four stiff legs sticking up, the pale underbelly, its shocking upside down, the drawer out and in its right shape, the bits of stationery. When she lifted it, it was lighter than she thought it should be and that made sense, didn't it, with all that emptiness in it. She rubbed her legs where they hurt, picked up the sheets of paper one by one, crouched beside her sister, looked her straight in the eye. 'Don't tell Mum, promise?'

And, as nobody mentioned the bruises, they weren't really there.

29

The thing with chickens is hierarchy.

He and Henry had always settled their children at dusk, hatchlings safe in their nests, and he had liked this mirror between work and home: the subordinate chickens roost earliest, the dominant last. And of all the things he could think of in these last moments, he thinks of this.

My mouth is dirt and blood. Someone hits and hits my chest, says something, urgent, and — and I can't see and can't speak but I know where I am, know the voice shouting, and that this is his track to his house, not mine.

I smell damp earth and chicken dirt, and there is no contract, no contract yet. And little Deebee not yet in school. Another year, there'd be a home with painted walls, a garden, the babies helping the way I helped my Da. What difference would it make to the world. One more year to make things right.

30

Even the tea trembled. Orla watched it in the cups, tried not to watch Cora's hips swinging under her sky-blue dress. Cora's feet stamped, and Orla felt the buzz through the floor, the chair, and in the backs of her legs. She lifted up her cup, sipped. Her lips fizzed with the tiny tremors. She drew the cup to her chest as if it were chattering from cold. Inside her chest felt like wings caught there.

Cora wore only skirts or dresses. She didn't seem to mind showing her dimply knees, fat calves, cracked heels. Orla's mother said heels cracked if you didn't wear shoes, but Cora wore thongs and cork wedges and strappy, backless sandals. Pain shot up Orla's legs when she looked at Cora's heels but she looked at them anyway, couldn't help herself, cracks in places where there shouldn't. It felt like staring at someone's tongue, the pink wet of it when they laughed. She hoped Cora might talk about the cracks one day the way she talked about a lot of things. But she didn't; and Orla wondered then if it was because Cora had seen her looking, and she felt suddenly a shame for them both.

When she had helped Cora hang nappies on the Hills hoist, Cora had said, 'Well, I've had my tubes tied.' And Orla had nodded gravely, as if she understood, handed her another peg. But cracks — and tubes, too, whatever they were — didn't matter when Cora danced in her kitchen in her sky-blue, or when she wore her stripy sundress with the bow under the bust to go into town. When she did that, even Orla knew no-one would be looking at Cora's feet.

She held her cup, watched Cora dance, felt the bee buzz around her heart. Then Cora lifted her foot, slipped off her sandal and waved it, saying, 'Come here, you little bugger! Just you wait!' and stomped after her son who was laughing halfway up the hall. Orla heard the front door open, imagined him on tiptoes, his small nimble fingers at it. She heard Cora's footsteps click-thump click-thump. 'Come here, I said!'

The wire door crashed open, Steele's feet drummed the veranda boards, tatata. Cora slammed the wooden door shut, click-thumped her way back. She leaned against the kitchen doorjamb, put her shoe back on. 'That'll teach him,' she said to the floor.

She turned up the radio and grinned so wide Orla saw black teeth in the back of her mouth. 'Listen to this!' Cora yelled, and danced again, her skirt flapping, her body wobbling, sunlight shuddering in her hair. Orla wished she were a woman with golden hair and her own home, a sunny table under her kitchen window. Cora closed her eyes, lifted her face and opened her arms, still grinning, and Orla looked down again at the shivering cups. She looked at Whit sitting by Cora's feet, gazing up at her, and Bettie who wiggled her bum, her face aglow, watching her mother as if she were an angel, no cracks or tubes or rotten teeth. Cora dancing made everything dance, even the tea in their cups and the bee's wings in Orla's heart.

Why, then, did she want to cry? She turned to the window. There was nobody there, just the fence and the side of her house, but if someone had been standing there, looking up at her, she knew they would love only Cora because, compared to Cora and even to Bettie still in nappies, she was just a piece of wood. A shy, shivery piece of wood. A smiling piece of skinny, pointy, sticking-out wood. Who won't dance even when tiny girls dance. Who stares through windows as if the street weren't empty, as if there were much more interesting things going on out there. Who picks up teacups to stop them spilling. Who has a something trapped and frantic in her.

Then, out there, in the driveway, she saw Steele, his head bowed, perhaps watching his toes as he walked. He looked even smaller than he really was, and when he looked up, she saw his cheeks were wet, his nose snotty. She turned to Cora, opened her mouth. He must have been banging on the door. The music was loud, too loud to hear him. Cora's eyes were closed, her arms still wide, her hips still swinging. Orla looked back to Steele. He stared up at the window, looked straight at her, his mouth open in a sound she couldn't hear.

The song became another song. Cora squealed, turned it up even louder. Bettie jumped up and down: 'Dis one! Dis one!' Orla replaced her cup, swivelled in her chair to turn her back to the window, and stared at Bettie's open mouth, at Cora's swaying skirt, at Whit's wide eyes, at the light in all their golden hair.

Later, while her mother was preparing dinner, Orla stood in front of her mirror, moved her hips the way Cora did. She had to frown hard to forget Steele's face. She remembered that, when Cora wasn't around, Orla's mother would roll her eyes at the mention of Whit. She'd say, 'Whit. Hah. That's a laugh.' And Orla would pull her mouth into the shape of a smile because she didn't know how to say that Whit was a just baby with a chubby white face and round blue eyes and a pink dummy stuck in her mouth.

Orla shut her bedroom door, watched herself dance in her wardrobe mirror. She shut her eyes, too, the way Cora did, and she danced and danced as if someone watching would love her.

~

When she turned the new key in the door each weekday afternoon, it only took a moment. Insert, lift slightly, turn to the
left. The lock would give, the door would swing and there it all
was again: the empty room, silent house. Deebee would push
in ahead of her and run — to her room, the kitchen, the toilet.
More than once she said she hated Mrs Thompson's toilet. Orla
didn't know what to say. She knew what Deebee meant; she
didn't like other people's toilets, either. But then she thought
about the toilets at school, and something fell away in her as
it had when she had seen her mother cross the street in her
flashing white slacks and disappear into the Thompsons' house,
and she hadn't been able to say anymore. Deebee had all that
open space in her, space that didn't know about teachers and
playgrounds and cheating and fights. That didn't know the mess
of school toilets, the pushing, the smell. She wished she still had
that space in herself.

It was just a moment each weekday afternoon: turn the key,
pray. Push the door, pray. Step in, pray. The clean air. The
silence. The second step in. His radio dumb on the mantelpiece.
Empty ashtray. Stillness, stillness. Take the key from the lock,
zip it back in its place, close the door. Remember that Cora is
just next door with a different scent, and cups of tea, and songs,
songs. Breathe. Breathe. Push it down. The cracks in the world.
The wings that beat.

31

Henry liked the walk through the city, the feeling of people going somewhere. She liked to look smart and smell sweet; she liked the department store windows she passed, and having her own desk, chair, phone. She liked clearly designated hours, tasks that finished; she liked having to take breaks, and adult conversation. She liked the orderliness of the office and the thought that she had colleagues. She didn't mind having to sometimes work late — the extra money was welcome and she'd call home quickly to tell Orla — but she worried even more those evenings on the later bus home, as the night drew in.

Still, when she was at work and she thought about home her throat would tighten. Several times a day she told herself they all had her office number — the school, Mrs Thompson, Cora. Sometimes she held a document, stared at it, but saw something else — a pile of laundry; Deebee crying; Dan lowering a newspaper he was reading to look at her.

'Henry?' She looked up from her desk. Her boss's secretary peered around the door. 'He wants to see you,' she smiled.

He got up, gestured for her to sit, closed his office door. 'I'm wondering,' he said, as he sat again, 'how you are settling in.'

Henry felt a jolt of alarm. She met his gaze. 'Is there something wrong with my work?'

He blinked. 'No! No — I'm sorry. No. Your work is excellent. I'm just wondering if you're happy here.'

She smiled. 'I'm very happy. Thank you.'

'Good.' He paused. 'And how you are coping, how are your children? It mustn't be … easy.'

She glanced at his hands resting on his desk. She liked his tie. 'Life isn't easy, is it. But —' She shrugged.

'No.' He cleared his throat.

She smiled brightly, said, 'You know how children are. They forget about things.'

He nodded. 'Mmm.' He opened and closed his hand. 'I was also wondering …' She looked at him. 'Perhaps you would like to have a drink sometime? Or, or a cup of coffee?'

She felt her mouth open a little in surprise. She smiled, met his gaze. 'Coffee would be lovely.'

~

On the evening bus, it was always good to sit, rest her legs, think her own uninterrupted thoughts. A cup of coffee, then. A surprise. She slipped her wedding ring around on her finger. A cup of coffee is just a cup of coffee.

Beyond the window, day was ending. She wished: if only Deebee wouldn't cry. As soon as she picked up her bag and keys it would begin, and be well away by the time she ushered the girl out the door, as they crossed the road, climbed the Thompsons' front steps, continue even as she shushed her, said it would be all right, all right, kissed her short brown hair, reminded her to be good. And behind her it grew louder as she descended the steps, as the Thompsons' door shut, as she walked back along the Thompsons' path to the road, her bag gripped tight, staring straight ahead, seeing nothing but her daughter's face. At first she had thought Deebee would get used to it, maybe even come to enjoy having children to play with. She used to be the happy one. It used to be Orla who cried. But weeks had become months, and still.

She alighted into half-dark and steady rain, walked briskly, the wind tugging her umbrella. Her heels clicked on the rain-slicked path. Rain dampened her skirt, her stockings and shoes. She shivered.

Rounding the corner into her street, a sound. She hadn't noticed anyone else get off the bus — but the weather, her hurrying. She glanced back: a dark shape, a man in a jacket, a briefcase in hand, collar turned up. She picked up pace, opened her bag, retrieved her key. She heard his footsteps faster and she broke into a run, could see her letterbox, her front yard, her porch light. Bless the girl for putting it on. She glanced over her shoulder again; he was jogging, along the grass verge so she couldn't hear him. She ran. Why hadn't he run faster, gained on her? She veered across her own verge. Her heels stabbed the grass. She was nearly at the path that ran down the slope of grass to her porch, her door. And her path shone red and slick. She shot a look behind. He was loping across the verge, still then yards from her. She stretched her arm out in front, her key gripped. Her heart battered. She dropped her open umbrella; it spun over the porch. She slid the key and turned it, burst through, whirled about, expecting him right there, pushing his way in. Instead, she saw him on the edge of the porch but turning away. All she really saw was his back: his shaggy wet hair, his swaggering stride as he strolled back up the path — her path — and onto the verge, disappearing into the rainy gathering dark. She watched, agape, then said loudly, 'I will recognise your walk.'

She closed the door, leaned against it, catching her breath, her eyes stinging, not yet facing her children who had shifted their gaze from the TV to her.

'Oh!' she said into the doorframe. 'What weather! I had to run from the bus!' She turned to them, smiling, smiling, smoothing her hair.

32

If Orla went to Cora's twice in one weekend, her mother would say, 'You spend more time there than you do with your own family.' And Orla would feel her cheeks flush, not being able to say what she wanted to say. So, if Saturday came and things were going well — if her mother wasn't angry, if Deebee wasn't annoying — Orla would hold off visiting Cora till Sunday. But if Saturday was bad, she would make an excuse, wander outside, step over the fence. Later, when her mother would ask her where she had been and why she hadn't sought permission, Orla would say she had been in the garden, Cora had invited her in for a cuppa, that she didn't think her mother would mind — she didn't mind, did she? — she had never minded before. And her mother would fall silent, give her a look.

It was always better not to ask first. If she did, she'd have to take Deebee, worry about her sister repeating words like bloody and bugger. But sometimes Henry seemed to see inside Orla's head, would say, 'You're not planning to go to Cora's now, are you?', and Deebee would start pleading. Orla would look hard at her mother then: 'Please, Mum, do I have to?' But her mother would say: 'Don't even start, missy.'

As always, Cora sang along to the radio as she made tea, put biscuits on a plate. Facing one another across the table, the sun through the window between them bouncing, dazzling. Cora slipped on her sunnies and grinned. Her kids played and fought, and now and then she'd swipe them, and Deebee would stand to one side, silent and watchful when she did that. Sometimes Steele yanked down his sisters' nappies and laughed and ran away while they bawled. Deebee would laugh, too, chasing him. Sometimes Steele pulled down his pants, jiggled his penis and ran, tugging his clothing back up, and Cora stomped after him, yelling he was a dirty little bugger. She returned, muttering, 'It's enough to make you go mental.' The first time she saw Steele do this, Orla laughed like a drain, as Cora would say, at the pale little thing she had never seen before. But the second time, Deebee did it too, wiggling her hips, her white mound on show, and Orla stood, cheeks aflame, yanked up her sister's shorts and took her home. Outside, Deebee whined. 'You laughed when Steele did it.'

'Steele's a boy.'

Deebee put her hands on her hips. 'But you laughed, Orly.'

'Shut up,' she hissed.

'I'm going to tell on you.'

Orla leaned in close to Deebee's face, squeezed her shoulders till she winced, whispered. 'Just shut up or I'll tell her what you did.'

Some days, nobody fought or bawled or pulled down pants.

~

One Saturday, Orla knocked on Cora's door and Cora called, 'You can't come over. Mum and Dad'll be here in a sec.' And a car pulled up in the drive, and Orla took her sister's hand, made her way back to the fence. A short round woman with a face nothing like Cora's got out of the passenger side and stood watching them. Orla looked back at the unsmiling face. She looked down to Cora's garden hose coiled near the woman's feet, remembered suddenly the man, truck, shouting, the car that came and went, this car, then looked up again. She tightened her grip on Deebee's hand, made her best smile: 'Hello.'

The woman stared. She looked like an apple: red hair, pink shirt, beige shorts and sandals. Her breasts and belly protruded. Her mouth a straight pink line; her limbs sun-freckled.

Behind her stood a tall man with lots of dark glossy hair. Orla looked at him hopefully; he smiled. It was easy to see where Cora got her looks. Orla glanced back to the woman, whose blue eyes were hard, unblinking, then turned away, ushered her sister over the fence.

In their own lounge room, Orla knelt on the divan and watched through the window. She knew Cora's parents lived close by, past the end of their street, at the top of the short, steep, daredevil hill. One day she would walk up that hill just to see. It wouldn't be hard to find their car. Cora had said they had a boat and a caravan and steep steps leading up to their front porch. Orla imagined she would stand on their verge, gaze up at their windows. She knew there would a wonderful view, had been to the top of that hill in her father's car, had glimpsed the miles and miles — the whole of the suburb and the whole of the next and the white sand dunes, the big sea. Yes, she'd climb to the top of their steps and stand on their porch, looking at the wide blue ocean, and imagine what it would be like to have a house, a car, a caravan, a boat, and see whether Cora's parents could look down on Cora's front yard and her own — the poplar trees in the day, the porch light at night. But now, with her knees on the divan, watching Cora through the window with her glossy father and apple mother, she felt a hollow in her middle, in the place where sadness lives.

Orla watched Cora stare at the ground, prod it with her toe; she watched Cora's mother's bottom lip move up and down and up, and Cora's father fold his arms as he stood behind his wife, his face turned away. He looked across Cora's front yard, beyond

Cora's house — to what? The house on the other side? Orla knew that the apple-woman hated her. She must have seen at a glance what Orla had done, her terrible unspoken wish, that she was bad, a bad, bad girl. Fear tightened her chest. Could only some mothers see?

She watched for a long time: Cora's prodding toe, the mother's mouth, the father's arms, his averted gaze. She could tell how Cora felt; it was all over her. And if she could see so clearly into Cora, she reasoned, others could see into her. The wind ruffled Cora's father's thick, shiny hair. The hairs on his arms glinted orange in the sun. She stared hard at Cora, at her tight mouth, her flushed cheeks. She sent a message to Cora. She flew it through the air: change your wish, she told her; change, change it.

Whenever a ventriloquist appeared on TV, Deebee hid. Their mother would say, 'There's nothing to be scared of; it's just a silly doll.' And Orla knew her mother was wrong. Silly wasn't the word for the way its mouth moved. Orla didn't hide when she saw the dummy because she knew how the trick worked. It wasn't the doll she needed to watch.

What could Cora's mother be saying all this time? And what on Earth was her father looking at, his arms crossed over his chest, as if he had nothing to do with it? Poor Cora. And then she thought about her own mother — always at work or in the laundry or kitchen; the remains of her lipstick in the corners of her mouth, her clutch bag under her arm, her keys in her hand, her pale, tired face.

Behind her, the floor creaked. Startled, Orla turned.

Her mother leaned her elbows on the back of the divan, rested her chin in her hand, peered out. 'It's none of your concern what goes on out there,' and gently shoved Orla's shoulder. 'You'd best wipe that nosey nose of yours.'

Orla smiled back at her mother smiling at her; her mother had always said that: nosey; nosey parker. When people are outdoors, she'd say, they look around to see who might be looking back, so wipe that nose. And although Orla smiled, she knew it was easy to look at others: as long as she kept quiet, they didn't have a clue.

In her room, on her rocking horse, she stretched her legs out on either side; it creaked beneath her. She locked her fingers in its mane and rocked a little, listened to it complain, remembered Nugget who'd never complained — had she been too heavy for her, as well? — thought about the ginger cat she sometimes saw on her way home from school, stretched out in its front yard in the sun. She called it, 'Puss, puss, puss,' and it trotted to her, miaowing against her legs. She had whispered to it, stroked it; it had rolled onto its back, offered its soft white belly to her. After several encounters, she had gathered her courage: 'Mum, can we please get a cat?' A cat, she had reasoned, was not as bad as a horse.

'Don't you think I have enough to do?' her mother had replied, to which Orla could think of no answer.

If it wasn't for that ginger cat, Orla thought, the rocking horse creaking beneath her, she would have hated Cora's ginger mother as much as Cora's ginger mother hated her. Cora's mother didn't purr, smile, say hello — even when Orla smiled, which is the same as calling, 'Puss, puss,' isn't it. Even kids know that.

~

Cora's house was back-to-front, the bedrooms at the front, then the bathroom, kitchen, laundry. She had identical rickety stairs from her back door down to what she called the undercroft, where she kept her twin-tub washing machine covered with a plastic sheet. Her proper laundry was full of nappies soaking in buckets or in wet piles on the floor or dry in baskets to fold and put away. But there was no man's shirt on the wall.

The lounge room was the last room of the house, its rear wall all windows. From there, Orla could look ahead into the high branches of the backyard eucalypts, the same trees she looked into from her treehouse. Kookaburras swooped, perched, their eyes bright, scanning. In the hills she had watched them hunt, diving and reappearing, reptiles wriggling in their beaks. Here, she only saw them jerk those big beaks open to laugh; they shook with it. In the late afternoons, the tree trunks flushed pink, orange. Dusk gathered them up, a handful of slender bruises: mauve, indigo, charcoal. Then swallowed them.

On wash days, Cora taught Orla how to fill up the twin-tub from the hose, how much Cold Power to add, how to turn on the machine. After a while she'd do it herself: turn the dial to 'off', yank all the wet clothes out of the washer, slop them into the narrow spinner, press down the lid so all the water came out, run the garden hose in there to rinse, repeat; she'd stuff the next load into the same wash water, turn the dial to start again; pull out the spun clothes and peg them so that they dried quicker, smoother, because Cora hated ironing and didn't everyone? Then she'd sit with Cora for a while in the sun, and Cora would wonder about whether to open a tin of spaghetti or of macaroni cheese for tea, and talk about her cousin Sally who, so her parents had told her, had some man trouble and was coming to stay but she wasn't sure when.

On wash days, Steele and Deebee whipped the walls of Cora's house with green twigs, threw honky nuts skyward. They fell on Bettie's head and she cried, or on their own heads and then one would cry and the other laugh; and Steele punched Bettie and she cried again; he poured sand on Whit and it got in her eyes. And Cora had to take off her shoe so much that she slapped her knees with her hands and said, 'Right! That's it!' and grabbed the hose and squirted the sand off Whit so she gasped and cried even louder. And then Orla would say, 'We better go,' but Cora wouldn't hear because she was wrapping Whit in a towel that had dried stiff on the line and cuddling her and blowing raspberries on her neck, saying, 'Who's my beautiful baby girl?'

At home Orla's mother sometimes said, 'What was all the noise about?' and Orla replied, 'Oh, that was just Whit,' and her mother rolled her eyes. And one day she looked at Orla and said, 'Poor Cora. She's very unfortunate.' But Orla was thinking about Steele, about what it was she didn't like about him, about how she was mean, a mean, bad, nasty girl because he was only four and who can hate a four-year-old? But sometimes she couldn't bear even to look at him.

Her mother stared at her: 'Did you hear me?' And Orla nodded. She had heard; she just didn't need her mother's ideas right now, not when she was worrying about Steele being four and hateful. She had heard her mother but knew she was wrong again; Cora wasn't unfortunate, she was lucky. She had her father, even though her mother was hard and sharp as an apple could be. She had a father with beautiful hair and a car, a boat and a caravan. She had a home of her own. She was in charge of it. Had Henry forgotten about what happened in the chimney — before the police, the zoo, the key that didn't work?

Orla had wanted to ask Cora about the man and that day, but she hadn't. Perhaps because Cora never asked Orla about her father, though Orla wouldn't have minded if she did. Nobody ever asked about him. Not at school, not at home, not anywhere. But if she ever did talk to Cora about her father, it would only be fair to let Cora talk about her husband, too, and, apart from wondering what had happened to make the noise come down the chimney, Orla wasn't sure she wanted to hear about him. Whenever she thought of him, she saw his bandy-legged walk, the way he had stroked his hair when he saw her that day he was working on the engine, the way he had winked when he smiled at her. She was pretty sure Cora was lucky that he had gone.

Orla had overheard her mother telling Kit that he was living with a woman up north. At school, Orla had looked in the atlas. There was a lot of world up north. Maybe Cora missed him like Orla missed her father. If she did, she never let on. And they were adults, Cora, Henry, Kit. She was a kid. And they must know what's best: not talk about things, pretend everything's normal, and that way it would be.

Before sleep, Orla lay on her side, looked at the line of books on her shelf, remembered her father carrying the furniture into her room, the shape of his back as it bent and straightened. Everything hurt when she thought of him but how could she not? And sometimes she thought she was forgetting his face. Already. Light from the lounge room fell in shapes on her floor. In the surrounding shadows, she could still tell the identity of her books from their size and the shapes of their spines: *My Friend Flicka*, *Thunderhead* and *Black Beauty*, *What Katy Did* and *What Katy Did at School*, an *Oxford Dictionary*, *Noddy*, *Treasure Island*, *Robinson Crusoe*, *The Swiss Family Robinson*, *Alice's Adventures in Wonderland* and *Through the Looking Glass*, *The Mystery of the Missing Man*. She thought about spines: book spines, people's spines, the sleek red spines of *Richards Topical Encyclopaedia* on the shelf in the dining room, and how sometimes, when she was reading, she disappeared into the story as if all spines were the same, and didn't even know it until a voice or noise and she was shocked separate and back into the world, blinking and queasy, as if despite appearances the world was not really solid at all, and the things that made it — houses, cars, trucks, bodies and clothes, beds, bookshelves and all the things adults say — are a big trick. She wondered if anything in the world was ever as it seemed, if there was anything that didn't crack or lie or shiver. Maybe people just agree on the solid world so they can stand in it and not fall down.

Before sleep there were things she tried not to think about: Heather and the viii; the galloping hooves; the chimney; the smell of horse; her father's smile; her fipel. Again and again she pushed them away, remembered instead Cora's shiny kitchen benches; the sun through her window; a kookaburra's eyes, its open, laughing beak; Cora's eyes closed in her dancing face. She listened to the TV, imagined her mother sitting in front of it, alone, and Cora alone, and Kit, as if that's what happens to women, eventually, even the pretty ones.

She remembered the way she had run from her bed in their other house, run from the monster wall behind her, the monster she knew would devour her if she dared to face it. She'd run breathless, heart battering, crouched in the cold hall, and her mother had heard her and turned: 'Come here, darling. What's the matter?' and let her curl up between her parents as they watched TV. Her mother was different then, in the night, after she and her sister had gone to bed. Softer, later tucking her in gently, telling her there were no monsters, that a wall is just a wall and doesn't have a life. And Orla believed her, felt loved and special. But she kept her back turned to it as her mother left and as, warmed, exhausted, she plummeted to sleep.

That night was a long time ago. Her eyes filled. She closed them. Tears leaked out. There were other things she tried not to think about, too, but that came anyway: whether they would ever have a car to go to the beach or the drive-in; move back to the hills; whether she would ever have a horse, grow bandy-legged; whether her mother would buy a twin-tub so she could show her how to use it; her mother's face when she asked Orla what she did at Cora's all the time, and whether her mother believed her reply: 'Oh, you know, have cups of tea.' Which wasn't really a lie but how her mother looked away then and shrugged, said: 'You could have a cup of tea with me.' Which wasn't true. Her mother didn't drink tea.

Orla got up, crept to the laundry, slipped the shirt from the hanger again. She stood in the shadowy space of her room. She pulled the shirt over her head, her arms sliding into its sleeves. She hugged it to her body, whispered, 'Dear God, I'll do anything you want if you just send Daddy back.' She caught sight of her image, ghost-like, in her mirror, climbed into bed. She said it, again and again, until she could believe she would wake in the morning to his voice in the kitchen, and run to him.

33

Kit blew smoke in a thin, high stream over Henry's head, tapped her cigarette firmly against the ashtray's edge. Henry sipped her whisky. The TV news was on in the lounge room, the sound just a murmur from where the two women sat, opposite one another at the table. On the divan, Orla was still and curled, looking past the TV, watching them. Deebee was already in bed.

Kit said, 'So what are you going to do?'

'What can I do?'

'You could move.'

Henry cocked her head towards the lounge room. 'I suggested that. She cried.'

'Did you tell the police?

'Are you joking, after the last time? What would I say — yes, officer, I can give you a description of his back?'

There was a long silence. Kit tapped her cigarette. Henry sipped. TV voices rose and fell. Orla looked from the women to the screen. There was trouble in Ireland, where her father came from. She was gripped by a sudden panic: had he gone back there? Trouble, too, in the Middle East. Orla remembered her parents talking about the trouble in the iya place, trouble that had driven them here. Was this the first peaceful place her father had lived?

Kit said, 'So, this solicitor thing. Do you really think you stand a chance?'

'Mr Featherstone thinks so.'

'He would. He wants your business.'

Henry leaned back in her chair. Her voice was cold. 'What would you have me do? Call State Housing?'

Orla sat perfectly still.

'It's nothing to be ashamed of. It'd be cheaper.'

'You're not living in State Housing.'

'But I'm working.'

'So am I.'

'What I mean is —

'What you mean is I should go cap in hand to the government.' She wrung her hands, made a face. '"Please, sir, I'm a poor widow."'

Kit glanced at Orla. She was looking at the TV. Kit smiled tightly at her friend. 'You need to be sensible. Is a court case sensible? You could lose, then what?'

'Mr Featherstone doesn't think I'd lose.'

She waved her cigarette. 'Mr Featherstone! Wake up, Hen!'

Henry thudded her glass on the table. Amber whisky sloshed and splashed. 'For Christ's sake! Wake up? Who are you telling to wake up? I hardly sleep, trying to work out a way to make a decent life. They've lost their father. You don't know what that's like. I do. He died because of the company. No-one can work day and night. Can you?'

'Sshh. Please. You said he had chest pains.'

'He was exhausted.'

Kit ground her cigarette in the ashtray, spoke quietly. 'I just think you're making a mistake.'

Henry's hand waved about. 'You want me to give up. You want the children to live in a dingy little flat, surrounded by other poor people.'

'There's no shame in being poor.'

Henry pushed back her chair. The legs scraped on the floor. 'You keep saying there's no shame, there's no shame. How would you know?' She stood. 'You have no idea what it's like to be poor. I grew up poor. I know what it's like. And I won't do it to my children. I won't.'

34

He wondered how he got there. Once he knew almost nothing about chickens, was unsure why he chose them. Because they're small, useful, don't ask for much? When he was a child — very young, before he began nursery school — his family spent a holiday at a coastal town. He could no longer remember its name. If he had stayed in Ireland, he could have asked his Da; if he had kept correspondence he could have asked Ma. Over the years he had wracked his brain but always there were the same three memories: holding his mother's skirt on a windy cliff, the sea roiling below; running along the sea shore, pebbles hurting his feet, glancing over his shoulder at his brother pursuing him, his thin feet and arms startlingly white, his grey trouser-legs flapping, his legs making long swift strides, his face grim-set and the sound of him over the pebbles; reaching to reach into a laying box, its dimness taking him by surprise, the glimpse of the layered peat and moss nest, the acrid stink of droppings, the hen's beady eye on him, its sharp beak, its low cluck cluck, his hesitation, his mother's voice, 'She won't hurt you,' then the flap of its wings, dust motes and feathers, its shriek that made his heart leap, its claws' scrabble on the timber struts, then look — the edge of something curved and pale in the nest hollow, the surprising heat of her egg in his hand. He had brought it carefully out into the light and stared at the bits of her — fragments of her dirt and feathers — and watched his mother scrape them off with her thumbnail. Whose hen was this? He only remembers one visit — he supposed the first — or did they only rob this nest once? What sense would that make with six to cook for?

He looked up, unsure now where he was, and into his mother's face: 'Ma, it's me, come home. Oh, Ma. I'm not one of those naughty boys, the ones down by the river. I'm not, now, am I?'

35

Deebee hated their smell, the way they stared at her. She hated their furniture, clothes, questions.

Every weekday morning she stood inside their closed front door, watching them, back pressed against the jamb, one of her hands twirling around the other, three times one direction, three times the other. Then the hands swapped over.

In front of her, their table and chairs, their kitchen, the tall, slim mother in her pretty dress and apron, chopping or mixing something on the bench. There were pictures on the walls: fields of trees and cows, little girls in ballet shoes, boats on stormy sea, boats at rest. There were shiny-framed photographs on shelves: old people; a bride; a baby; a family in front of this house — mother, father, daughter, son. There were pots full of plants by the windows, their leaves thick and green. Alongside the table was a gleaming piano.

The daughter, Suzie, and the son, Johnny, stood in the kitchen behind the mother. Johnny's arms hung at his sides, a wooden block tight in each fist. Suzie held a doll to her face and chewed its yellow hair. Without taking her eye from Deebee, the girl sidled up to her mother. 'Why is she here again?'

'Sshh,' the woman said, sharply. She half-pirouetted, leaned forward, held out a plate of cut fruit. Her children dropped their toys, filled their hands with apple and orange. 'Would you like some, dear?' she smiled, stepping closer, holding out the plate to

Deebee, who shook her head, hands moving faster. Three times one, three times other.

'It's nice outside,' the woman sighed, turning away. 'Why don't you go out and play.'

Deebee stood on the back porch, watched the two chase one another. Round and round and round. They squealed. They ran to the back fence. She stepped out after them, stood in sunlight.

36

Mr McIntyre was as good as his word.

He and Mrs West turned up again one Sunday morning. Their car was new, spacious and perfectly clean. The smell made Orla feel sick. She had to sit in front between them. As he drove, Mr McIntyre's thigh pressed up against hers, his belly rubbed her side. 'Sorry,' she whispered, inched away, tried to make herself smaller, felt Mrs West edge away to make room. Mr McIntyre smiled briefly, looked straight ahead.

Henry and Deebee sat in the back. Mrs West spoke over her shoulder to them, her voice loud in Orla's ear. On the sand, Mr McIntyre set up the umbrella, opened three fold-up chairs. Henry took hold of Orla's arm: 'Look after your sister.'

Mr McIntyre said, 'Don't worry, I'll look after her,' and Orla heard her mother say thank you, ran away from them all, suddenly free, down the slope to the ocean's edge.

Sea foam popped and vanished. Other feet appeared alongside hers, big feet she didn't recognise. She looked up, squinting. Mr McIntyre wore black racing bathers. His belly was round and tanned. Her sister stood on the other side of him. She was holding his hand. Orla craned to look at the side of her sister's face. Deebee was looking at the sea.

Orla raised her hand to her eyes, squinted up at Mr McIntyre. 'You have to carry her.'

But Mr McIntyre held out his hand to her and smiled, said, 'I can take the both of you.'

His hand was big like her father's but different — shorter, wider, harder. The wind blew tough from the land behind, blew froth off the edges of waves, blew as if it could blow all of them out to sea. Orla held tight, jumped into waves, turning her face away. He pulled them up so their feet dangled and they shrieked and kicked. He laughed loudly, lowered Orla till her feet touched bottom. Deebee clung to his flexed arm with both hands. And then they were suddenly past the waves, walking on firm white sand, the sea shallow and clear, the same light blue as Mrs West's eyes.

He released Orla's hand. She jumped up and down in the shallow water, splashing, floated awkwardly on her back, her heels and bottom bumping along the sand. She stared up at the sky. How she must look from up there; could God see her here? Was He looking at her in her body, small in all the endless.

She stood. A short distance away, Mr McIntyre sat cross-legged in the shallow water on the perfect sand, the sea shifting calmly around his hips, Deebee sat in his lap. Orla moved closer, tried to sit beside them but the sea tugged her and she tipped sideways, her face going under, her legs splaying above her in the air. She felt his hand inside her thigh, slide up and cup and squeeze then let her go in the moment before she spluttered up, righting herself, her eyes and ears all water. As if from a distance, she heard him laugh, say something like, 'Careful there, little lady.'

'Where's your mum?' Johnny asked.

'At work.'

'Where's that?'

Deebee shrugged. Above them, the Thompsons' Hills hoist squeaked; their white sheets flapped and shuddered.

Johnny stared. 'How come she doesn't stay home?'

'Dunno.' Slabs of sunlight opened around their heads and closed again.

'My dad's at work.'

'Sshh,' his sister said. 'She doesn't have a dad, remember?'

Deebee looked at her. 'I have a dad.'

'No, you don't,' Suzie said. '*Our* dad told us.'

'Where does your dad work?' Johnny asked.

'I do so have a dad.'

Suzie tipped her head to one side. 'Well, where is he, then?' Deebee twisted a dolly peg into the lawn. Suzie looked at her brother. 'Told ya,' she said. Deebee pounded the peg with her fist. After a while, Suzie stood, smoothed her skirt, said, 'Come on. I'm thirsty.'

When Orla arrived at Cora's, Sally was sitting at the table. In Orla's chair. Orla smiled at her tightly. Sally gazed back silently, took a long drag of her cigarette.

'Hi,' Orla said, glancing away and back.

Sally nodded, narrowed her eyes. Blue smoke drifted from her nose. She tapped her cigarette in the ashtray, taptap. On the table in front of her, a bottle of nail polish. Her fingernails were long, hot pink.

Orla hesitated, then sat in the spare chair, the one that turned its back on the kitchen, that looked straight out the window: so much sunlight, a big piece of blue above the red roof of her home; the shaded red brick wall, a window; inside the window, the grey blur of venetian blinds. She stared at the smudge of it, pictured once again the room: below the window a telephone table the colour of creamed honey, the black bakelite telephone with its chrome dial and black numerals on white background, the thick black fabric of its cord.

Behind Orla, Cora stood at the kitchen counter. She talked to Sally about people Orla didn't know. Orla imagined herself home, on the other side of that window there, in that other kitchen, her bare feet cool on its lino tiles, her hands on its yellow bench, the yellow cupboard doors around her and above. She remembered the rough feel of the lounge room's charcoal carpet. It would be quiet there: her sister napping; her mother doing something, as usual, in the kitchen or laundry. No radio; no TV; no conversation.

Cora set the teapot on the table, sat in her usual chair. Orla cast occasional curious glances at Sally on one side, smiled often at Cora on the other as they chatted past her. On the tabletop the Benson & Hedges packet and lighter shone gold in the sun; light flashed along one edge of the nail polish bottle; its hot-pink lid, hot-pink liquid; the three lime-green mugs glowed; the aluminium teapot shone. She studied the pattern, pale as spider web, in the table's red formica, ran a finger along its cool, solid aluminium edge.

Sally had short dark hair, a small round face, a little nose. She seemed older than Cora — the way she half-shrugged her shoulders, half-smiled, the way she tapped a cigarette neatly from its packet. Cora had said that Sally worked at a dress shop in the city, and Orla had imagined that she would dress like Cora. Instead, she wore jeans and tee-shirts. Today, a leather jacket hung on the back of her chair. When Sally leaned forward, Orla caught a trace of leather scent. That warm, good, saddle smell.

Sally talked about a man with a motorbike. Orla didn't look at her. She didn't know about boyfriends or going out. All she knew was that Sally was also seeing a man with a car. A few nights before, she'd heard wheels on gravel, an engine switching off and even before she was fully awake she was out of her bed and running on tiptoes, heart pounding, opening the front door. The porch was cold under her feet. She was ecstatic with belief: God had heard her at last.

The driveway gravel hurt. She stopped. The porch light behind her threw blocks of light into the dark garden. There was no car. 'Daddy,' she whispered. This was — she looked hard into the carport, the driveway, the night — this was impossible. She had heard it. But there was no car. But the wheels. The engine. She took a few more steps along the driveway, her hand out, feeling for cool smooth invisible metal. 'Daddy.'

She looked at the street. She rubbed her eyes. Overhead, the wind whooshed through the poplars. Her heart. There. As her eyes adjusted. There, in Cora's driveway. In moonlight. The glint of it. A car. The wrong car, but of course it would be. The company had taken his car back. Wrong car, yes, and wrong house. Maybe someone else had driven him in their own car, turned into next door's driveway. An ordinary error.

She heard sounds. Behind the wind in the trees, behind her racing heart. From the car. A low voice. Again she whispered: 'Daddy?' Crept closer. The sound. Slow, quiet steps. Her stinging feet. Another voice — higher. She froze. A skinny moon shone. The car's roof and windows. She stared. No heads in there. Just sound. Her skin prickled. She was hot and cold. Were they voices of ghosts?

She took a last step. Through the driver's open window, the front seats empty. Then some movement. In the back. A shape, undefinable, moved. Became the shoulders of a man, a little moonlight on him. She frowned. Below the line of his shirt, the pale skin of his buttocks. The muscles in them clenched, released, clenched. Under one of his arms, the side of a face — Sally's, she now realised — her head turned away from him, her eyes closed, mouth open, her small nose clearly outlined against the dark upholstery. One of her arms stretched back over her head, hand bent at the wrist, its open palm pressed against the inside of the door. Her other hand held the back of the man's neck. One of her legs was drawn up high. Its calf glowed whitely. Her hot-pink toes, spread wide against the car's rear window, made small squeaks against the glass. The wind moaned in the trees. Whimpering sounds from Sally's mouth. The man's voice deep and growling. Aw. Aw. Aw. Aw.

She crossed the porch, closed the front door quietly. She curled up tightly in her bed, listened to the wind and thought about all the wrong things: wrong house, wrong car, wrong man. She knew she was wrong, too, for going outside, wrong for seeing. She wiped her face with her sleeve and thought about Sally's toes and Sally's voice, the man's clenching, growling, and she pushed her hand into the soft warm place in her pants. The car started up, its wheels crunched, its headlights swept across her room. Just like the last time she had seen her father.

The next morning she woke sickly tired. Her mother brought her orange juice. Deebee sat on the floor with her cars, said, 'Are you sick?' And, when she didn't answer, 'You sick, Orly?' And she said of course she was, what else, and Deebee said she felt sick every day, and was heaven really up in the sky, and which star was Daddy on and why can't you see the stars in the day. Orla said, 'Play somewhere else.'

Orla remembered of all this while she sat between Sally and Cora, listening to them talk about the man with the motorbike. Sally slid the nail polish bottle over to Orla, said, 'Give it to Cora.'

When Cora opened it, the strong smell made Orla dizzy. She watched Cora paint her stubby nails, wipe the pink off her skin with a tissue, wave her wet fingers in the air, breathe hard on them. Orla slid the bottle back to Sally. Sally looked at Orla and said, 'You wanna go?'

Cora said, 'Her mum'd go mental.'

Sally gave a sideways smile. 'Suit yourself.' And she twisted the top of the bottle down hard.

Orla said, 'I don't think she'd mind.'

But Sally laughed a bit and said, 'Nah, she's right.'

Cora lifted her breasts and let them rest on the table, reached past Orla for the B&H. Orla watched her flip open the pack and pull one out, clamp it between her teeth. Nothing touched her wet nails. Sally stretched her arm out in front of Orla, flicked open the lighter. Cora took a small puff, blew the smoke out quickly.

Sally laughed, 'Bum suck,' and blew a smoke ring. Orla looked at Cora then, but Cora just lifted her chin, opened her mouth, let a small blue cloud drift out.

Orla looked straight ahead again. The sun pounded the roof of her house. She heard Cora say, 'If you ask my mum and dad, maybe they'll lend you their car so we can take the kids to the beach.' Sally shrugged one shoulder, took a drag. Through the window, Orla saw how black the TV aerial was, black as something burnt sticking up out of her house, reaching to the pounding sky.

Sally said, 'Hey, you want one?' Orla turned to her. She was holding out the open pack of B&H, her eyes narrowed: 'How old are you?' She looked at Orla's chest. 'Got your rags yet?'

Orla looked at Cora again but Cora just gazed back mildly, sighed out another high blue cloud. Orla tried to smile; her cheeks burned. She shook her head a little as Sally laughed, closed the pack. Whatever they were, Orla was pretty sure she didn't have them.

39

Deebee could see home from a number of places: their kitchen table, their driveway that ran alongside their house, their front garden. It sat still all day, hunched over, sleeping: the empty yard, the venetian blinds closed like eyes shut. Only the poplar trees moved, although once she saw a cat walk over the roof. Not her cat but it could be. All she needed to do was pat it.

The Thompson kids raced their trikes up and down their driveway. Deebee watched them from the sunny front lawn, waited for a turn, wished she had her own trike. She stood for a long time, grew tired of the waiting, looked away from them to the road again, her dozing home, the trees, Cora's front yard. Steele was by the tap. Deebee lifted her hand to wave but Steele wasn't looking; he was picking up the garden hose. Deebee saw the silver arc of water shoot into the air. She watched as Cora's parents' car turned slowly into the drive. She heard the screen door slam open and closed, slapslap. She saw Cora's mum and dad get out of the car, go inside. The abandoned hose writhed and glistened.

She walked to the edge of the road. She stared at her house, then walked again, walked into the road. Easy.

In her sandpit she buried her cars, dug them up, put her eye to the fence but the cake lady and the dad weren't there, and their back door was shut. She heard the Thompson kids shouting for their mum, and she climbed the back stairs, made herself small in a sunny corner. There were flies on her arms and legs and face. She closed her eyes, swiped at them, and listened to them buzz. A crow called slowly.

And then she cried. Because Mrs Thompson held her hand too tightly as they crossed the road. Because Mrs Thompson crouched, looked hard at Deebee with her pretty face, shook her shoulders, said she must never, ever do that again, that her mother would be very upset, that she could have been killed by a car. Because Mrs Thompson hugged her then and said it all again, her voice trembling.

40

More days passed and the hard, white light of summer came. In the lengthening evenings Orla lay on her bed, stared out her open windows at her narrow slice of eastern sky turning mauve and green. When at last the sun set on the other side of the house, all the rooms would begin to cool and she would listen to her mother make the dinner. But now, as she waited, the wind had sprung up strongly from the desert, the air full of eucalypt and then bushfire smoke. She turned over on her bed so that she faced the window, breathed it in, tried to imagine a world in which everything she had been told were true, that her father really was never coming back, and she tried to look into that future, the endless repetition of days unfolding the way they always had: sun rising, crossing, setting, long darkness coming in. A straight line of days waiting for her, days becoming smaller and smaller the further ahead they lay, harder and harder to discern, until they were so tiny they didn't look like days at all and disappeared off the horizon's edge. She tried to imagine all the walking to school, the walking home. The key, the door swinging open into silence.

Later she would tell her mother it was the song, that she immediately knew that song, had heard it on Cora's radio, and that the song, like a message, arrived clearly through her sleep, made her open her eyes.

He stood outside her open window, looking in. His mouth was in the shape of smile but not his eyes, she would say later. No, Mum, his eyes weren't smiling. He held his hand — his right hand — near his face, and in his hand was a small transistor radio, facing her, not his ear, as if he had wanted it to wake her. She had opened her eyes and looked right at him, saw him clearly though she didn't know, at first, the meaning of what she saw, and she closed her eyes again, for a moment, for just a moment, she would say, agitated — and so it puzzled her that, when her startled eyes flew open once more — immediately, she thought, just a moment later — he, the radio and the song were gone.

She leapt from her bed, from her room, through the laundry, and was at the kitchen door, making a sound: 'Aaaarrrr. Aaaarrrr.' Both hands gripping her mother's arm. Her voice shook as she spoke. Then, alarmed: 'The window! The window's still open!' And her mother went to close it as Orla paced the tiny kitchen, chewed her nails.

'It's all right,' her mother said. 'Sit down. I'll get a pen and paper, and we'll write down everything you saw, and tomorrow we'll tell the police. Now that we have a description, they'll have to take it seriously. What was the song you heard?'

'Cat Stevens,' she whispered, eyes wild.

'The song's called Cat Stevens?'

'No. He's —. It's —. Cat: see, ay, tee. Stevens: ess —'

'I know how to spell it.'

In the corner of her eye, Orla saw a movement. Deebee in the doorway, her big eyes, her fingers, and Orla smiled briefly at her, looked back to her mother, said, 'The song's "Moon Shadow". You know.' She sang the first line, her throat tight, voice a wavering string.

Her mother nodded, wrote it down. 'What did he look like?'

Orla shook her head, flapped her hands, put them over her eyes. She leaned in close to her mother, whispering. 'He — he looked like — he looked like Satan, like pictures you see of Satan.'

Her mother watched Orla closely, frowning, her pen over the page.

'His eyes, they were. The way he. His, his mouth, Mum. Like a smile but, but it. And his eyebrows were, they were.' And she drew a vee on the table with her finger.

Henry nodded. 'Hmm.'

~

Later, Orla asked her mother to tuck her into bed, to double-check the windows, shut the blinds.

'There,' her mother said. 'No-one can get in.'

'Are all the other windows closed?'

Her mother sat on the edge of the bed. 'Yes. Always. Now sleep.'

'Mum,' she said, her eyes filling. 'His face.'

Her mother sighed heavily, looked away. She picked at the bedspread. 'It's not his face you have to worry about.'

'What do you mean?' her voice wavering.

'Never mind,' her mother replied. 'His face can't hurt you. Go to sleep. I'll leave the lamp on.'

Orla looked around. Lamplight softly filled the corner by her bed. What was it then, if not his face or the way he smiled at her, that could hurt her, that she should worry about? What could be worse than the way he had looked at her? She watched for a long time, but nothing moved.

41

Some weekends, Kit came to visit with her wide straw hat and leather gloves. This time she said: 'The lawn is going to pot. You'll have to run around with the hose.' And she smiled, stroked Deebee's hair.

Deebee smiled up at her. 'What does going to pot mean?'

'It means no-one's looking after it.' Kit kissed the top of her head.

Orla watched but didn't smile. She wasn't sure it was something to smile about. She looked away, so they couldn't see her face. Deebee was too little to know anything about smiling but Kit was old. Orla frowned at the lawn. The mower man still came but, when he mowed, the air billowed dust and bits of brown grass. Weeds towered in the beds. Their seeds drifted in the sun like tiny feathers.

Kit pulled on her gardening gloves, tied her big straw hat under her chin. She said, 'Weeds don't stop growing just because there's no-one to pull them,' and worked on her hands and knees. Orla sat cross-legged and silent beside her, grasping the thick, prickly stems of weeds at ground level, as she had been taught, and between her thumb and finger, and twisting them till their roots gave. She carried a handful to the drum. When she dropped them in, minute scraps of burnt paper flew up and she touched one with her finger as it floated past her. It crumbled to dust in the air. She grabbed at another; when she opened her hand there was only a smudge of soot.

In the front yard again, Orla handed Deebee the rake. In her peripheral vision, she watched her sister wrangle it, catch weeds in the tines, and wave the rake in the air, furious. Soil and limp weeds flew. Her father and sister, the rake and drum, the weeds, the leaves: all these thoughts made her blurry. Her fingers hurt. She scraped the weeds' stinging hairs out with her nail, listened to Kit, sometimes answered. Her throat ached; her heart pounded. She concentrated on breathing. She wanted her sister to take the rake and go, to be alone with Kit to tell her about the man at the window, his face, to ask what her mother had meant. But Deebee followed them as they worked; she bashed the lawn with the rake, threw it, sat on it. She gathered weeds in her hands.

When they reached Orla's bedroom window, they were right where the man had stood, and it was not like on TV; there were no footprints, no scrap of cloth on the hibiscus bush. It was as if he had never even been. She watched Kit dig her gloved fingers into the earth, deep where the roots were. Her jaw ached from clenching.

Kit chatted, as if she had no idea. Then she stood, stretching, and smiled. 'See? Better already.'

Deebee carried into the house a big red hibiscus and a spray of honeysuckle. Kit filled a clean jam jar, arranged the flowers, placed it in the centre of the dining table. The hibiscus stared back obscenely. Orla couldn't stop looking at it, a big red kiss. The honeysuckle trailed like a veil. At the laundry sink they scrubbed their hands.

42

The Earth turned and so the sun crawled overhead. Because, Orla knew, everything was always spinning no matter how it seemed. Schooldays crept to weekends and visits to Cora's, crawled towards the end of the school year. Monday. Pains in her belly. Cracks in the world. Not talking to Heather. Not looking at her. Coming second in her class instead of first. The knock at Mrs Thompson's door. Deebee's face, the key, the prayer, the empty house. Coming third. Thinking of Heather and pushing it down. And the thoughts coming back back, and what she had done to make Heather do. Fingers in her ears. Concentration. Cracks in roads and footpaths, in netball courts; in desks, rulers, veranda boards. Hard praying. More of it. And Christmas coming. When anything could happen.

She sat outside, against the wall on the sunny side of her house, where there were no windows, no garden beds, just sand and a few bits of lawn and the tall, wide red brick wall at her back, she and the wall hidden from the street by the trellis fence with the jammed gate wild with honeysuckle. As long as Deebee wasn't in the sandpit with her cars, as long as the old man and woman next door weren't in their backyard, she had the wall, its sunny world, to herself.

Up in the hills, in her street, an old man had lived in a shed behind a neighbour's house. Kids from the street had watched him feed bits of mince to a kingfisher which cocked its head and blinked its eye, its iridescent chest breathtaking in the sun.

Watching the man's shaking, wrinkled hands had made her recoil a little, wonder how some people could live so long, become so ugly and old.

Sitting now, with her back against the sunny wall, she made all the noise she had to make, all the noise her mother hated, and then she wiped her face with her clothes, let the sun beat down on her. She watched a trail of ants, hugged her knees, dug her hands in the warm sand, listened to it crunch between her fingers.

What if everything she had been told was just a story, or a trick, like a play, she wondered. What if people who died just went to another part of the world, like a room behind a wall, a secret room, the kind she had seen on TV. Like the rooms on the other side of the wall she leaned against, the bathroom, her bedroom, the inside of her house so different from the outside, and so close, that she could reach her hand through the wall and touch it. No-one could tell what was on the other side of the wall just by looking at it from where she sat. All that, just because of a wall. She turned to face it. Just above her head, a lizard sunned itself. From all around, birds twittered. Her father had made things fly through the air and pass through walls and wood. She placed her palm flat on the bricks. They were rough and hot. She closed her eyes. She pushed. Not hard. She slipped through. As if, under her touch, they turned to butter. Her hands felt the coolness of the other side, of the rooms there, her bedroom, the bathroom. And then she brought her hands back again. Calm and empty.

～

It was a Saturday when she saw.

By midmorning, the day was too hot, and she and Deebee had been a while in the paddle pool; the sun bit their shoulders, the air already so dry it hurt. She had gone inside, passed her mother in the laundry. Lino cool beneath her feet; cold fridge air on her face. She filled a glass from the chilled jug, its handle soothing in her hot fist.

Cold washed down her gullet. She gasped, gulped again, gazed over the rim of the glass, through the kitchen window, into the backyard. Deebee was out of the pool, her arms and legs still shining wet, feet leaping lightly over the grass. She was laughing as she darted, raised her arms, pushed at something, gesticulated, her fingers nimble as birds. Sun played over her skin and her mouth moved in what Orla recognized, with a jolt, was a stream of language. And Orla stood unblinking, glass poised by her chin. Then she stepped back and a little to one side, in case her sister felt eyes on her and looked up, in case the act of watching broke the spell.

Orla's first unblinking thought had been to wonder what Deebee was doing, but this had rushed through her in an instant and evaporated. She knew what she was looking at, had seen it many times, at the beach, the pool, the front yard, and just there, in the backyard, right where her sister was now. She had heard it from all her watching posts: on the seashore, her beach towel, her bed, the treehouse. That excited laugh, and her father laughing back; the particular tone they kept for one another. She had watched them together there, right there on that grass where Deebee now danced and spoke. And, still watching her sister, she could see the game, hear it clearly, too, in her own head. As if their father was really there. With Deebee.

Her vision swam; she turned away.

All along, she realised, her sister had had the thing Orla had longed for, and had kept it all to herself.

~

On Monday morning, Orla stood in line behind Heather outside their classroom door. She stared at the small blonde pigtails above each of Heather's ears, the pink hair bobbles on pink elastic, pearlescent scalp in the line of her part. Orla leaned close: 'Hi, Heather.'

Heather turned. Her blue eyes blinked. She smiled back. 'Hi.'

At recess, they walked the edge of the bitumen playground, dodging games of chasey, elastics, marbles, skippy. They walked side by side, just like real friends. It was so loud, so full of shouts and screams, it was impossible to speak.

~

At dinner, Deebee said, 'What's a cinema?'

Their mother looked up. 'A place you go to watch films. Why?'

'Can we go to watch a film?'

Henry looked at Orla. 'This is your idea, I suppose.'

'Can we?' Deebee grabbed her mother's arm. 'Please.'

Her mother shook her head. Deebee turned to her sister.

'We could catch the bus to town one day,' Orla said.

Henry opened her mouth and closed it again. She looked back and forth between them, frowning. 'Where did this come from?'

'Mrs Thompson said they're going to the cinema. In the holy days.'

Orla snorted. 'Holidays, dummy.'

Their mother shot Orla a look, put down her knife and fork, took Deebee's hand, patted it. 'You'd get lost.'

Orla scowled. 'I'd look after her. I look after her here.'

But their mother didn't reply. She picked up her cutlery, cut her food, put it in her mouth.

Later, passing her mother seated at the table, Orla stopped. Henry had opened the evening paper, spread out the Entertainment pages. Orla peered over her mother's shoulder. She had seen the inside of cinemas in films on TV: big, shadowy, smoky places, rows of seats, handsome men in suits, women with perfect hair and lips. All kinds of things happened there: people cried and laughed and talked, held hands, kissed. Sometimes women minded if the men saw them crying. Sometimes it didn't seem to matter. The films were full of planes and ships, bombs and deserts, jungles and elephants. Men punched each other. The music was wonderful. Orla had heard her parents and Kit talk about films they had seen before she was born, films full of women with names like Greta, Lena, Marlene. Once she had heard her mother tease her father about one called Ingrid. But Orla thought that couldn't be right: the only Ingrid Orla knew was the one Heather had whispered about months ago, the one who lived down Orla's street, who went in the backs of cars with boys. Orla had nodded solemnly, although, at the time, before Sally, she wasn't sure what Heather meant. But she had understood. It wasn't what girls were meant to do if they wanted to become stars.

The Entertainment pages advertised all the city cinemas: The Grand, The Metro, The Piccadilly. Were children allowed, Orla wondered, in these places where so many things can happen?

Her mother ran a finger lightly across the cinema ads as if she was stroking them. Quietly she said, 'I could have been a film star once. I had a contract.'

Orla turned to her, agape. 'What? In America?'

Henry gave a half-smile. 'No. Egypt.'

'Oh.'

Henry shrugged. 'I couldn't get a passport.'

Orla frowned. She had seen her mother's passport in her dressing-table drawer. Dark blue. British. 'But —' she started. Then, 'I didn't know you could speak Egyptian.'

Her mother shrugged. 'Arabic.' And turned away.

Orla tried to imagine her mother's tired face in a film but she couldn't.

~

That evening, when Deebee was asleep with her head on her mother's knee, Orla took a deep breath, turned to look at Henry in the TV light. 'Mum, what's an Arab?'

Her mother looked back at her. 'Why do you ask that?'

'Daddy was writing about it.'

She sighed. 'Oh. That. Those Arabs are people who live in Palestine. That's where your father and I met. It's not called Palestine anymore. It's called Israel.' She shrugged. 'He was there during the war to keep the Arabs and Jews apart. They were fighting each other and then they started to fight the troops, as well. It was a very dangerous time. A lot of men were killed.'

Orla bit her lip. 'Did anyone Dad know get killed?'

'Many.'

'Who?'

'Oh ...' She waved her hand. 'Men he worked with.' She looked back to the TV, frowned. 'Friends.'

'With knives?'

'Knives?'

'Were they killed with knives?'

Henry turned her frown to this strange girl she'd been given. 'What kind of question is that.'

'He was writing something about knives.'

Her mother sighed again. 'Sometimes knives. But mainly guns and bombs. Hand grenades. Other things.' She shrugged. 'It was a war.'

'Like on TV.'

'Yes. No. Not really. Oh. I don't want to talk about this.'

~

The following weekend, Orla heard her mother call, found her in the laundry, up to her elbows in bubbles. The room smelled like flowers.

Her voice was light. 'Now listen,' she said, lifting something dark and plunging it again. 'I want to tell you something. I had dream that I'm going to die at fifty-two.' She straightened, pushed her hair back with her arm and smiled. White suds clung to her ear. Orla stared. 'You'll be nineteen,' Henry explained, 'so it will be your responsibility to look after your sister.'

Orla blinked.

'All right?' There she was, looking at Orla, smiling again.

Orla's head jerked, a kind of nod she couldn't quite control.

Her mother turned back to the sink, pushed her hands deep. 'And I've made arrangements for you both to go to live with my sister in Nottingham when the time comes.'

Orla frowned at the side of her mother's face, at her hands pulling at the bundle, at her fingers squeezing it. 'All right,' she said and retreated to her room, lay on her bed, stared at the ceiling. Her mother had a sister. Her mother had a sister she had never talked about. I have a sister, Orla thought, and I talk to her. I talk to her even though she's just a kid. I will be nineteen. That's grown up. How will it feel to be grown up?

She tried to imagine it but she didn't know anyone who was nineteen. She tried to imagine sixteen but couldn't do that either. She couldn't even imagine what it would be like to start high school.

She knew where Nottingham was; she had watched *The Adventures of Robin Hood* on TV. England, she knew from the school atlas, was on the other side of the world, much too far to go for an aunt no-one talked about. If they had to live with an aunt, she thought, why not Kit? Did it really matter that she wasn't their real aunt? It had never mattered before. If I refuse to go, she wondered, would Deebee have to go alone? Do people take other people's sisters away? Is there someone who does that for a job, arrives in a car and knocks on the door? Orla imagined opening that door, speaking back to them: 'I'm nineteen. You can't come in.' She imagined them barging past her the way men do on *Z-Cars*, grabbing Deebee, pulling her into their black shiny car. A man in a suit and a hat would say: 'You can stay here, Miss, or you can come with your sister.'

Better never to even open that door. Better just to disappear. After the funeral. Or before. Do we have to go to the funeral? We didn't have to go to Dad's.

Orla thought carefully. After her mother died, she decided, she would phone Kit, swear her to secrecy, bring down the suitcase from her mother's wardrobe, pack it quickly for Deebee and herself, call a taxi, tell the driver to go to an address. It would be the address of a flat she had found in the newspaper and phoned about, the way her parents had rented all the houses they had lived in. It would be a flat like the ones she had seen from the bus: pink brick walls, a sliding glass door to a balcony strung with laundry. She would learn to type, get a job. On weekends they would visit Kit. They'd be happy. But university — what about that? She pulled her pillow over her head.

~

In the kitchen, Henry watched her hands do things. Blade steak, carrots — only two carrots now — and four potatoes. A couple of tomatoes. Large. An onion. Large. No celery, still.

Things change; things stay the same. One person less makes a hole, a smaller meal, makes a three-quarter family that isn't quite. No husband, no father, only two-thirds the meat.

When the hole is a child — God forbid — a family is still a family, for how many children does it take and a family is made with only one, and everyone around has more than one or can make another. And a child eats so little there would be no gap or barely one; the amount of meat would be the same, wouldn't it. When the hole is an adult, though, and a man, the gap's man-sized, and the world sees nothing but that gap, can't tear its gaze from it.

Woman-sized — God forbid that, too — and how would any man cope with children? Everyone feels sorry. They rally; they understand when he sends them to relatives and orphanages. Because he works, he's tired, needs time to himself, likes a drink, and it's better they're not with him because he'll find another woman, sure as eggs, and she'll be cruel to the dead woman's kids and, anyway, God knows what he might do to his kids otherwise.

A man-sized hole, though, and strangers wonder: what did she do to drive him away or into his grave? Look how she's let herself go; she's a bitch, she's a nag. Henry wasn't blind. She saw their faces: a woman on her own should be watched; she's sex-starved, she's trouble.

The knife, the board, the pile of vegetables. The heel of her hand. The downward pressure, the resistance, the crack. The surrender, the split.

Behind her, the window, the afternoon breeze. Outside, the children in the blow-up pool. The sun edging west forever and ever, amen. And this was it. This was all anyone had. Soon shadows would cover everyone. Like earth. She rinses the knife. She looks out. Orla spreadeagled, her face to the sky, as if she owns the whole world, the low hills of her baby breasts Dan didn't live long enough to see. She'll soon learn the truth about life, that being a woman is disappointment. And Deebee there, crouched on the edge of the silvery water.

The phone rang, made Henry start, the knife clatter into the sink. She glanced at the clock as she dried her hands: late afternoon. She walked across the room, breathing, breathing, the tea towel against her belly. She knew what this could be, had been waiting, trying not to think. Her knowing hand shook; she lifted the receiver. 'Hello.' Reached for the nearest chair, gripped it, listened, sat. Curled over, one elbow on her knee, head in free hand. Her voice gone.

Later, she stared at the receiver in its cradle. The clock ticked. She didn't feel the way she thought she would, wasn't sure she felt anything. She didn't know what that meant. She picked up the phone. The dial tone was loud. She called. It took a long time for the dial to rattle its way back, over and over. Surely the children could hear what she was doing, even from outside.

Surely even Cora could. Surely the whole world could hear and would come to the door to ask what has happened.

When Kit answered, Henry said, 'It's me.' Hot tears stung. She closed her eyes. She gasped.

Kit's voice shrill. 'What's wrong? The children?'

'No, no, it's all right,' she replied, her voice high as a girl's. 'Everything's all right. Just listen, listen — I won, Kit. I won.'

43

Orla had reached the old church on the walk home when someone called her name. She turned. It was Derek, running to catch her.

'Hi,' he said.

She blinked, pulled her mouth into a smile with no teeth. 'Hi.'

'Can — can I carry your bag?'

Her face flushed. Was this what she thought it was, this thing she had seen on TV, read in books? Except the boy wasn't Derek, was nothing like him, and the girl was nothing like her. 'Sure,' she said. She held out her bag. She was already worried: he was smaller than her.

She watched him hoist it onto his free shoulder and they set off down the short hill. She glanced sideways. He looked like one of the mules she's seen in Westerns, loaded with possessions, mules that follow one another quietly, nose to tail, mules she always felt sorry for.

'What do you think of choir?' he asked.

'It's okay. I mean it's good. I like it.'

'Me, too.'

They walked, then, in silence. She could hear him breathing. Two bags would be heavy, she thought. She said, 'It's my favourite thing, actually.'

'Me, too.'

She glanced at him again. He smiled at her.

The sun felt warm. The scent of cut grass. A faraway motorbike. Their loud syncopated footsteps. She said, 'You know where you were that day when I saw you, is that where you live?'

'Yep.'

'I just live in the next street.'

'I know,' he replied.

She regarded him from the corner of her eye. 'How do you know?'

'I've seen you.'

Her throat tightened. 'Where?' she said.

'Walking.' He smiled.

'Oh.'

'In the mornings.'

'Oh.'

'Across the oval.'

'Ah.' She swallowed. She hadn't walked that way since —

'I didn't follow you or anything.' There he was, beside her, with that smile.

She looked away. 'No. I didn't — I don't — ' Her cheeks burned. 'It's just that, well, if you've just seen me at the oval, how do you know my street?'

She turned her head to look at the home of the ginger cat. The yard was empty. In the moment before he answered she wished she could tell him how it purred when she stroked its white belly, and that he wouldn't think that was weird. She wished she hadn't given him her bag. She hoped he didn't want to come to her house. She'd have to explain about collecting Deebee, about them being at home alone, about all the rules.

'Well, not just at the oval.'

'Oh.' She looked down at her feet, at all the pavement cracks they were stepping on.

'You know, just around the place,' he said, hitching her bag higher on his shoulder.

'Oh,' she said.

They walked the remaining half-block of footpath, through sun and into shade where the wind blew colder; the hairs on her arms stood up. At the corner, in sun again, the path ended. She gestured ahead, said, 'My house is just there.'

'I know.' He flashed her a smile. Those bright eyes. He handed over her bag. 'Bye.'

She saw his cheeks were pink. She turned away. 'Bye,' she said, felt her heart beat in her throat. From behind, she heard him: 'See ya tomorrow!'

~

The next day Orla asked Heather, 'Can I come to your house after school?'

The girls stared at one another. Heather's face flushed. 'Okay.'

Heather's mother turned from the sink to the kitchen door and smiled at Orla. She had a peeler in one hand, a potato in the other. 'Hello,' she said. And Orla was struck by the resemblance between mother and daughter: same skin, hair, nose, smile, eyes the blue of her gingham apron. How strange, Orla thought, to know how you'll look when you're old. Orla listened for sounds from other rooms but there were none. So, Orla thought, Heather's father wasn't there. She supposed he was at work; she felt relieved. Other kids' fathers — their fingernails, whiskers, cigarette smoke, voices, all the creases in their faces when they smiled. Heather's older brothers didn't seem to be there, either.

The girls sat at the kitchen table, drank milk, ate Milk Arrowroot biscuits topped with chunks of butter. Heather's smiling mother wrapped up the potato peelings in newspaper, said, 'Why don't you play with Orla in your room?'

The window and curtains were already closed; as they entered, Heather shut the door behind them, too. Then she crossed the big, dim room, while Orla stood just inside the door, surveying: two single beds with white-painted iron bedheads and frilly white bedspreads, one near the door and the other near the window. She wondered who else slept there. A white festooned dressing table: brushes and pins, necklaces, earrings, pretty boxes and bottles, bracelets and vases, paper flowers and long feathers. On the floor, a big white wooden box overflowing with toys; a smaller one bursting with comics and magazines; over there, a huge, fully furnished doll's house; and there, a small round table set with a miniature, painted china tea set. And, staring from every surface, blonde, blue-eyed dolls in pretty dresses.

Heather stood at her dressing table with her back turned while Orla gazed from one doll to the next. She had never seen a room with so much stuff. She didn't know Heather liked dolls so much.

When Heather turned she had something long and white in her hand. She pointed to one of the beds and said, 'Take off your clothes and lie down there.'

Orla glanced nervously at the door. 'What if someone comes in?'

'They won't,' Heather replied. Orla frowned. How could she be so sure?

She turned her back and undressed quickly, lay stiffly on the bedspread. She tried not to watch Heather take off her clothes, too, then turn and walk towards the bed. But, as she drew closer it was impossible not to see that her face and arms, and her lower legs, were beige and freckled but the rest of her, everything, was milky white. Between her legs was a plump white mound. She had tiny breasts, but not a single hair down there, and Orla held her legs tightly together, embarrassed.

Heather knelt beside the bed, her small pink nipples at the Orla's shoulder. She held up a white peacock feather. Orla stared at it. She had never seen one like it before. Heather said, 'Close your eyes,' and Orla did as she was told and felt the feather on her arms and stomach and thighs. It was nice but all she could think of was footsteps, the door, the aproned mother in the kitchen, and how had Heather even thought to do this? Heather stroked her with the feather for a long time, up and down, and there was no sound other than Orla's heart, their breathing, the floorboards creaking beneath Heather's knees, the tiny scrape of feather on her skin.

Then Heather lifted the feather. Orla opened her eyes. Heather was standing, her hand at her side. She said, 'Now we swap.' The feather was at a right angle, pointing at Orla like an accusation. Heather's plump mound was suddenly too close and white.

Orla sat up. 'I have to go.'

She dressed fast. Heather didn't say anything, just dressed, too. Orla stopped at the kitchen door. Heather's mother turned around again, wiped her hands on her apron and smiled. Orla said, 'Thank you for the milk and biscuits. I have to look after my little sister.'

Heather followed Orla to the front porch. 'See you tomorrow,' she said.

'Yeah,' Orla replied, leaping down the steps, not looking back.

~

As always, Mrs Thompson smiled and took Deebee's hand and closed the door so Deebee could never be sure which way her mother went, and so she stood there, her binoculars clamped under her arm, and looked around at the Thompsons' kitchen which was just the same as every morning, its windows and pictures and indoor plants all swimming the way her father's face had done at the pool after he'd said, 'Hold your breath and jump!' and she had, she had, she had closed her eyes and leapt from the edge to her father's arms but there was only quick air and water and she was down, under, flailing, eyes open, looking up to the bright swimming blue of the sky, to her father's face, reaching reaching her straining fingers, kicking all the water aside, her cheeks puffed out hard, holding her breath, her lips closed tight, a blowfish girl, her father's face so far away and bending strange, her father's mouth laughing stretched, her father's laughter like a storm, the water banging into her, and then the grip of her father's hand and she burst out, blinking, into the air, was lifted into her father's arms, clinging, a monkey girl, her own hands swiping, swiping the pool from her face.

Mrs Thompson said, 'Suzie has something to show you,' and the kids ran ahead, and she followed them down their wobbly passageway, her hands twirling, three times one way, three times the other, trailing after their voices, legs, the back door slapping open against the veranda wall, her sandals stepping off the back veranda into the hot bright, onto their green lawn, following them under their Hills hoist, under its pink basket full of pegs and hanging, into the big cold dark of their shed.

'Look! Look!' they said, so she squinted until she could see. A bird. A bird bright and slim as a leaf, a bright leaf-bird in a cage; green-chested, yellow-necked, speckled green and yellow wings opening closing above its back, squawking, tipping its head and peering. She moved closer to its dot of an eye.

'What is it?' she asked.

Suzie unlatched the cage. 'Look!' Johnny said. 'It's tame!' And it was, its feet like the roots of tiny trees. It gripped Suzie's pointer finger and she brought it out and held it close to Deebee's face. It yawned. Its claws were sharp. She saw its curved, pointed beak.

'Will it bite me?' Deebee said.

'Nah, it's just a budgie,' Suzie replied.

'You can touch it,' said Johnny.

So she lay her own pointer finger on the top of its head.

Suzie put her free hand on her hip. 'Mum said you have to name it.'

Deebee stroked it carefully. She smiled at its face. Its feathers were the softest thing; she pressed down and she could feel its body there — its skull, warm and hard, round as a pebble. Just like Daddy's when she was on his shoulders, her knees and fingers clinging to him. She lifted her hand from it, placed it to the side of her own head. Just like hers.

'So,' Suzie said, 'what are you gonna call it?'

'Da —' Deebee began. She took her binoculars from under her arm, put them to her eye, trained her gaze on the bird. A smudge of green, a huge eye, a movement, a piece of Suzie's skin.

Johnny screwed up his face. 'What?'

Deebee heard the cage door open, the bird flutter. All she saw were smears of colour. 'Daniel,' she said, turning towards the cage. Its bars were big and close and blurred and far apart.

Suzie snorted. 'What a dumb name.' She latched the cage door.

Deebee turned the binoculars towards Suzie. She felt their hard plastic eyepieces in her fingers. Through them she saw the strange fat mess of Suzie's hair. For a moment she imagined raising them up, bringing them down on the top of her head.

44

When she thought about it afterwards, Orla couldn't remember how they had travelled there or where it was located. She could remember only that it was a place of new roads and kerbs, expanses of yellow sand and sunshine, of new-planted buffalo lawns. A moment in which the future looked possible. Although that day she gazed intently through the window as they took roads she didn't recognise, and although she looked as if she was seeing everything they passed, bequeathing it all to memory, it was in fact her teetering excitement that kept her fixed as if on a dangerous cliff, silent, her hands tightly clasped in the nest of her lap, her mind a cinema of images, all the whirling possibilities of return. If this could happen, then anything.

There was a breakfast bar in the kitchen, a large linen cupboard near the laundry door, interior walls of exposed brick, ceilings of exposed beams. It felt modern: naked and daring, spacious; it made Orla's skin tingle. Deebee was loud and rushing, wide-eyed.

Their mother grinned back at them. 'With the compensation and a small loan, this is the one I should be able to afford to build. Do you like it?'

Deebee jumped up and down. 'Our house! Our house!'

'On our block?' Orla asked. 'Really? Really?'

Her mother gave a big, slow shrug. 'I don't see why not.'

Orla's heart thumped. She pointed. 'Can I have that room?'

Her mother laughed. 'I don't see why not.'

That night Orla lay awake: back to her friends; gumnuts underfoot and coffee-rock sliding; boulders and stretches of hard-baked clay radiating heat; and trees, trees, the smell of them, their bark and sap; lizards basking; trails of ants, the orange hills of their homes; running from the possibility of the searing bite of sergeant ants, from the look of hairy caterpillars; rooted to the spot by a herd of sudden brumbies; the sound of snakes, cicadas, the crush of eucalyptus leaves; soft rain-soaked litter on forest floor, its slippery, winter treachery. She couldn't stop smiling, squeezed shut her eyes, tried to sleep. And, she told herself, when her father returned and didn't find them where he had left them, he would know exactly where to look.

~

The bank's linoleum was green and shiny; a yellow light gleamed overhead. The manager was grey-haired, grey-suited. His large desk shone, his blue eyes regarded her. Later she would realise he looked tired but, as she sat opposite him, her bag in her lap, all she could think about was how exciting this was and how straightforward, really, and how he would see that. She fingered the pearls at her throat and smiled.

He watched her. 'What can I do for you, Mrs — err …?'

'Blest,' she said. And she told him: the block of land paid off, the appointment with the builder, her husband's death, her job, the compensation win, the cost of a more modest house than they'd planned, her children's need for a home of their own, that stability. He listened politely, nodding. She glanced at the nameplate on his desk, said, 'So, as you can see, Mr Murdoch, I only need to borrow one thousand dollars of the eleven thousand for the house, that's all. And the land is worth four thousand, too. I'm working full-time and paying rent, of course, so repayments won't be any trouble.' She smiled brightly.

He looked at her steadily. 'And who is your guarantor?'

She blinked. 'Guarantor?'

'Yes.'

'I'm sorry, Mr Murdoch. What's a guarantor?'

'Someone who will guarantee the repayment of the loan.'

Henry frowned. 'But I'll guarantee the repayment. I'm working full-time. Did I say that? And there'll be fourteen thousand dollars equity. As you can see, I just need one thousand.'

'I'm sorry; you will need a guarantor. It's bank policy.'

'No, no, *I'm* sorry, Mr Murdoch; I don't quite understand. When my husband and I discussed our home loan with you, there was no mention of a guarantor, so I'm puzzled. Is this a new requirement?'

'No. It's not new. There was no need for a guarantor when your husband was alive.'

'Oh.'

'The guarantor must be male.'

'Male?'

'Yes. All banks in Australia require this.'

'But I don't have a male guarantor.'

'I'm sorry, but banks don't lend money to a woman without a male guarantor.'

'But I — perhaps I'm not making myself clear.' She leaned in. 'I own the block, and the compensation will pay for all but one thousand dollars of the cost of the house. There's no chance the bank will lose its money.'

'I'm sorry. I understand that. You will still need a male guarantor.'

She sat back, pressed her lips together. 'Could — couldn't the bank make an exception in this case, given I'm in such a strong position — financially speaking. After all,' she felt her face flush, 'even if I weren't able to make the repayments — which would never happen because the loan is small and I'm working five days a week and the repayments wouldn't be any more than the rent I'm paying — but even if that were to happen, the bank could just sell the house and get its thousand dollars. There's no chance it could lose.'

He paused, looked hard at her. 'I'm very sorry, but that will not be possible. It's bank policy. Surely there is someone you could ask? A brother, a cousin, a — a friend?'

She felt herself stiffen. 'No.' She gathered her bag with both hands. 'No friend. And I have no relatives.' She stood. 'Thank you for seeing me,' she said, her voice cold as she turned to the door. Behind her, the scrape of his chair, the shuffle of his feet, his voice saying something. Her heels clicked loudly across the floor.

Outside, the sunlight was shockingly bright. She shielded her eyes with her hand, looked this way and that along the street, unsure for a moment just where she was.

45

Christmas was close. Which was impossible. Orla retrieved the box of family photos from the hall cupboard, found some taken the previous Christmas, the last one in the hills, the last one with him. They were all so normal: her sister, her mother and herself standing around, looking into the lens as if they had no idea. She frowned at the faces, the walls, the carpet, curtains, tinsel. She remembered she had come home from school and told her mother there was no Santa. Her mother had said, 'If you don't believe in Santa Claus, you don't get any presents,' in a singsong voice, and she had understood what that meant, that they were all in it together, the joy of the game, the choosing of belief. And so she had pressed her face to her bedroom window on Christmas Eve, peering up at the stars, because she had heard the sleigh bells, she knew she had, and she had shouted, and her mother had come, and had smiled at the bedclothes, avoiding Orla's gaze as she tucked Orla in.

Orla studied the photos and all she could see was that everything was ordinary. Her father wasn't in them. Sometimes Kit took the photo but, otherwise, he was almost always behind the camera. If she thought of the moments the shutter clicked last Christmas or on birthdays, she could only see his hands, legs, torso, the way he stood, the sun on his hair. Always a camera, black and silvery, in the place where his face should be.

More of December passed. She waited for her mother to say something. When Deebee mentioned Christmas, their mother looked from her to Orla, and nodded but didn't speak. Orla didn't speak either; the words she had planned and stored just fell away. Instead she made a list for a Christmas at which her father would appear. God, who saw everything, would tell him it had been quite long enough. There was a block of land to build on. There was no male guarantor. There were men who looked at and touched her. And there were men in a spaceship circling the moon. She had seen it on TV, heard about it at school. It was hard to believe everything. She had peered out of windows at night — her bedroom, the lounge room. She had stared at the moon, but couldn't see a spaceship. She understood some things, though. She had learned her lesson. She was bad. She would be good. Her friends were waiting. Deebee said she always felt sick. Even though. Even though Deebee talked and played. So much to talk about when he came.

The world rewards patience; the world rewards; the world —

Buy tree

Decorate

Buy presents

Wrap them

Buy food

Cook

She left it on the kitchen bench. Simple. If a spaceship is orbiting the moon.

Her mother called her. Orla's heart pounded. She wished she hadn't. Shouldn't tell her mother what to. She stood back, muscles tensed, watched her mother's face as she scanned the list again, watched her hand as she slid the list aside, as she turned to the stove and said, 'Was that for me?'

'Sorry.'

She stirred something with the wooden spoon. 'Can you set the table instead of delivering cheek?'

Oral hesitated. Only five days left. And it had to be perfect. For when he came home. Or why would he bother. She squeezed her hands together and made her legs walk to the cutlery drawer. She took a deep breath and opened it. 'Mum, do you remember how you said if we don't believe in Santa Claus we don't get any presents?'

'Yes.'

'Is it the same this year?'

And her mother turned her head and looked at her, pushed hair from her face with the back of her free hand. 'Of course.'

'I thought so,' Orla nodded, lifting four of everything.

46

The last school day of the year was like the day after the earthquake, everyone laughing and jumping about. They cleaned out their desks. Orla found piecrust wrapped in paper, a mouldy orange. She held them close to her body, walked quickly, watched the floor, dumped them in the classroom bin. Back at her seat, she glanced about. Her desk smelled strange. She rubbed her fingers on her clothes.

The bell went; everyone ran. She put up her own chair and some abandoned ones. Suddenly there was just her and Mr Woodland, at his desk, writing. She could hear the scratch of his pen. A breeze blew through the windows. Kids shouted as they ran across the oval. She picked up bits of paper, crossed the room with them. She watched her teacher in her peripheral vision, wondered what it would be to have a job like his, wondered if she could ask. She dropped the rubbish into the bin. She couldn't see her orange but she could smell it. He looked up, smiling, said, 'Thanks, Orla. Merry Christmas.' Looked down at his papers again.

At the door, she glanced back. It wasn't right. She should have been happy. She should have been leaving for good. Now there would be another year. She wanted to tell him. She wanted to tell him how things had been, how they had changed, but that they'd be better soon, that at Christmas her father would come back. And so another year and they'd build their house and then high school would be in the hills. With her friends. She raised her hand to him, lowered it. He didn't look up.

It was hot. Her bag was heavy. She walked along the edge of the school oval, crossed the road, passed the church. The page he had been writing was more interesting than she was. She could understand his being sick of his class, of those fighting boys and talking girls. But was he really sick of her, too? Summer already felt long.

~

Next morning she woke early with the remains of a dream, a half-remembered image: the shape of a man walking away from her. She stared at her bedroom ceiling. Then she got up, went to the linen cupboard and opened it. She lifted down the box. It was lighter than she thought it would be. She put it in the middle of the lounge room floor. Deebee stared. 'What's that?'

Under the cardboard flaps, gold and silver tinsel. She stepped back and smiled. 'Christmas.'

Deebee jumped up and down, shouted. Their mother appeared, stared at Deebee, the box, Orla. 'What are you doing?'

Orla spoke carefully. 'Please, Mummy, may I put it up?'

Her mother waved her hands about. 'On what?'

Orla remembered with a thud. She stared at the tinsel. Her sister shouted, 'Christmas tree! Christmas tree!'

Orla's eyes prickled. She couldn't look at Deebee. Their father had always brought home the trees in his car, put them in garden pots filled with soil. How could she have forgotten? She grabbed her sister's arm, hissed, 'Shut up!'

Deebee yelled. Their mother took a step towards them. 'Don't speak like that to your sister!'

She let Deebee go.

Her mother said, 'Who do you think you are? Don't you dare speak like that to anyone!'

'Sorry, Mum.'

'Don't apologise to me!' She stepped closer; her finger stabbed the air. 'Apologise to her!'

Orla took a step back. She looked at her sister, quiet now, her fingers in her mouth, her round eyes looking at their mother. Orla lifted the corners of her mouth into a smile. 'Sorry, Deebee.'

'No!' Their mother stamped her foot. 'No!'

Orla stepped back again. She kept her eye on her mother, heard her sister start to cry, heard her mother say, 'Apologise properly for what you said, that awful word!'

Orla opened her mouth. A small sound came out. She couldn't remember an awful word, dug her fingernails into her palm. Maybe should could find it there. She looked at the floor. It wasn't there either. 'I'm sorry for speaking to you like that, Deebee,' she said. Her voice was going from her, running away, ragged and distant, and she hated the sound of it. She glanced up. Her mother was staring hard at her and shaking her head, turning away, and Orla knew what her mother had seen, the deep inside part of her, where she had left her window open for the prowler to look through, where she hadn't cleaned her room when her father told her, and where he had gone away because of her; the part that kept rotting food in her desk; the part that had wished her own mother dead.

Orla swiped at her eyes with the backs of her hands. She closed the lid of the box. Deebee sniffled. 'Are we going to get a tree, Orly?' she said. 'Are we?'

Orla couldn't look at her. 'Just shut up about the tree,' she said quietly.

After breakfast their mother stacked the dishes in the sink, turned on the tap. 'Get dressed,' she said, without looking at them. 'We're going to town. The bus comes in an hour.'

~

Orla sat behind her mother and Deebee. She watched Deebee's hand slide open the window, her neck stick her face out. Hot wind poured in. The bus roared, jerked, an angry thing. Orla leaned against her window's metal frame, cool against her cheek. Light so white it hurt. Up a hill past a house with a big circular lawn, a circular rose bed in the middle, a sprinkler on a spike dead centre in the rose bed; the bushes festooned red, pink, yellow; the lawn around the rose bed thick and green; for oh a moment the scent of the air like coming rain.

Then fast along the highway, past factories and big, vacant, sandy blocks. The bus slowing. Orla's chest tightening, pleaseGoddon'tlethemsitnexto. Her mother's face to the window, shoulders stiffening, and Orla knew she gripped her clutch bag in front of her with both hands. But Deebee just stared at them, the stream of passengers on their noisy way to the back seats, even though Orla poked at Deebee with the toe of her shoe. Hard. It made no difference to Deebee's big eyes, open mouth, her twisting in her place to watch. Orla turned away, studied the glass in the window so she didn't have to see those born wrong-headed, misshapen, limping, gripping their small school cases. She stared out at the black road, the passing cars, as if it were beautiful out there, as if she couldn't hear the elongated, too-loud speech, as if she were deaf to the randomness of luck.

Then the highway became straight and fast. Hot air blasted in, the roar of the wind in her ears louder than her thoughts. She squinted through the screen of her lashes at the trees grey and fuzzy along the verge. The sky was blue and exhausted. Someone behind her grabbed the back of the seat and pulled themselves up. She glanced back. A man was settling himself now across the aisle; he caught her eye with a glare. She closed the window a bit, too late, so he would see she understood her mistake. The rest of the way to town she lifted her legs a little, one at a time, to let the sweat under them dry.

~

In Boans there were glowing yellow lampshades on the walls. The floors gleamed. Light rippled like cream over the marble counters. And Orla remembered a poem Mr Woodland had read them, holding up the book to show them the way the words ran like a ribbon down the left-hand page, illustrations in purple and yellow and midnight blue like a river on the right. A highwayman, masked, on a black and galloping horse; a zigzag of yellow moonlight across a moor, whatever that was. All through Boans, the big metal blades of fans rotated, each whole shiny contraption fixed to marble pillars. Orla trailed behind her family, watched the fans buzz and turn, this way and back. She looked at the ladies who stood beside the cash registers she passed, slim ladies with pale skin, long eyelashes, perfect hair, who stared into the middle distance and did not look back.

Henry pressed coins into Orla's hand. Deebee pressed her face against the cabinet-glass, watched the machine squeeze out pale batter rings, jiggle them along a conveyor, drop them into hot deep oil where they bobbed and sizzled. Orla turned to smile at her mother, but Henry was gazing at the cosmetics counters. Beside her, Orla felt her sister jiggle and looked back at the cabinet. On its other side, a pimply girl turned donuts with a long-handled wire scoop. Her thin hair was pulled straight back from her forehead into a high, tight ponytail. Her blonde eyebrows were plucked into thin, pale lines. Orla studied her:

bright blue eye shadow, dark blue mascara, pink lipstick. The girl scooped the donuts, two at a time, held them as yellow oil dripped into the bubbling vat. She upended her scoop to drop them, brown and glistening, into a tray of sugar, pushed them about, flipped them, lifted and slid them into a paper bag. Then she nudged the paper bag across the counter, and Orla pushed the money back to her, smiling. The girl's gaze slid away. Patches of oil grew on the brown paper bag. Deebee kept close to Orla as they walked, watched the oily bag swing hotly from the ends of her fingers — the glorious scent of it — while Orla ran the fingers of her free hand along the timber balustrades, gazed deeply into the swirling patterns of the marble steps they descended, at the shape of each stair, its curving and widening, heard the sound of her mother's heels ahead, and thought of Cinderella arriving in her gown, everyone turning to look. She believed she had never seen such a beautiful place. At the bottom of the staircase, strings of coloured lights led the way past rows of dolls with wavy hair and blue, wide-open eyes, past shiny yellow Tonka trucks with thick rubber wheels. Orla slowed her pace to allow space to open between her and the others. Her mother took Deebee's hand and strode on. Deebee glanced back at the hot paper bag.

But, when it came, there was no mistaking it. Orla hesitated, pressed her lips together, then edged forward, saw her mother's hand resting on the top of her sister's head, women in hats turning to look, clutching their gleaming handbags to their sides.

Orla thrust the paper bag at Deebee. 'Here.'

But Deebee just looked, shook her head, kept wailing. Orla held the bag out to her mother but Henry was glancing about. Orla looked where her mother was looking but there was nothing other than the faces of some passing women: no children in a

queue, no photographer in his red bow tie, shaking a teddy bear.
The Santa stage with its red crepe trim, its strings of coloured
lights, its empty Santa throne.

Their mother fixed her gaze on a sales assistant. 'Excuse me,' she
said, waving. 'We've come to see Father Christmas. Can you tell
us when he'll be back?' The woman stared. Orla watched her
take in the scene: her mother's dress, fixed smile, small wailing
child, older girl with her arms crossed, half-turned away. The
sales assistant shook her head and shrugged, tidied the papers
in front of her. Orla stared at the gleaming floor, the paper bag
limp and gaping in her hand. She heard her mother say, 'Never
mind, darling, we'll leave him a note under the tree.'

Deebee wailed, 'But we don't have a tree!'

Orla turned her back. She didn't have to look to know just how
her mother would be smiling.

The pavement radiated heat. Deebee tugged two fistfuls of her
mother's skirt. Henry prised the fabric from her daughter's
fingers, stepped away, looked up and down the street. No taxis.
In a singsong voice, she said, 'Making a noise will just make you
hotter.' Deebee cried louder.

Orla pointed to slim shade beneath a shop eave. 'Can we sit
there?'

Her mother frowned. 'I beg your pardon?'

Orla sighed and looked away. Her eyes prickled. 'May we sit
over there, please, Mum.' When there was no reply, she pointed.
'In the shade. Against the wall. Just over there.'

Her mother shook her head, pulled Deebee awkwardly up to her
hip but Deebee slipped till she was clinging like a monkey to her

mother's leg. Henry unhooked her arms and stood her back on her feet, stroked her head. Deebee made a long loud sad sound.

Orla glared at the shaded shop front. Her feet were sore. She stepped forward, hoisted her sister up and Deebee clambered, clung tight to Orla's neck. Orla staggered. Her mother frowned. 'Whatever you do, don't lean on that glass. It's not safe.'

So Orla leaned against the bricks. She felt the back of her dress scrape. Had she made a hole in it? The bricks were hot and rough but they held them up.

When the taxi came, the driver opened the doors for them, put their parcels in the boot. Henry sat in front — she must have forgotten — so Orla slumped into the back seat with her sister. If she opened the window and let the air blow hard into her face, maybe she would be all right. Maybe. The car smelled of cigarettes. That smell stirred something, a kind of sickness, and stilled something else.

All the way home, they were driving into the sun. She stared out the window, as the car lurched and swayed, her eyes half-closed against the flickering light. Like the films her father would screen against a blank wall, all the pictures of the iya place. Along the highway, the afternoon shadows were longer, the air a different colour. Otherwise it was like a film running backwards: city streets, highway, factories, homes and gardens. No-one spoke. Once, her mother turned to look at her as if she were going to speak, and Orla looked back. She watched her mother glance about — doors, floor, upholstery. When her father was at the wheel, her mother usually said something like, 'Make sure your door is locked properly, Orla.' But this time she just looked as if she couldn't quite believe what she was seeing and then faced ahead again, held her hand up to her eyes to shield them from the glare of the sun.

Deebee slept, her head sweaty on Orla's knees. Orla wanted to sit up, high, higher, to get above the sideways movement of the car but she didn't want to wake Deebee, so instead she stretched her legs out slowly, pushed her feet into the space beneath the driver's seat, pressed her toes to its underneath, remembered she'd once tapped her father's seat like that when she was young, before the car sickness, and had kept tapping, sending him a secret message — I love you best — watching for his smiling eyes to appear in the rear-view mirror. But when he had looked at her he was scowling and she had felt ashamed, pulled back her feet, pressed her hands between her knees, folded up her chest, made herself small, stayed quiet and still. Now she gazed into the back of the taxi driver's head, the wrong head wrong hair wrong colour, and her thoughts were loud, and one word only: 'Daddy. Daddy.' Nausea rose.

She wound her window right down and the wind shouted in her face. After a while, she turned back to see her mother looking at the driver. He held his wrong chin high to keep his wrong eyes shaded by the wrong sun visor. The top half of his wrong face was shadowed, the bottom half brightly lit. Black hairs curled from his neck. Orla imagined how he must look from where her mother sat, his whiskers sticking out of his sunlit skin the way they would appear on her father at the weekends. That must be what she was staring at.

The taxi driver lifted Deebee from the back seat and carried her to the door, handed her to Henry. He fetched their shopping to their porch. Henry said, 'Thank you so much.'

He smiled, said, 'Merry Christmas.' His eyes were dark and kind.

Henry smiled. 'Yes. And a Merry Christmas to you.' But he was already walking away. Henry held Deebee to her hip with one arm, listing. Deebee's head hung dumbly on her mother's shoulder, her limbs dangled. Henry jiggled the key in the lock with her free hand. Orla wrapped her leg around one of the metal veranda poles, watched the man reverse onto the street, drive off without looking back.

She carried in the parcels, heard her sister cry briefly in her room, their mother hush her. Back in the lounge room, Orla and Henry stood silent, gazing down at the bags of shopping. Henry fanned herself with her hand. 'Open the windows.' Orla dashed from room to room to let the sea breeze pour in.

When she returned, her mother was kneeling over a long box. On its lid, a picture of a lit-up Christmas tree, a mum and dad, a boy and girl. They had neat brown hair and white smiles. Her mother took out strange wrapped shapes. As Orla watched her, she thought: wherever her father was, he must know it was a plastic tree or none. He didn't have his car keys and, anyway, there was no car anymore so he couldn't get them a real tree the way he always did. Besides, all the roadside stalls would have sold their trees by now. Or all the good ones, anyway. That's what he always said.

When he comes home, she thought, watching her mother tear the wrapping from the pieces of tree, it will be like this: he'll knock because he doesn't have his house key either. I won't run. I'll walk. Fast as I can. Open the door. He'll smile, say, 'Hello, Tweety.' My eyes will sting. I'll unlock the flyscreen door. My hands will shake. I'll say, 'Mum got a plastic tree.' He'll say, 'That's all right.' Mum will call, 'Who is it?' He'll raise his finger to his lips. Ssshhh. He'll step inside, his eyes shining, the way they did after he had written about the Arab and the knife. Later he'll say he doesn't mind anymore if I cry. But I won't cry because things will be different, happy, and I'll tell him so, and he'll kiss the top of my head. 'That's my good girl.'

Her mother looked up. 'Get the Christmas decorations.' By the time Orla brought them to her, Henry was clicking together the tree's base. Orla pushed aside the coffee table, sat on the floor beside her. The tree's limbs were different lengths in that deep fairytale green. She stared at the colour of it, remembered the slick surface of the penguin pool. The breeze rattled the venetian blinds and shook the poplars; the quiet click of her mother's work as she put together the frame of the tree. Orla handed her the fake limbs one by one. Sometimes it looked like her mother's eyes were wet. Orla kept glancing at the side of her mother's face, unsure. Around them the afternoon shadows deepened.

47

He will push me away, pick himself up, easy, like a handkerchief, swipe at his mouth with the back of hand, look at me and say, 'What the hell?' He will be indignant. He will be ashamed. He will turn away his face away and spit out the dirt on his tongue. In the dark we won't see the blood in it.

When the ambulance arrives, he'll be sitting at my table. My wife will appear in her dressing-gown, woken by the noise. He'll apologise. He'll drink tea with plenty of sugar. She will say it's good for the shock. He will grin and thank her, polite and sheepish. The young lads will still be there, trembling: 'Bloody hell, you scared the shit outta me, 'scuse my French!'

48

Early light slipped like spirits through her blinds, sparkled on her ceiling. She sat up. Her walls glowed. The world hushed. No wind, no kookaburra.

Last time she had seen the light-spirits she had been so young she had thought the worst thing that can happen was that mothers use fipels to paint bathroom floors. Now she pressed her fists into her eyes to forget and to remember, in the same instant, all the mornings riding Nugget, the sitting beside her father in his car, watching the world rush past: streets she knew well becoming streets she didn't; houses becoming traffic lights then grey-brown river, green fields, overhanging trees — the world in flux; the way their life had been in the places they'd lived — transient, unstill; how moving house changes everything; how returning could change it all back again — forest, lizards, stones, scudding cloud, the cold creeping shadows of a winter garden, its wet red clay; how if you don't believe in Santa, then; how at Christmas, anything.

She dressed quickly. Now, she knew, a sound you have never heard before can enter a house and a body, change everything, make you pray, sleep, wake, pray, sleep, wake, pray pray pray. Now, at last. At last. She pulled her best dress down over her head. The most important thing today, she told herself, was to keep control. No crying, which was easy because there'd soon be no need for any more of that. And no running. She already knew what running does.

She brushed her hair, pushed in a hair slide, scrutinised herself in the mirror, slid it out, pushed it in again. She stood in her doorway, took a deep breath. Her hands gripped the front of her best dress, then gripped one another.

The tree, thick with tinsel, stood where her mother had placed it, in the corner between the fireplace and the window, where the lamp once was. Parcels were piled at its foot, red paper patterned with green leaves and Santas ho ho ho-ing.

Her heart thumped; breath came in small. There was no-one else in the room. But what did she expect? He would hide. In shadow. Behind the tree. In a box. She took a step. Another. She had been good. Had tried to be a, Jesus loved the. She moved so close that her breath. He had shrunk himself. Had become a present. The tinsel quivered. Could see her many selves in its gold and silver. She stared. Behind the tree. Charcoal carpet, grey wall. A triangle of shadow — empty, quiet. Early sun slanting in. She stared. All the versions of herself staring back. Let me present. He will present himself. Be present. Her present.

From behind, her mother's voice. Orla felt her hand lift itself, her fingers grasp a decoration, gold and shiny as the light-spirits. Hold it lightly. Jesus the light of. 'The tree looks nice, Mum,' she heard herself say.

Her mother leaned in, kissed her cheek: 'Merry Christmas.'

'Merry Christmas,' she said, and closed her eyes and swivelled herself to kiss her mother back.

Feet thump, and then her sister and mother kneeling, holding parcels in their hands, her mother saying, 'This one's for you, Deebee.'

Orla sat on the divan's edge. She felt the frame press into the backs of her legs. She watched her family on the floor in front of her, she watched the door of her parents' room. It's all right, it's all right. The day is early and Jesus is. She listened. For other sounds: running water, the clink of a spoon, the rustle of sheets, a floorboard's creak.

Instead her mother's hands appeared, holding something red, green, white. Behind it, her mother's mouth smiled. Orla looked at her mother's eyes which were not smiling and made a mouth-smile back. 'Thank you.' Her mother turned to Deebee. Orla rested the redgreenwhite on her knees, her hands on top of it. The air was full of her sister's shouts.

Another redgreenwhite, another smile. She put the two on the divan beside her, worried at one with her fingernail — pick, pick pick. How loud sticky tape is. Worried at it till she folded back the redgreenwhite to reveal the edge of *Green Grass of Wyoming*, slid it out. The cover so pretty her stomach ached: farmhouse, wind-swept grass, a sky as big as the one she knew. She opened it. There were illustrations. Its scent filled her. She stroked its pages, closed her eyes, lifted it and pressed its smooth surface to her cheek.

She stood, moved one foot at a time until she was by the kitchen sink, filling a glass, sipping. Beyond the window the world was new and waking. There had been no mischief in her mother's face. Her mother could have been an actress but she was not a liar; no, not like me, Orla thought, gazing at the bruised line of the sea.

Behind her, voices rose and fell. An intention formed and settled, wordless. She breathed deeply, rested the glass quietly in the sink, ran on her toes across the dining room and through her parents' door. She did not look back.

The bed was empty, the sheet kicked away. No-one stood between the bed and wardrobes, the bed and dressing table, the bed and window. Two more quick steps and no-one crouched on the other side of the bed, ready to leap up, surprise her. Swivel left, two more steps and she tried a wardrobe: the mechanism clicked. Her stomach flipped. She closed her eyes, pulled at the door.

Once, her father had explained lightning. They were sitting in the car at night, waiting somewhere for their mother. It was raining. He said two clouds, the energy, the electric arc. Her father had made something fly through walls. And the handle of the wardrobe turned so easily for her now. Because he could do anything. Arabs lived in him. Knives and shadows. Her body shook. She had been as good as, was sorry for every, for making him hit, for being a. She had learned. She would be better, better, even better. And Christmas. A miracle. Anything could. Because Jesus.

She pulled open the wardrobe door, opened her eyes and blinked. Then she opened the other door.

Later she'd remember she'd run. She'd run when she knew, she knew what would happen if she did. For a moment her heart hurt so much she had to curl herself over with the pain of it.

~

And after that it was her mouth, of course. It was always her mouth, its stupid. Had a life of its own, her mouth, noisy, always giving her away. She tiptoed back quickquick, past the table, the kitchen bench, the TV, mantelpiece, the stern dial of her father's radio. Quickquick up onto the divan, turned, sat, legs drawn up, one fluid movement; pressed her stupid mouth hard against her knee to stop, to put it in its place, show it who's; peered over, her arms wrapped tight around herself, holding, holding. No-one looked. Which was good. Very good. Which was what she'd hoped. She shouted in her head, 'It's all right. It's all right. He'll knock. I'll run, I'll walk, I'll fly through the air.' Hello, Tweety.

Deebee tore open her presents. The loud rip of it. Orla dug her teeth into the skin of her leg as she watched because this is how you keep it in bottle it be a full bottle a bottle full of things inside with a top you press down hard and this is how I won't won't won't so no-one looks no-one guesses no-one notices a thing.

She watched her mother's mouth read the gift tags, watched it move the words up from somewhere deep and push them out, rivulets of words, as if words are nothing, nothing at all, as if everything was normal and there had always been just the three of them.

Deebee held a toy tractor in her fist. It gleamed in the middle air. Behind it Deebee's eyes shone like treasure. She leapt and ran through the house with her treasure-eyes and her toy. Orla heard her happy voice, her feet fast-thumping. The vibrations buzzed the floor. Her mother swivelled her head to watch her go, raised her voice: 'Love from Daddy, kiss kiss.' Orla pushed harder, felt the edges of her teeth against her knee. The smooth stretched-tight skin. Her nose pressed flat against her kneecap, then slipped itself sideways, squashed against her cheek. Her breath roared through her mouth. Press. Hard. Breathe. Hard. Press. Hard. Harder. And her front tooth popped through as if she were a plum, juicy underneath, and she was surprised, the texture, the slippery, the blood that filled her mouth as if she were a cup. For a moment, her tongue floated warmly, an island. She swallowed and there was pain, of course, but the pain was a tender thing and she was calm and salty as the sea.

Deebee reappeared, pushing the tractor across the floor. Its wheels rattled. Their mother smiled. She said, 'See? Daddy hasn't forgotten you.'

Orla's toes gripped the edge of the divan like short, squat fingers. She heard her mother say, 'He hasn't forgotten you, either,' and heat shot down her neck and arms like a cartoon shock. Maybe, she thought, she was a storm, had clouds in her, a bolt of lightning. She unclamped a hand, held it out, let her mother put the parcel in it. Her heart bashed. She peered at the label: With love, Daddy, kiss kiss. Something stabbed one side of her head. She winced, swallowed again, licked her lips, saw her blood well, her mother's mouth in a smile. But just her mouth. So. No smile in her eyes. So this. 'Thank you,' Orla said. So this is what. In her mother's eyes a plea.

So this is what we do.

With love, Daddy, kiss kiss.

The blood trickled. She licked it.

If you tell yourself something long enough, it's easy to believe it.

Once she had overheard: 'I always sign her report. Why don't you sign it for a change?' So her father had written: 'Very satisfactory' in his small pointed writing, not like this writing, this big, loopy, running-off-the-lines that had shouted back to her teachers: 'Good girl!' or 'I am very proud of my clever daughter!!' Words she never heard her mother speak.

Orla picked open one end of this parcel. Inside her head she imagined herself excited, smiling, saying, I wonder what on Earth it is? Like a real daughter and a good one. Like the daughter on the Christmas tree box. She tipped the parcel up and another book slid out with the sshh of the sea and she caught it easy in her other hand, made sure her face looked the way it should.

On the cover: four girls sit close to their mother, all before a blazing hearth. The mother is small and neat, blonde, calm. Three of the daughters have the shape of breasts beneath their dresses. The youngest flat-chested, in plaits. *Little Women*. Orla glanced at her mother who watched Deebee unwrap a small telescope, and said, 'You can look at the stars,' her fingers twitching. Who watched Deebee crash her truck and car together, shouting: 'Get out! Get out of my way!'

Later, in the kitchen, Henry opened and closed cupboard doors. Pans clanged on the sink and stove. Orla took her presents to her room, set them beside her on the bed. She lay rigid, listened for footsteps on the path, a knock at the front door. She felt tired. The day grew hot. When she woke again, the house smelled good. The light through her window was hard. She closed the blinds.

Her mother was bent over, peering into the oven. She glanced up at Orla, black smudged beneath her eyes, some colour in the corners of her mouth, hair stuck to her forehead, her dress stuck to her body. She basted the turkey and potatoes. Orla backed away from the furnace of it and into the laundry. The concrete cooled her feet. Her mother slammed the oven door, whisked something on the stove, the fork scraping the pan's insides.

Sweat stung Orla's eyes. She rubbed them. 'Can I do something?'

A car door thudded and Orla gasped, had begun to run before she could think. Behind, her mother's voice: 'Oh, no.'

Deebee yelled, 'Somebody's here!' But Orla was already across the lounge room, knowing, flying, knowing who it was, but still, still. Was the first at the door, wrenching it open.

Kit smiled. Orla stared. Deebee pushed past, waving her truck, shouting, 'Look what Daddy gave me!'

Kit brought in her bag and basket, a standard fan. Kit stroked Deebee's hair. 'Aren't you lucky.'

Henry appeared, dabbing her face with a tea towel, smiling at the fan. 'Merry Christmas,' she said. 'You're a life saver.'

Kit opened her arms and Orla walked into her, into the rustle of her, the softness, and breathed her in. Deebee threw her arms around their legs and squeezed. Orla felt one of Kit's arms slide down to her sister. Over their heads Kit said, 'Hello, my children.' Then, 'Merry Christmas.'

'Merry Christmas,' Orla mumbled against her. She felt Kit's hand stroke her back for a moment, then let her go.

~

There was still time, Orla thought. There was always time. Hour after hour. Another fork, knife, spoon, and Orla closed the cutlery drawer.

Crisp turkey; ham glazed with pineapple rings; browned potatoes; cauliflower au gratin; a bowl of peas with butter; a jug of soft stewed apples, a jug of gravy. Henry and Kit looked everywhere but at one another. The fan blew hot air over everything. Henry's chair scraped the floor as she stood, lifted the knife and sliced open the bird's white breast. No-one mentioned the cutlery and plate at the head of the table. Kit sipped her whisky, or swirled it in its glass. Sometimes Orla caught its scent. Sometimes her father had smelled like that. The fingers of Kit's other hand, long nails frosted peach, smoothed the white tablecloth. The glasses gleamed, the water jug silvered with condensation. Orla's legs stuck to her chair. Her mother said, 'Pass your plate.'

Deebee said, 'I'm hot,' and rested her forehead on the edge of the table. Orla fiddled with her red Christmas cracker; its crepe paper crackled. A blast of the fan lifted Henry's hair from her face as if she were running. Orla gazed at the window behind her mother's head. Outside was quiet, the light intense and the leaves of the cape lilac shimmered.

~

Later the girls lay spreadeagled on the lino. The women's voices rose and fell: 'And what did your sister say?'

'I don't know. I haven't heard from her.'

'Oh.'

'I got a card from Ireland, though.'

'And how are they?'

If Orla turned her head the right way, she could see the belly of
their dining table, her mother's pale leg. Kit's feet eased from her
shoes. The fan turned and trembled through the floor. Deebee
slept. Orla's eyes were heavy. Her mother's voice was far away,
calling. Then her father was with them, in his usual place at the
table. His teeth shone when he smiled, his cutlery shone in his
hands, the hairs on his arms and legs shone too, his feet jiggled in
his thongs and, when he laughed, he dropped his gaze and reached
with one hand to smooth the hair on his head. She smiled. No-
one, she knew, could guess how much she held inside.

~

That night, in her bed, raised voices woke her. As she opened
her eyes, she remembered only briefly the image of trees, their
branches close and tangled. She rolled onto her back, her heart
pounding, lay stiffly, strained to hear what she couldn't quite
make out. She should get up but the thought of it made her shiver,
clutch her sheet to her chest.

She started. A movement at her door. Deebee with her eyes wide.
Orla lifted the sheet for her sister to climb in. The sound of the
front door opening, closing. A slow car approaching, idling, a car
door slamming, the car moving away. Long silence.

For the rest of the night she was restless, drawn over and over
to wakefulness by a scratching at her window. Rigid and pressed
between Deebee and the wall she would open her eyes wide and
listen. Something — someone — was there, just there, on the
other side. So close that, any moment, he might have found he
could reach through and touch her.

In the morning she and Deebee sat at breakfast. They watched
their mother's face and knew better than to ask.

~

The next afternoon, Orla watched her mother at the sink. She knew she hadn't imagined it, and she had looked everywhere.

'Mum,' she said.

Henry glanced up. 'Yes?'

She took a breath. 'Where is Daddy's writing?'

'What writing?'

Orla hesitated, frowned. What did she mean, 'what writing'? 'You know — the story he was writing. With his typewriter.'

'Oh, that,' Henry said, watching her hand work the peeler again. 'I burned it.'

Orla grabbed the edge of the bench. The floor lurched. Her mother's hand gripped the wet potato to stop it slipping; she peeled in quick, sure strokes.

Orla opened her mouth. 'Why?' The word thin and high.

Her mother shrugged, wrenched on the tap. 'He spent so much time on that writing, and for what? All the hours I had to keep you quiet. All that time he could have spent with me.' Her voice trembled. Her thumbs rubbed hard at the potato under the stream of water.

There was no wood stove in the kitchen, no traces of fire in the lounge room grate. 'But where?' Orla said. She hated the whine in her voice. 'Where did you burn it?'

'Outside, of course, in the drum.'

In a breath, Orla saw again images jagged and fleeting: the treehouse, holding her book to her face like a shield; below, her father and sister raking the leaves. The wind shaking the skinny she-oak; a line of small bright clouds spinning across blue sky. The thin sharp stink of smoke. Laughter. She saw her hand reaching for fragments of burned paper that flew into the air, turned to soot on her fingers. The drum. Of course. Where else.

All evening, her voice shouting in her head: While I was at school. Before she started her new job. While Deebee was asleep. No, Deebee helped, dropped the papers in, watched the match flare, held Mum's hand the way she had always held Dad's, watched smoke rise, turning away as it stung, laughing about it, Mum saying, 'Don't tell Orla.'

When I came home that day — which day was it? — they must have looked at one another. Did Mum wink? While I was sitting still, praying, shoving thoughts down, learning sums, words, days cracking open. Hold Deebee's hand. Pray. Look both ways. Pray. Turn the key. Pray. Push. Listen. The stillness. Walls and floors. Breathe. The scent. Emptiness. Heart, just wait. Stand still. A moment of pain and it passes. Just like yesterday. The day before. Already Deebee filling everything with noise and running, don't don't just don't think about it, his knock, her own hand, trembling with relief and love, opening the door for him. And all the while.

All the while.

That night her dreams were words she couldn't read, and she was suspended just above the earth, swimming through smoke, breathing it in, each breath feeling as if it was her last. She was peering over the rim of an ordinary bowl, a glass, desk, drum, to find them wide and black and bottomless as she fell.

49

Once, before the war, he had loved a girl from his street, with thick hair and lashes, and skin like cream. In his last days home, in those thrilling, sleepless days before he waved his family goodbye at the station, travelled to London for weeks of uniforms, salutes, drills, lectures — in those days, believing that life would be long and good, so much better than it could be at home, an adventure if only he could get out now, now while he was young and had the chance, find it elsewhere, anywhere at all — he had held the creamy-skinned girl as she wept, had promised he would keep himself safe, write every week, return.

'Do you not think all the boys say that,' she'd sobbed.

'Aye,' he'd whispered, 'but it's been going more than three years now; there can't be much left. I have to go before it's done.'

In those few days, her resolve had wavered. She allowed touch she had once forbidden. On the last night, walking, their breath frosting the air, he had stopped under a network of autumn limbs, kissed her mouth, ear, throat, opened his coat and drawn her to him, pressed forward until she was caught, backed up against a tree. This time she didn't push him away. She was rigid, silent. His hands fumbled at her clothes. She didn't help him.

He drew back, looked at her face. 'Go on, then,' she'd said breathlessly, barely audible. Nightlight caught the edges of her cheek, her eyebrow, the frightened wetness of her eye. But, for reasons years later he could no longer recall, he had stepped back from her, buttoned his coat, turned up his collar, thrust his hands in his pockets. They had walked the rest of the way in silence.

At her door, he had barely looked at her. 'Night,' he'd said and walked on. Fool, he told himself. Fool.

A wish passed through him, light as a breath. He stared up through the trees, at all those stars. A moment ago he had known that up there in those other worlds there was no time at all between then and now, nor an inch of space between his boyhood home and this, between his tongue and her nipples' taut heat, his cock and the shy curls between her thighs. All he had done in the twenty-five years since amounted to a tidy sum and nothing. He would go home now, return it all if he could; he would burrow beneath that girl's skirt, begin again.

50

Before Christmas, when Cora's parents had come in their car, taken Cora and the kids to their holiday house, Orla and Deebee had stepped out onto the porch to watch them pile their suitcases into the boot, had waved at them and they'd waved back, and Deebee had said, 'Have we ever been to a holiday, Orly?'

'On a holiday. I don't think so.'

'Can we go?'

'Don't ask me.'

'Can we?'

Orla watched Cora's parents' car drive away.

Deebee said, 'Can we, Orly?'

Orla turned away. 'You're so stupid. What are you asking me for?'

Henry's boss had closed the office till after New Year, so for days Orla was able to lie in her room, reading or gazing out the window at parched lawn, verge tree, quiet neighbourhood houses, strip of relentlessly blue sky. If she needed to, she had only to follow the sound of water to find her mother: hand-washing clothes in the laundry; pushing the steaming iron; peeling vegetables in a part-filled sink; dunking the hot spitting pan; rinsing out the kitchen sponge. No sound of water meant she'd look to the Hills hoist to find her mother with a basket.

Each day, some time after breakfast, Orla would breathe into the narrow valve of the paddle pool, taste the odd tang of plastic. She and Deebee would stand in it, the hose running over their feet, or sprawl in it through hot afternoons, rolling in tepid water, sun moving steadily across an almost white sky, until the sea breeze, strong and cool. Then they'd lie like lizards on the warm concrete path, and Deebee would ask questions and Orla would say I don't know don't ask me how do I know and how and how and yes yes heaven's there but you just can't see it until you die does that make you feel better yes everyone is happy there and God can see us of course He can He sees everything everything you do so you better be careful not to do anything behind my back anything you know I wouldn't like and stop annoying me by asking stupid questions and don't you remember I told you all this yesterday what's wrong with you you're so stupid. There were other things Deebee didn't ask about because she didn't know, things Orla wouldn't have told her anyway, about the cracks and the praying and the biting and that it was her fault and that it didn't matter where he was she'd rather be there with him, even if he really was dead, than here with the two of them.

When hunger or the cooling afternoon drove them indoors, they watched TV Westerns, which pleased Deebee, or musicals, which Orla preferred because Westerns meant beautiful pinto or appaloosa ponies with their ears pricked, loping along trails or across hilltops at sunrise, or galloping quarter horses, their cowboy riders whooping down rocky slopes, horses falling in battles with Comanche and Sioux. It wasn't really the falling — she could see how trained the horses were, sliding in like a softball player. It was the way there was no end to them, these stories their father loved. They just went on without him.

~

One night Orla woke to her mother lifting her head from her pillow, her voice gentle: 'Happy New Year, darling.'

'Happy New Year, Mum,' she murmured. The way she knew she should.

The rim of a glass against her lips. 'Champagne. Sip.'

She opened her mouth. The bitter fizz. Screwed up her face, lay down again, closed her eyes.

Her mother kissed her cheek. 'Go back to sleep.'

As she fell back into slumber, Orla heard her mother's footsteps fade. Against the dark of her eyelids she saw the darker shape she knew from dreams, the shape of a man walking ahead of her, his figure forever smaller and more distant.

~

Cora and the kids came home, their skins darker, hair blonder. They waved and smiled. Next morning, Henry swiped lipstick across her mouth, clicked shut her bag. She said, 'There's plenty of bread. There's butter and vegemite and peanut paste. Make sandwiches. There are oranges. Peel them. Don't use a knife. Promise me. Don't open the door to anyone.'

Orla nodded, glanced away. Her mother took hold of her chin, stared hard at her. 'Promise,' she repeated.

'All right! I promise! I know all this, Mum!'

And the days were longer again, quieter. They looked forward to the evenings.

And then it was the weekend again and Cora invited them over now that she had settled back in. She made coffee, Nescafé; Henry sipped it politely. Orla tipped hers quietly down the sink, flicked on the jug, used a tea bag, listening to Cora recount everything they had done in Mandurah — the beach, the estuary, the crabbing, the shops. Orla avoided Whit and Bettie underfoot, heaped sugar into her cup and stirred for ages for the pretty tinkling sound, watched it swirl swirl smooth as a dancer's skirt.

~

Later, her mother would look at Orla and say, 'Why did they go in that way? How did they know we weren't home?' At which Orla could only shake her head because it didn't make sense, none of it, did it, because they had been at Cora's table, the three of them, overlooking their house, overlooking the window the robbers were supposed to use, had been sitting there with Cora bouncing Bettie on her knee and Whit on the kitchen floor behind them, clattering things from cupboards. Henry had smiled at Bettie and stroked her chubby arm, had let her fingers be grabbed by sticky hands. And every time Whit crashed a pan on the floor, Henry had pursed her lips or given a long sideways glance, and eventually Cora had turned: 'Put those bloody things back!' Again and again, Steele and Deebee flashed past the kitchen door, chased one another through the house and outside, waving sticks and shoes, yelling.

After the police had gone, the three of them — Orla, Deebee, Henry — stood side by side, stared at the windows in their lounge room and above the telephone table — all still demure, intact — and at the shattered front door. Scattered over the dark carpet, shards of glass twinkled under the light like stars.

When they had left Cora's, Henry had hurried home, relieved, thinking of dinner. Orla had trailed behind. Deebee and Steele were standing silent at the low fence, watching Henry. 'Come on!' Henry had called over her shoulder as she pulled open the screen door. And, turning back, key at the ready, she had seen it, the smash like a mouth aghast, the inside of their life dangerously framed. For a moment Henry imagined herself just stepping through because it was her home and she had a right but she stepped back instead. All that jaggedness. She slid in the key and opened the door. She turned to them. 'Stay out here, understand?'

But Orla followed her mother in, hesitant at first and then close behind, stepping over glass, watching Henry, taking cues from the way she peered around corners, looked into all the rooms, her fists clenched, not speaking. To Orla, everything was the same except the door and the air. The air seemed to hold its breath. Like shock. Then Deebee was alongside them, talking, 'Who broke the door? Who broke it, Mummy? I didn't, Mummy. I didn't. It must have been Orly,' until Henry ordered for-God's-sake-get-her-out-of-my-sight, and Orla sat on the back stairs with her elbows on her knees and her chin in her hands, while Deebee smashed a stick against the steps, the railing, the landing, the closed back door.

Once the police had gone and they had stared at the untouched windows, and the sky had started to dim, Henry collected the shards in a wad of newspaper, wrapped and placed it all in the outside bin. She turned on the lights and vacuumed; the girls, still in shoes, directing: 'There! There!' She pushed both armchairs hard up against the empty doorframe, and leaned the mop and broom against them so that, as she explained to Deebee, 'Anyone who comes in the night will crash into the chairs and fall over and hurt themselves and make such a huge noise that we'll all wake up. And they'll get such a fright that they'll run away.'

Deebee's eyes were round. 'But what if they don't run away?'

'Then we'll whack them over the head!'

'What will we whack them with, Mummy?'

Henry smiled. 'Well, the broom and mop, of course! Whack, whack!'

Orla helped her mother hang a sheet on the door and, once the girls had gone to bed, Henry dragged the spare mattress into the space in front of the armchairs. If he wanted to come in he would have to get past her first. She lay awake a long time, slept briefly, fitfully, a blanket pulled over her face to keep out the porch light, the desert wind flapping the sheet as it rose strongly in quiet hours before dawn.

Next morning, she phoned in sick, called a glazier listed in the Yellow Pages, straightened the room, washed the breakfast dishes slowly. Deebee hugged her mother's legs, closed her eyes and held on, giggling, as Henry shuffled between bench and stove, wiping everything clean.

In the afternoon, a car door slammed. Deebee turned away from cartoons and scampered up the divan. Through the blinds, she yelled. 'The lady's here!'

In the kitchen, Henry frowned. 'What lady?'

Orla followed her mother to the front door. Footsteps approached down the path. On the doorstep, a woman with a suitcase, peering through the flyscreen at Henry staring back. Orla looked from one to the other. It was like looking at a slightly off mirror. Deebee pushed her way in front. The suitcase woman looked down and smiled. 'Well,' she said. 'You must be Danielle. Hello.'

'No, I'm Deebee,' she replied, sticking out her chin. 'Are you the glass man?'

'No, I'm the flesh and blood woman,' she laughed.

Deebee cocked her head. 'Then why are you here?'

'Sshh,' hissed Orla, glancing again at the woman's chin and nose, eyes, hair. 'Can't you see?'

'Well.' Henry turned the door lock. 'I suppose you'd better come in.'

~

Deebee sat on her own bed and watched the flesh and blood woman lift her suitcase onto the spare bed along the opposite wall. The springs groaned. Orla leaned in the doorway. Their real aunt, in Deebee's room, unzipping her suitcase with a sound like fabric tearing, flinging it open.

'It's so kind of you to allow me to share with you, Da — er, dear. I think we're going to be chums.'

Black shoes placed beneath the bed. A dressing-gown — pale green with peacocks — on the back of the door. Their real aunt opened Deebee's wardrobe, hung up three dresses, a cardigan. She slipped a nightie beneath the pillow. Against the suitcase's dark-red lining, a pale, bulging toiletries bag, a pile of underwear the colour of sand.

'Hm,' she said, picking up a red paper bag by its handles and swinging it. 'I wonder what this is?'

At the table, the girls sipped their milk. Deebee's feet thunked against the table's leg. Henry brought the teapot, two cups and saucers, a small jug of milk. 'Do you take sugar?' she asked.

'Oh, yes.' The real aunt winked at Deebee. 'Two naughty spoonsful.'

Deebee grinned back. Thunk-thunk, thunk-thunk.

'Now let's see,' the real aunt said. 'There was something I was going to do. What was it?'

Deebee bounced in her chair. 'Our presents!'

Henry traced the pattern on the tablecloth. 'Sshh.'

'Oh, yes!' And the real aunt opened the paper bag. 'This one's for your mother.'

Henry smiled with no teeth. 'Thank you but you shouldn't have. Really.'

'Nonsense. Now. This is for someone called Danielle but ...'

'That's me!'

'... I've been told there's no-one ...'

'Me! Me!'

'... by that name here.'

'Yes, there is! I'm Danielle!'

'But you told me your name was Deebee.'

'I have two names! Give it to me!' Deebee stretched out her arm.

'Don't be rude,' her mother said.

The real aunt lifted the parcel into the air and frowned. 'Are you telling me the truth?'

Deebee eyes filled. She looked at her mother.

Henry's voice was cool. 'My girls always tell the truth.'

The real aunt made a strange laugh, lowered the parcel close to Deebee. 'Oh, it's all right, dear. No need to get upset.'

Deebee hid her head in her arms, her arms on the table. The real aunt nudged her hand with the parcel. 'Here it is.'

'Say thank you,' Henry said.

In the silence, the real aunt gave Orla her gift with a quick, tight smile.

'Thank you,' said Orla. 'Aunty.'

'Harry,' said the real aunt.

'Harriet,' said Henry. 'She means Aunt Harriet.'

The real aunt made another laugh. 'No, no, please. Let's agree on this,' she said, stroking Deebee's hair. 'If I call you Deebee, you call me Harry.'

Orla looked at her mother. Henry was holding an open pink box that said 'parfum', she was running her thumbs over a small bottle nestled in its small bottle-shaped hollow. Deebee was staring at the face of a bride doll, its wide-open eyes and pink lips. She tipped it up; its eyes shut. Orla hooked her fingers under the lid of the slim black box; it opened with a snap. A wristwatch glinted palely against red satin.

Harry reached for it. 'See?' she said. Orla heard the faintest click. 'This is how you set the time ...' She watched the hands spin. '... And this is how you wind it.' Another click and the tip of her aunt's thumb and finger rubbed over the tiny winder with a little whirr. She pressed the watch to Orla's ear. The clear loud tick of it.

'Now you'll always know the time,' she said, smiling, turning Orla's hand to expose the pale inside of her wrist, fastening the metal catch there.

From outside, the crunch of wheels on gravel. Deebee running ahead, holding the doll by its foot, its skirt flapping around its ears, its perfect white bloomers shining.

The glass man's boots were loud. He stood framed by the surround of the empty door, an open wooden box full of tools in one hand. 'Well,' he grinned, as Henry let him in, 'no needta ask where the problem is!' He smiled at Orla and Deebee who stood aside, watching him, still and silent. 'You girls a bit shy, eh?' When he set down the box, Orla saw its handle had been made slick and dark from his fist. He whistled softly through his teeth as he worked, measuring, gouging bits of glass from the frame. From the table, the clink of cups as Henry and Harry sipped tea, their low voices.

'You got my letter, then.'

'I did. And I immediately thought, Harry, you're more use there.'

'Ah. But it took you a while.'

'There's the cat. And work. And Dot.'

'Isn't she grown up now?'

'They're never grown up enough for us to suddenly leave. You'll see.'

'Hm.' Henry tried to imagine it, pursed her lips. 'You could have phoned, though, in that time.'

Harry replaced her cup into its saucer. 'I could have. And I wonder what would you have said.'

'Don't come.'

Harry looked at her sister, shrugged and smiled. 'Well.'

'I would have said what I said in the letter. That I need a thousand dollars. I would have said just send it and save yourself the journey.' Henry smiled. 'How much did it cost to get here?'

Harry lifted her cup and sipped slowly. In the silence, Henry drummed her fingers on the table's edge. 'How long are you staying?'

'That depends.'

The glass man called out, 'That's it for now.'

The loud scrape of Henry's chair and her hurried steps into the lounge room. He was standing with his toolbox in his hand, grinning again. She blinked at the clean empty frame behind him.

'I'm gonna havta cut it ta size and bring it back,' he said, his hand on the screen door.

'Oh,' Henry said, reaching to open it for him. 'When will that be?'

'Ah, coupla days?'

'Oh. Can't it be today? It's just that ...' She trailed off, unsure what she should say. Surely he could see.

'Nah, sorry. We're flat out.'

~

Orla's eyes flicked open. She stared at the shadowed ceiling, her body as tense as a gecko she had once watched — small, frozen beneath her gaze, changing colour and pattern so it could disappear where it stood with its strange, spread feet. She strained to listen. Other rooms. The house breathed differently. A new body dreaming on the other side of the wall, turning over in sleep. She listened beyond, for the sound of yet another body sawing open the cardboard her mother had sticky-taped over the front doorframe, but there was nothing. Whatever had woken her had gone. She could hear the watch on her wrist, her hand close to her face, her heart pulsing in her ear.

She thought of the glazier, his big, rough hands, the lines around his eyes. Muscles moving beneath his skin. His smell. She hadn't recognised the tune he whistled. But the breathy sound of it, the tip of his tongue wet behind his teeth. He had glanced at her a few times, smiled at her. And kept smiling at his hands as he worked. She hadn't been able to take her eyes off him.

She got up, paused at Deebee's door. Her sister's limbs glowed in blue street light. In the shadows of the opposite wall, Orla couldn't make out if the dark tangle was Harry or merely a memory of her shape. From the door to the lounge room, she saw how the porch light behind the venetians illuminated the carpet in thin stripes. Light leaked around the edges of the cardboard. She stepped and a floorboard creaked. From across the room, Harry's voice: 'Hello, there.'

Electricity shot through Orla's chest; she gasped.

'Sorry.' Harry fumbled with the switch on the standard lamp. The room filled, golden. 'I didn't mean to frighten you.'

'I couldn't sleep,' said Orla, squinting.

'Neither could I. It's still daytime where I've come from. Shall I put the kettle on?'

Orla shook her head. 'We have to be quiet.'

'Oh, well.' Harry smiled, patted the edge of the divan. 'Maybe we could just talk for a minute.'

Orla looked at her aunt's face, the lamplight slanting into it, the deep shadows. Its colours and shapes, all the separate parts were so like her mother's, but somehow the whole of it was different, full of something that looked like twinkling. She crossed the room.

Harry leaned forward, rested her elbows on her knees. 'How is school?'

'It's the holidays.'

'Oh. But it must have been strange. To go back to school. Was it?'

Orla shrugged.

'I just mean to say — well, it must have been a terrible shock.'

Orla didn't look at her. In the edge of her vision she saw Harry clasp her hands together in front of her. Her fingers were long and white. 'I've been wondering whether you might like to come to live with me. I, I have a large house, plenty of room.'

Orla looked at her. 'But ... what about Mum and, and Deebee?'

Harry smiled. 'Oh, they can come, too, of course, if they like. There's a good school close by, where my daughter went. The bus comes past our gate. You would each have your own room, like here. There's a big garden with an orchard and a tennis court. Do you play tennis?'

Orla shook her head. There was a tennis court at school with a high fence and gate. She had never seen anyone use it.

'I have a nice car, and we could drive around on weekends. There is a lot to see where I live. And in the holidays we could go to France or Italy or Spain. You could learn languages. Would you like to do that?'

Orla watched Harry's pale cheeks, dark eyes, the frame of her short dark hair against her face, the lines near her eyes, the folds around her mouth when she smiled. She smiled a lot. An orchard? A car? She knew the meanings of the words but it was hard to make sense of them. She blinked. 'Would Mum and Deebee come to Spain, too?'

Harry chuckled. 'If you like.'

Orla nodded: if I like. A thought passed through her. She wondered if she was asleep, if she had walked into a dream in which someone who looked like, but was not, her mother was sitting where her mother had sat, in the same lamplight, saying more impossible things. Because that's what happens in dreams. She took a breath. 'What about Daddy?'

Harry was silent, blinking. She leaned back in the chair and studied her niece's face, the sunken darkness around her eyes, her eyelids heavy with sleep, tousled hair. Very gently, she said, 'What about him?'

Orla looked down at her own hands, curled quietly there in her lap. She was surprised how easy it was. 'When he comes home,' she whispered. 'He won't know where we are.'

After a while, Harry said, 'Oh,' then reached out and took Orla's hands. 'Oh,' she said again, and she stroked Orla's thumbs lightly with her own, not looking up, and in the silence Orla felt the warmth of her aunt's fingers, watched the small movements of her aunt's thumbs, the soft scrape, skin over skin. From beyond the window she heard the rustle of the night wind through the poplars. Harry said, 'I knew your father a little, met him a few times many years ago. He seemed, he seemed like a very nice man, and I, I just don't think he would leave his family, stay away from you and your mother and your sister, the people he loved most in the world and who love him too, so very much, I know, if he could help it.' She lifted her gaze and met Orla's. 'Do you?' she continued. Her eyes glistened. 'Do you think he would do that?'

Orla's mouth opened but she didn't know what to say so she closed it again. Her real aunt's eyes were red and wet and what did she mean? Orla shook her head a little because that was what Harry wanted, wasn't it, and because — well, Harry was right, because no, no, of course he wouldn't, he wouldn't just stay away and let everything. Would he? And her throat felt as if someone was squeezing it between their big rough hands. Enough to, enough, it was hard to breathe, but not enough, not quite enough, if she stayed very still, very quiet, not quite enough to, to make her die. And she loved him, she loved him very much, she loved him so so much that she thought if she moved now, right now, if she nodded or spoke, if she tried to tell Harry how sad she was, how very, those hands would close her throat and everything in her would stop. She would die then. And when he came back she wouldn't be there.

A sound came out of her, the long low sound of something falling for a long time into a deep hole and finally hitting bottom. Something she had no idea she had been holding.

51

In the morning she woke again.

The clatter of dishes. She stood. Her head hurt. Walked past Deebee's door and glanced in. Blinds open. She squinted against the room bright with sunlight. Two pink feet poking out from beneath the blanket on Harry's bed.

Harry's bed now.

When their mother left, they didn't go down the back stairs; they sat on the divan, side by side, staring the TV in its sleeping face. Deebee said, 'Is she ever going to wake up, Orly?'

And Orla shrugged and turned away because why ask her, why ask her anything, because what does she know, everything she thinks turns out to be wrong.

And then it's gone nine and the day already breathless. So she filled the pool, lay in it, stared up at the hard blue of morning. Beside her, Deebee zoomed cars, twirled and swooped them. Water scattered silver in the sun. Orla watched her sister's small back, the shape of her ribs beneath her bathers. A small bruise bloomed on her arm. Orla prodded it. Deebee pulled away, 'Ow,' scowled over her hunched shoulder. Orla prodded again.

'Don't!' Deebee scrambled out of the pool, cars dripping in her fists. Her eyes glittered.

Orla looked her up and down. She was so thin. Such a cry baby. Orla trailed her fingers through the water, watched light ripple over the pool's blue skin. She said, 'You were outside with Steele that day. Remember? How come you didn't hear anything?'

She glanced sideways at her sister. Deebee was very still, head bowed, gripping her trucks as if she wanted to murder them. Suddenly Orla was filled with certainty: her sister had nothing to say because — because all it takes is a whack with a stick. She smiled to herself, lay back in the water and closed her eyes. So. Now she was sure. She was not the only bad one. Deebee did bad things, too. Burnt things, broke things, lied.

The sun lit the inside of her eyelids brilliant orange. Water lapped loudly and resettled. Nearby a magpie warbled. Still no reply. She half-opened an eye. Deebee was staring at her, jaw clenched, eyes narrowed. Orla saw her sister draw back her arm, and she opened her mouth. Saw Deebee fling her arm forward, tried to turn away.

A giddying pain. Above an eye. She clutched at it. When she opened her other eye, Deebee had gone. Blood dripped from her elbow. Beside her, the truck was sunk, upside down, like a real wreck. In the water, her blood curled and twisted.

She climbed the back stairs, opened the door slowly. No sound. In the bathroom, water dripped from her bathers, puddled on the floor. She ran the tap, splashed her face, dried it carefully with a towel. In the mirror there wasn't much to see. She pulled her fringe down over that eye. It looked okay. She didn't think her mother would notice, but she had no idea about Harry.

Deebee's door was ajar. Orla tiptoed; the floor creaked. She listened. The soft, even sound of Harry's breathing. She put her face close to the gap between the door and frame, and there was Deebee, crouched on the floor, jammed between wall and door. She thought she should step round, sit alongside her sister to speak, but instead she put her mouth up to the chink. 'You better come out,' she whispered. She pressed her eye up to the crack. Deebee looked, recoiled. 'Come out,' Orla hissed, 'or I'll tell.' She widened her visible eye, heard her sister sob, stand. Deebee came slowly around the door, shivering, her fingers in her mouth. Orla grabbed her shoulder and shoved her into the laundry. Hard enough to hurt. She opened the back door and shoved her out, closed the door behind them, smiled at her sister's weeping face. Not quite hard enough to make her fall.

~

From the treehouse, Orla heard the back door squeak open. She looked across the yard. Deebee was still in the sandpit; her face still pressed up to the picket fence. Orla heard Harry before she saw: 'There you are! The house was like the *Mary Celeste*! What are you looking at?'

Deebee turned to her. 'What's the Mary?'

Orla watched Harry lunge, wiggling her fingers at Deebee's neck. 'A ghost ship,' she laughed. 'Now. Where's your sister?'

Deebee shrugged one shoulder, stabbed her fingers in the sand. 'What's a ghost ship?'

Orla called, 'Up here.'

Harry stood at the base of the sheoak on a blanket of its dry needles. She looked small down there, looking up, and for the first time Orla saw a line of white along the part in her hair. Harry raised her hand to her eyes. 'It's so hot, I thought you'd be in your pool.' She grinned.

Orla stared at her. 'We've already been in.'

'Oh. Is it always so hot here or is this especially for me?'

Orla narrowed her eyes. 'It's summer.'

'Yes. So,' said Harry. 'Shall we have breakfast?'

'Mum gave us breakfast.'

'I see. Well, second breakfast, then. And, after that, we'll do something.'

'What?'

'We'll go out.'

'Where?'

'You tell me.' Beneath the awning of her hand she kept smiling.

~

When Harry reappeared with her wet hair plastered to her scalp they were sitting at the table, waiting, because, Orla reasoned, it's not every day that an aunt turns up, a real aunt, one you didn't even know about for most of your life, one you have no idea what to do with, who stands there smiling at you in the morning, insistent, saying, 'Shall we make pancakes?' One who lets you break the eggs, sift the flour, beat the batter. Who hands you the egg slice and asks you to turn the strange, half-baked thing. Who laughs when, wet and pale, it slips to the floor.

Later, Harry called a taxi. Outside the shops she told the driver to wait. But still Orla pressed her fingers together. What if he left anyway? How would they get home? From the greengrocer Harry gathered dusty potatoes, fat strawberries, hairy Chinese gooseberries. 'Boozeberries,' Deebee called them and Harry threw her head back and laughed too loudly. There were still-green bananas, silverbeet, tomatoes. From the grocery store: more eggs, more bread, more butter, more cheese. A leg of lamb and a bundle of pork sausages from the butcher. Each time, she opened her purse and asked Orla to pick out the money because, she said, she couldn't make head nor tail of it.

When Henry came home this time, there was no-one watching from the lounge room window. A pot of potatoes was boiling on the stove. On the bench, a bowl of lettuce and chopped tomato. The table was set. Harry was wearing Henry's apron. Deebee was washed and in her pyjamas.

A knock on the front door and Cora's voice: 'Yoo-hoo!'

Henry let her in. In the kitchen, Cora said, 'Sorry, didn't know you had visitors.'

Deebee grinned up at Harry. 'She's not a visitor, she's an aunty.'

Henry said, 'This is my sister, Harriet.'

Cora smiled broadly. 'Oh yeah.' She looked from Harry to Henry. She nodded. 'Yep. I can see that.' She put her hands on her hips. 'Listen, I can't stay. I just wanna tell you there was a guy in my backyard.'

Orla looked from Cora to her mother and back again.

Deebee said, 'Who was it?'

Henry said, 'What? When?'

Deebee tugged her mother's skirt. 'Who was it, Mummy?'

'Last night,' replied Cora. 'I rang Mum and they came and got us.'

Orla looked at her sister and aunt. Deebee's voice: 'Who, Mummy?'

'I gotta go,' Cora said. 'Dad says just keep the windows shut.'

52

Orla woke in the night, knowing what to do, carried a chair from the dining table, placed it dead centre. When she sat, she had to slide the chair back to allow the drawer enough space to open fully. Behind her, Henry's breathing didn't even change.

Moonlight through the window, and there it was, opened like a road in front of her, all silvery blue and shadowy, and then, as she lowered her head to look into it, a long darkness in which she knew lay everything.

Her arms slipped in. Easy. Her fingertips feeling nothing but space, space and her head followed, just as she'd imagined it would, the tunnel expanding like time to accommodate her: shoulders, hips, sliding. Like Alice, she thought. Like birth. Or the reverse of birth. Was she slipping back, or was time? To all the places she knew. All the life already been. How can she go forward, go anywhere but back, when the past is all we see? Future a creature always approaching, striking us always from behind? Like death, she thought. Yes. Which she knew was gathering behind her, had been gathering since she was born, just as it had gathered behind him. He had felt it close. She had seen he had. She had felt it, too. Though she couldn't name it. And now she had slipped herself into something else she couldn't name and what propulsion is this? Death or life. Where he had gone. Where he still was. Ahead or behind. All his stories there with him. Waiting for her.

She smiled. Relieved; unafraid. She moved effortlessly. At last. And in every direction. That feeling. Her body rising on a weekend morning to a quiet house, knowing he was in the next room. Hello, Tweety. Her body rising in the saddle, rising to a trot. Her mind rising to a question, her mind raising her hand to answer it.

He would be so pleased.

~

She opened her eyes. Time had passed. She walked slowly through the shadowy house, touched the doors and walls, the furniture. Yes, she thought, it looks the same. But something, she knew, had changed.

53

At dinner, Deebee turned to look at Harry. 'Are you rich?'

Orla heard her mother sniff. Harry smiled. 'I don't think so. Am I?'

'Yes,' Deebee said.

'That's enough,' said Henry. 'Eat your food.'

Orla watched Deebee chew, swallow, turn to Harry again. 'Are you going to stay with us when we move to our new house?'

Harry took a mouthful, shook her head. Deebee made a small sound, looked to her mother.

Henry said, 'Your Aunty has her own house.'

Deebee frowned. 'But there's lots of room!'

Harry half-smiled again. 'Well, isn't it lovely that there is.'

'But I want you to!'

The two women made the sounds of laughs. They didn't look at one another. Harry said, 'Who will look after my house and my pets and prune my roses?'

'Oh.' Deebee hid her face in her arms.

Henry brought ice cream in two small bowls. She caught Orla's eye, said, 'Go sit next to your sister so I can sit next to mine.'

From the wrong side of the table, Orla watched the two women leaning over a piece of paper, their heads almost touching as they examined it. Henry smoothed it with her palm. Orla frowned at its upside downness. 'What's that?'

Henry didn't look up. 'The floor plan. Of the house. Remember? The one I showed you?'

Orla peered. She thought she recognised the porch, the placement of the front door, the lounge room's shape. She saw Harry frown.

Henry said, 'Shall we have coffee?'

'How much is this?' Harry asked.

Orla looked from her aunt to her mother. Henry pointed at something on the page, said, 'It has a linen cupboard here. And a broom cupboard.'

Harry tapped the plan with her finger. The sound of her nail was sharp. 'Is it big enough — as the girls grow?'

Henry pressed her lips together.

Harry leaned back in her chair, looked straight at her sister. 'Won't it look small? On your land?'

'It's a quarter-acre block.'

'Oh.'

Henry smiled quickly. 'That's normal here.'

'Oh.'

Orla looked into the film of ice cream in the bottom of her bowl, the coarse weave of the tablecloth beneath her hand, the tiny flower print of her cotton dress; she remembered tennis court, car, holiday, Spain; remembered from somewhere — was it the encyclopaedia? — black-and-white pictures of Spanish horses, their raised hooves, arched necks. She gazed into the lounge room, the charcoal carpet, grey venetians, grey divan. Her cheeks burned. In the corner, Henry's empty chair. Alongside it, the lamp. In her mind she saw: the bedrooms, bathroom, laundry; the cardboard over the front door; the dingy carport; the back stairs; the paddle pool.

Across the table, her mother was rolling up the floor plan, saying, 'Anyway. There it is.' Then, 'The girls loved it.'

Deebee jiggled up and down in her seat. 'When can we live there?' But Henry had moved away.

Harry blinked at her nieces, gave them a little smile, turned towards the kitchen, spoke loudly. 'Why don't you let the girls come to stay with me? Just for a while, at least. Until — you know.'

There was a moment's silence. Henry reappeared. She was frowning. She stood near the table and looked at Harry. From the kitchen, Orla heard the sound of the jug beginning to rumble. 'What do you mean?'

'A holiday. To see. They might like it!' She smiled at the girls across the table.

'What do you mean: "Until — you know"?'

'Well — until you decide.'

'Decide what?'

'What you want to do.'

'I want to build the house.'

'Yes, but you can't, can you. The bank won't lend you the money.'

Orla looked at her mother. Henry folded her arms across her chest, stared steadily at Harry. 'But *you* could.'

Harry turned to the girls again. 'You'd like a holiday, wouldn't you?'

'Yes!' Deebee beamed.

Orla looked from her aunt to her mother. Henry's gaze shifted from Deebee back to Harry. 'Girls,' Henry said, 'bed.'

'But I want a holiday, Mummy!' said Deebee.

Harry leaned across the table. 'Remember what I told you, Orla? You'd like that, wouldn't you?'

'Girls,' Henry growled.

'What about me?' Deebee whined.

'Girls —'

'I want a holiday!'

Orla stood, grabbed Deebee's arm, hissed. 'Come on.'

'Ow! Mummy! She —'

The jug whistled softly. Henry spoke through her teeth. 'Go. To. Bed.'

Orla pulled her sister by the arm, squeezing.

'It isn't dark yet,' Deebee whimpered.

Orla pushed her to the end of the passageway, pushed her into her room, stepped in behind, shut the door, leaned on it.

Deebee glared. 'You hurt me!'

'Good.'

'I hate you!'

'Good.'

'It's not fair! I want a holiday!'

Orla took a step, raised her open hands. 'No-one's going on a holiday.'

'But I want to go on a holiday!'

Another step. 'God!' Her hands cutting the air. 'Will you just.' Another. 'Shut. Up. About. The holiday!' A third and she was there, at Deebee. She pushed. Watched her fall back. The look of surprise. Her head missing the edge of the bed. Her back hitting the floor. Her head continuing. Hitting and rising. A bounce. The thwack of it.

~

'Mum.' Orla stood in the lounge room, her heart banging in her throat. She had closed her bedroom door but she could still hear Deebee wailing. When she could she had leapt to her, hugged her, apologised, stroked her hair, but the look in her sister's eyes — fear, distrust — and she just kept pushing Orla away, crying, till Orla said, 'I'll get Mum if you promise not to tell her.' And Deebee had hit Orla then, hit her head and face, and Orla had backed away, saying, 'If you tell on me, I'll tell on you,' and pushed her own fringe back to expose the nick above her eye. And she had wondered where her mother was, had expected her to burst in any moment, shouting. But she hadn't. And now that Orla was standing in the lounge room, she understood.

'You're just like our mother!' Henry shouted.

Orla stood very still, clasped her hands in front of her.

'Don't you dare!'

Orla closed her eyes. Mum, she thought. Mum.

Henry yelled again. 'You think you're so much better than me!'

'Don't you dare say —'

Mum.

'What? The truth? That you look down on me? That the two of you always —'

'Don't bring her into this! This is nothing to do with her!'

Henry snorted. 'It has everything to do with her. Why do you think I got out as soon as I could?'

Orla turned her head to look at the window.

'Because you don't know what's good for you.'

'Because nothing I did was ever good enough for her, and now nothing I do is good enough for you.'

Through it, outside looked good. She closed her eyes.

'I'm just —'

'I don't want to hear it.'

'— trying to give you advice.'

'I don't want your advice. I just. Want. Your money.'

She remembered another day, a big blue sky, her mother wanting to drive somewhere.

'I have a large house! A large garden!'

'I need my own house, not someone else's.'

'Think of the girls.'

'I am thinking of them!'

'I have everything to make them happy.'

'They're happy here.'

Harry gave a strange shout. 'Really? You know, don't you, that Orla thinks her father will come back.'

Henry shook her head a little. 'You'll say anything, won't you. Anything. To get what you want.'

Orla opened her eyes, her hand on the front door lock, opened it, too, stepped into the cool air, her face hot, and everywhere the dulled light beginning to colour.

She walked up the path, turned right, continued past Cora's, past houses she rarely saw full of people she didn't know. Fat rain thudded on the pavement, road, her back. It fell harder, on her head. She felt it trickle down her scalp and neck. She rounded the corner, past Ingrid's house, past Derek's, past the street that lead to Heather. There were cars in driveways, cars slickly wet and empty. Quiet yards. Her clothes stuck. Dogs barked behind front doors. The world a blur. She shivered. A car slowed, passed, its brakelights bright. It stopped. She watched it, without turning her head. As she drew alongside, the driver's window opened.

'Orla?'

She stopped. Mr Woodland. From last year. He remembered her. She raised her hand a little then lowered it. She took a step towards him.

'You all right?' His brow furrowed. 'Need a lift?'

I don't know, she thought; then, yes. She smiled a little, stopped at the edge of the road, shifted her weight from foot to foot.

She saw him reach and throw something from the passenger seat into the back. He turned his gaze to her again. 'Get in,' he smiled.

Water dripped from her. Her teeth chattered. 'I —' She glanced up and down the street. 'I'm soaked.' She shook her head a little.

'Get in,' he insisted.

Somewhere deep began to shake. 'I — it's not far. It's — it's okay. Really.'

'Please. I can't leave you here. You direct me and I'll take you home.'

In the passenger seat she trembled. She pushed herself up against the door. He put the heater on. The hot air made it hard to breathe.

'So,' he said, pulling away from the kerb. 'Which way?'

And it wasn't that she had planned it. At first, she had no idea where they were going.

'Turn left,' she said. In that moment, the only thing she knew for sure was that she didn't want home. 'Over the hill. Then turn right at the bottom.'

'How are the holidays going?'

She shrugged. 'Turn left and keep going.'

'Been doing anything fun?'

She took hold of the window winder. 'Can I open it, please? I feel sick.'

'Of course.'

Cool air rushed against her skin, through her hair. She heard his voice, light-hearted. 'I thought you said it's not far.'

She turned her face further into the wind streaming in. The sun was re-emerging and, as they moved, light flashed from the roads and footpaths, the car bonnet, the leaves of trees. So bright it made her close her eyes. Open. Close. Open.

He pulled up in the beach car park. She looked ahead at the sea, big and restless and blinding.

'Orla.' His voice was stern. 'You have to tell me your address.'

'Yes,' she said, as she opened the door. 'I will. I just want —' She stepped out. She heard a car door slam behind her.

'Want what? What's wrong?' He was at her elbow.

'To go to the sea,' she replied.

His footsteps behind. Him saying something she couldn't quite make out. The breeze strong, pulling his words away. It tugged at her clothes. She walked into it, knew she should stop, apologise, get back in the car, tell him where she lived. But where was that, really? Every time they found a place, they moved. Or when she thought they were going to, they didn't.

Cresting the dunes, she could see the swell, waves rising, crashing. The boom of it. White water for fifty yards. Now the wind so strong it blew her inside out. Where was her hat, the one with the green ribbon, tumbling, spinning, that other version of herself chasing it down, the one that didn't know anything. Where was the car, and Mum and Dad and Kit calling, waving. Goodbye, Orla. Goodbye. Is that what they were calling. Where was Deebee, tiny and curled, her face full of tears, her mouth full of sand and wailing sorrow, her small arms clinging, her small arms hitting and pushing Orla away.

The sand looked wet but, underfoot, the thin, damp crust broke to reveal dry, warm sand just below the surface. She thought: that means it's still summer, isn't it, despite everything. And that —

She lifted her hand to shield her eyes; she stared at the sea.

It roiled. There was no-one out there. In the sky, a single gull, unsteady, buffeted. Appearing and disappearing against the glare. The white open underneath of its wings. On the surface of the sea was spit and fury, the sun angling, flashing. Flashing so she had to close her eyes. And that he's dead. Really.

'Orla.'

She turned, blinking. He's not coming back. I will never ever see him again.

'Are you all right?'

She looked. It was her teacher Mr Woodland, his face creased. She nodded.

'What's your address?'

So she told him.

~

Outside her house he stopped the car on the side of the road. She closed the door quietly, walked slowly through the carport, waited till she heard the sound of the motor fade, then made her way back to her bedroom window, peered in. A shape in the bed. She tapped. Deebee sat up with her startled face, opened the flyscreen and window. Orla scrambled in. It was harder in this direction. Bricks scraped; the edge of the window frame dug.

'Raining,' Orla said, changing out of her damp clothes. Deebee stared without speaking. Orla sat on the bed beside her. 'What did you tell her?'

'Nothing. She didn't come yet.'

'Oh. Well. If you promise not to, I'll read you a story.'

She opened *Thunderhead*. '"Within the firm walls of flesh that held him prisoner the foal kicked out angrily. He did not want to be born … Here was quiet darkness … Here was security … food … warmth. Here was — in some dim way he felt it — love and protection from his mother's heart. He would not be born."'

Orla stared at the page, the creamy paper greying in failing light, the print harder and harder to see.

Deebee said, 'Is he a prisoner?'

Orla shook her head. 'He's inside his mother's tummy.'

'Will he have to stay there forever?'

She shook her head again.

'But why is he angry? It sounds nice there.'

In the edge of her vision, she could see her sister's head on the pillow, her eyes watchful. Orla kept her gaze on the page. 'It doesn't matter whether he's angry, or whether he wants to stay. We just get born. It just happens. Just like we grow up. Just like we get old. That's it.'

'Just like we die?'

Orla stroked the lines of words with the tips of her fingers. 'Yes,' she said. And then she read on.

~

At breakfast, Deebee looked from Orla to her mother, eyes wide. 'What's that?' she mumbled, her mouth full.

Orla prodded her food with her fork. Thunder rattled the windows.

'It's just a storm. It'll pass,' their mother said.

Orla watched her plate. 'Where's Harry?'

'Oh.' Henry paused. 'She had to leave.'

'When is she coming back?' Deebee asked.

Henry didn't reply. Sudden rain fell on the garden, the roof. Orla listened. It sounded like applause. She dug her nails into her thigh till it hurt.

~

In the night, a movement in her room. Orla opened her eyes, sat up, gasping.

Her mother's voice: 'It's all right.'

Orla rubbed her face with the back of her hand. Henry was perched on the end of the bed, her face profiled in light. Something in her hand glinted. A glass. 'What's wrong?'

'You were having a dream.'

'Oh.' Orla smelled whisky.

'It's all right.'

'Sorry.'

'What did you dream?'

Orla looked down. Her hands felt heavy on her bedspread. She stared at her fingers. 'Oh, I — I was in. The sea. With someone. I don't know … It was fun and then. It. It was too … deep and I couldn't. I had to swim and swim. I was scared and I was. By myself. And the waves were … Sorry I —'

Henry patted Orla's foot, 'It's all right.' She took a sip. There was a long silence. Then, 'Listen, darling.'

Orla felt a stab of something. When did her mother call her darling.

'I've been thinking …'

Orla stared. 'About what?' She could see her mother's lips pressed together.

'Harry told me she spoke with you. About going. To live with her. For a while.'

Orla's voice was a whisper. 'Yes.'

'It might be best.'

'What? Why?'

Henry looked down, into her glass. He hair swung forward a little.

'Why, Mum?'

'Because … otherwise … I can't …' She turned to Orla's shocked face, turned an open palm to her.

'*Please*, Mum.'

'I need help. I can't do it all. Not by myself.'

Orla gripped her mother's hand. It was clammy and cold. 'But you're not by yourself. I'm here. And Deebee.'

Henry made a sound, shook her head. 'No. Look. She's right. She has everything. And it's beautiful there.'

'But I want to stay here.'

'You'll have nice clothes, nice school, nice friends.'

'But I want to stay here.' Orla's hand squeezed.

'You'll have a horse.'

She opened her mouth but nothing came out. She shook her head.

'Here you'll have none of those things.'

'I don't care.'

'Well, I care.'

'But what about me?'

'This is all about you! When have things *not* been about you?'

Orla lifted her mother's cool hand to her face, pressed the back of it to her forehead, the way her mother would do when Orla was ill. 'Please, Mum, I want to stay with you.'

'For pity's sake, I'm just trying to do my best! Why must you always contradict me?' She pulled her hand away.

Orla's mind raced. 'Mum, Mummy, listen. The first night she was here, I woke up, I went out into the lounge room, she was just sitting there, where you sit. She told me then that I should live with her.'

Henry nodded, took a sip.

'She said it then, Mum.'

'And what did you say?'

'I —' Orla pressed her hands together. Then, 'Mum, listen. She said she just came to visit us, to help, but she always wanted to take me away. That's what I'm saying.' But there was so much else to say: the way they had swerved to miss the dog; the way he had hit her, right here in this room; the zoo clock and penguin pool; being a little lady; Sally in the car. She wanted to say how it was all her fault, wanted to explain; the cracks in things, what Heather did.

Henry said, 'She wants to because it's best.'

'It's not. It's not. Who is it best for?'

'For you. For the future.'

Orla's heart pounded. Her voice was shrill. 'Why don't you ever listen to me?'

Henry turned to her daughter. 'I don't have to listen to you. I'm your mother.'

'You're a liar,' Orla spat. 'You say everything's about me but it's about you.'

'I'm your mother and you'll do what I —'

'You want me to go because you don't like me. You've never liked me.'

'Orla, that's —'

'You probably planned it together. You probably asked her to come and get me.'

Henry gave a small laugh. 'I didn't. But maybe I should have. I hope she hasn't changed her mind now that she's met you.'

Light haloed the top of Henry's head; the outline of her hair shone. Orla couldn't see her face, her expression, but from her tone she could imagine it. 'You're not my mum! You're not! I hate you!' she shouted. 'I've always hated you!'

Henry stared at her daughter. 'Do you think I don't know that? Do you think you're the only clever clogs around here?'

And it came out of Orla's mouth as if it belonged to someone else. 'I wished you were the one who had to die.'

In the dim light, the daughter she barely recognised — her round, wet, darting eyes. For a moment, Henry didn't speak, let pain slice through her. 'Ah,' she said, gripping the mattress, steadying herself. 'Ah.' She stood. At the door she held onto the frame, turned back. 'Harry said something else, too. She said you believe Daddy will come back.'

Over there, on the other side of the room, Orla didn't move.

'That's not true, is it?'

'No.' Orla's voice was so small. As if she was afraid of it.

Henry nodded briskly. 'I didn't think so.' She turned away. 'Don't worry about dreams. Go back to sleep. Don't think about them.'

For a long time, Orla felt cold, listened to her thumping heart, the quiet of the house. Later she stirred again, rising to the surface with an image: Kit, a shell to her ear, 'Iya'. She turned over, opened her eyes and closed them; felt, for a moment, something outside cast a shadow, blocking out the streetlight she had thought, in her dream, was the sun.

~

To tear a page from her grade six maths pad. To write:

Dear Aunt Kit,

I hope you are well.

School starts soon.

How is your garden? Ours has gone to pot again. I look after Deebee when Mum goes to work. She wants me to take her to a cinema to see a film.

Mum wants to send me away. Can I please come and live with you? Please don't write back because Mum might see it.

I still remember you and iya.

To steal a stamp from her father's desk, to slip around the corner to the post box one weekend afternoon, to hold it in her hands and make a wish. To kiss it once and drop it through the slot.

54

Before breakfast one morning, Deebee asked, 'Do you like night time?'

Orla shrugged, picked at her nails.

'I don't,' Deebee continued. 'Everyone goes away at night.'

'Don't be stupid. I'm still here. So are you. And Mum. Cora. Mrs Thompson. And all the kids. So. How do you explain that?'

'All the *nice* people go.'

Orla scraped her fingernails along her arm, made thin white lines. 'Yeah, well, I guess we're stuck with each other, then.'

Later, Henry frowned, lifted Orla's fringe. 'What on Earth did you do to yourself?'

She saw her sister looking sideways at her, and shrugged. 'Banged it.'

Their mother leaned closer. 'On what?'

Orla waved her spoon. 'The back door.'

'That's the trouble with you running in and out from that silly pool, getting water everywhere, making everything slippery. You're the eldest. Be more responsible. If something happened to you what would your sister do? And don't wave your cutlery.'

'Oh, I dunno,' Orla replied, poking at her cereal. 'I think she'd be all right.' She turned to Deebee. 'Wouldn't you?' Deebee scowled.

'Don't say "dunno". Only stupid people say that.'

'Stupid,' Deebee said.

'Door,' Orla muttered.

Their mother thumped the table. 'That's enough!' she shouted. 'Another word and I will tear that pool to pieces!'

In the silence, Orla concentrated on breathing, on swallowing the lump in her throat. She pushed more food into her mouth, glanced at her mother; Henry's face was closed and hard.

Deebee poked her toast with her knife. Their mother said, 'Eat', without looking at her. Deebee tore off a corner and put it in her mouth, pouting. Orla wanted to say, 'Why are you making that face?' But she knew why. All the nice ones go. And they were still here, no car, no trips to the beach or pool. That paddle pool was all they had. She didn't want to lose it. She swallowed past whatever the stuck thing was, thought about the ocean, remembered the way their father had carried Deebee on his shoulders out to sea. Her little fingers holding on. The fear on her face. Their father oblivious. She should have called out, run to him, warned them both.

She tried not to think of the dream.

Deebee whipped her head around and glared at Orla. 'Stop it! Mummy, she's kicking me!'

For a moment, Orla didn't understand. Then her mother was standing over Deebee, her hands a blur and all Deebee's limbs drawn up in front of her body, her face; the air full of hitting and their mother growling through her teeth, 'What — did — I — just — tell — you? What — did — I — just — say?'

As if from a distance, Orla saw her own arm swing in front of her sister like a gate. She felt her mouth move and heard a long, wordless sound. In the next moment her mother was upon Orla, at her head and shoulders, her voice shrill, 'You think I don't mean it? Is that what you think?' Orla covered her head with her elbows, her hands, wished herself small, smaller, small enough to roll away; wished herself jagged, broken glass to cut her mother's hands; wished her father was there to say, 'Stop! Stop that!', to let Orla climb onto his shoulders, to take her with him out to sea, to never, never come back.

It hurt, she thought later. But it always hurts. And at least they still had the pool.

~

A sunny afternoon, and she heard it from somewhere behind, beyond the cubby house. She sat up in the pool. There it was again.

She put her face close to the fence and smiled through a gap in the pickets: 'Hi.'

'A guy's coming to measure up for some new blinds on Saturday,' Cora said. 'I have to go out. I'll try to take the kids with me but — I dunno, it's Whit's nap time. Can you let him in?'

Orla glanced over her shoulder. Deebee was sitting in the pool, watching. She turned back to Cora, smiled broadly. 'What time?'

She spread her towel quickly on the warm path and lay on it. Deebee said, 'What did Cora say?'

'Nothing,' she replied. She opened one eye, peered at her sister, watched her as she threw her cars into the water.

~

Cora had left the screen door unlocked and the main door propped open. The teapot sat on the kitchen bench by the electric jug. Orla pulled the lid off the tea caddy; inside its red plastic body, the tea was dark twists. They rustled like the piles of dry poplar leaves in the driveway in May, piles she had trudged through, crunching them beneath her shoes, piles that Deebee had kicked and kicked at until she fell over.

Cora always bought Robur tea. Orla loved its indigo wrapper, the squeak of its leaves when she squeezed the packet, its scent. New boxes of tea, she thought, smelled like earth, sounded like a forest full of birds.

Everything was quiet. She waited. When wheels turned onto the gravel, she went to the front door. In the kitchen she measured three scoops into the pot. The handle of the scoop was varnished wood; it was short and wide and said Ford in shiny chrome lettering that suddenly seemed beautiful. She knew three was right because Cora had taught her: one for each person, one for the pot.

He carried a small black case and settled at the kitchen table, in the place where Orla usually sat. He set his case on the floor. She knew how the room looked from there, how the sun felt, too, so close to the window, the warmth all along his side. She knew the view outside: the strip of sandy ground about ten feet below, the picket fence between Cora's house and hers. She knew that, if he looked through the glass, back towards the road, he would see Cora's driveway. He would see his small yellow van, the tops of the poplar trees. And, if he just stayed where he was and turned his head to the right, looked directly through the window, on the other side of the fence was Orla's house, plain as day: the dining room window, the one robbers were supposed to choose. She knew her mother would be in the kitchen and her sister would be playing, probably on their lounge room floor, just as she had been a little while before. She thought of all this while she waited for the jug to boil. The telephone was beneath the robber's window, silent on a small laminated table the colour of honey. When the phone rang in her house, everybody jumped.

All the light from Cora's window made part of the man's head disappear. Even so, when he looked down at his hands in his lap, she could see he was balding. She wanted to say, 'You're not old enough to be bald.' But she didn't: she knew words were more powerful than most people thought; it was always safer to keep quiet, to pretend she knew more or less than she really did. And for a moment she felt relieved to be a girl — at least she wouldn't lose her hair like that. And she was right; he was too young. The hair he had was black, his skin pale and smooth. Orla studied him. He was slight, not much taller than her. His hands were slim and still and clean. He wore long dark trousers, shiny leather lace-up shoes and a white nylon shirt, buttoned cuffs, open collar, no tie. She could see the shape of his singlet beneath his shirt; it made her think of her father, of how he dressed when he went to work. Her father had been balding, too, but he was old. She wondered: when I take him his tea and sit there, on the other side of the table, will the light make me disappear, too? Or will it gleam in my hair, prettily?

He stared a long time into his lap. The electric jug rumbled loudly on the kitchen bench between them. Then he looked up at her. She smiled, looked away.

He said, 'Do you have any brothers or sisters?'

She looked back at him. Now he was smiling. She said, 'A sister. She's a lot younger than me.' The jug began to boil, water leapt from its spout. She turned it off at the wall, pulled the cord from it, filled the teapot carefully. Through the steam she could see he was watching.

'And a mum and dad?' he said lightly.

She took a steamy breath, settled the jug on the bench, picked up the teapot lid. 'Just a mum.' Her voice sounded strange to her. She stared at the teapot. In the curve of its belly, she could see the room all out of shape. She looked down at the bench so he couldn't see her eyes. 'Dad died.' She stood very still. He didn't say anything. People usually didn't.

He asked, 'How old are you?' School would soon start again and she'd be not too far from high school. She felt grown up. She was in a house alone with a man she didn't know. She had sneaked out of her home to do it. She was making the man tea. She looked at him. He had turned in his chair so he was facing her. She liked that.

She told him: 'Twelve this year.' He nodded and stared. His hands were clasped loosely in his lap. She looked away, lifted the teapot and poured. She said, 'How do you like it?' Just the way Cora did.

He smiled again. 'White, thanks. No sugar. I'm sweet enough.' Cora always said that, too, and hearing it made Orla smile, breathe easier. She set the teapot down gently, crossed the room to the fridge. In the corner of her eye she saw his head turn to follow her. She closed the fridge, swung to face him, milk bottle in hand, looked at him and smiled, kept turning, returned to the bench. She heard him shift in his chair, and glanced up. He had turned back to the table. He rested his still-clasped hands on its edge; he stared at them. He said, 'It's hard being young, isn't it? Your mum still treats you like a kid. Adults don't really understand you. I know.'

She picked up a cup in each hand, carried them slowly. She didn't want to make a mess. She put the cups on the table. He reached for his; she slid it closer. 'Thanks,' he said. She sat in Cora's place, watched him take a sip. She said, 'I got a Beatles record. I saved up for it. But Mum doesn't like me playing it.'

He nodded, sipped. 'When did you say Mrs Muntz would be back?'

'She's wasn't sure. She said you could just measure it all while I'm here and then call her about it.' She lifted her cup. Inside, the liquid still swirled from the way she had stirred it.

He took another sip. He smiled at her and she smiled back. He said, 'It's bad when they won't let you do what you want — like playing your music. They just don't understand. They want you to be what they want you to be, do things they want you to do.' He shook his head. 'It makes you feel such a lot of stress, like screaming sometimes. Do you ever feel like that?'

She stared at him, at his lovely eyes. How did he know? She nodded.

He peered into his cup. 'I know a way,' he said, 'to get rid of all that stress, make you feel relaxed.' He looked straight at her. 'It's called sex. Have you heard of sex?'

She nodded again. She sat very still.

He said, 'I could show you, if you like.'

She blinked at him. He leaned forward, lifting his cup with two hands, resting his elbows on the table. 'Wouldn't you like to get rid of all that stress?'

She stared. She saw his hands loose and easy around his cup. The chair pressed into the back of her thighs, the edge of the table pressed the bones of her arms, her cup was hot against her palm. Without taking his eyes from hers, he lifted his cup to his mouth and parted his lips to sip.

She looked down at her tea. It was perfect and pale. She listened. The house was silent. She had no idea when Cora would return. The phone didn't ring. No-one knocked at the door. The front porch was empty. The lounge room was empty, and all the bedroom doors were open — they were always open — and so were the front and back doors. There was a breeze blowing through. She knew the laundry basket was empty in its usual spot at the top of the back steps. In a while Cora's washing would be dry. She had planned to bring it in.

She thought of her mother in their kitchen, her mother who thought she was in her room. Orla hadn't told her because — because she felt grown up, because she wouldn't let her play her record, because she only drank coffee, because she made her feel like screaming.

He didn't speak. He just looked down at the table, drank his tea. Orla listened, but there was only the wind in the trees, the air pouring through all the rooms, the empty yard, the silent street. Slowly she turned her head so she could see outside. There was her house, so close, the venetian blinds open at the window. But, just as she knew before she had turned, from where she was sitting, at the table with the man with dark, thinning hair and lovely eyes, she couldn't quite see in.

She said, 'I think I heard my mum call me.' She looked back at him. He looked up at her. Nothing passed across his face. She said, 'I better go and see what she wants. I won't be long.'

He stared at her, nodded. Orla pushed back against her chair. It squealed on the lino. She stood. Then he stood, too; his chair scraped back, and he stepped towards her. She stared at him. His mouth smiled. His teeth were white and even. He took her hand, his palm dry and smooth against hers. She watched as he raised it to his lips and kissed it. 'You're so beautiful,' he said. She felt herself blush. Her heart banged. He let go of her hand and it felt new and strange at her side. She turned to the kitchen door; she walked. Her breath was shallow; she listened but there was no sound behind her.

She ran through the carport, ducking past the robber's window, into the backyard; she peered around the corner of the house and up at the kitchen. No-one. But, at the bottom of the back stairs she stopped: the sound of water from the laundry sink. So she ran back, sprinted across the front lawn to her bedroom window, clawed it open again, climbed in the way she'd left. She pulled the window closed in its frame.

She stood looking: the glossy white furniture, her bed against the rose-pink walls, the neat way it sat on the purple shag pile. The shiny, curvy animals stared at her from the top of her chest of drawers: the dog like a girl, a bow in her hair; the horse more muscular, more theatrical than any horse could be; the cat so pleased with its red bow tie. Suddenly she saw how stupid they were: ugly, childish. She glanced into the corners of her room. She opened her wardrobe, looking into all the spaces where someone could hide. She wasn't sure what she was looking for but everywhere was emptiness.

She stared out the window. The yellow van still in Cora's drive. When she had looked him in the eye and lied, he had gazed back at her as if she were telling him the truth. She had looked away then, certain that any moment he would see inside her, spot the deceit, the shame. But now, she was starting to see, lying was easier than she had ever thought. And the longer she waited, the more she began to think she must be good at it.

Then she heard the van door, the motor, the reverse up Cora's driveway, the loud crunch of gravel. From between her venetian blinds she watched him pull out onto the road, drive away.

Orla slipped through her window again, walked slowly through Cora's house. Everything was just the same, though she wasn't sure it should be: Cora's pink satin bedspread was still smooth; Steele's shoes side-by-side under his bed; the kitchen floor still bare and clean. The air silent. The teapot cold. He had rinsed their cups, left them upside down on the draining board.

She peered into the girls' room, all light and pink, bed, cot. Whit asleep. On her back, arms and legs splayed, mouth slightly open, breathing evenly. Orla stood very still, looking at her.

She sat at the kitchen table. The house breathed in and out.

~

Wheels on the driveway. She stood. A car door slammed. Another. Voices. She sat again. Cora called, 'Yoo-hoo!' Kids' feet running. When they saw Orla, they stopped, stared. She stared back. Steele said, 'What are you doing here?'

The sound of Whit crying. Orla followed Cora to the bedroom. Whit's face flushed and sweaty. Cora lifted her. 'Yep. Soaked,' she said.

From the doorway, Orla watched Cora get down on her knees, lay Whit on the floor in front of her, open the nappy. 'Did the blinds man come?' she asked, without turning her head.

Whit's plump white belly, her tearful face. 'Yeah,' Orla replied. 'I — I think he's gonna call you.'

'Okay. Ouch. Bugger,' Cora said. She lifted a hand. A drop of blood swelled on the end of a finger.

~

Her mother was still in the laundry, leaning over the ironing board. Henry straightened, smiled thinly, set the iron on its heel, pushed her hair from her face. 'That was a quick nap.'

'Yeah. I'm ... I just woke up.'

Her mother smoothed a pillowcase with her hands. She picked up the iron again. 'Please don't say "yeah".'

Orla looked at her mother's face. It was tired, she could see, but there was no trace of the lie she had just been told. Orla's heart folded over: she could have just stayed in her room, stayed there to think about what had just happened; she didn't have to find her mother just to lie to her. Her head felt thick, her legs shaky. She leaned against the doorframe and watched her mother iron. After a while, she took a breath, made her voice bright: 'What are you doing, Mummy?'

Her mother frowned. 'What does it look like I'm doing?'

Orla bit her lip, shifted her gaze from her mother's profile to her strong grip on the iron, the white pillowcase smooth and steaming. She kept her voice steady. 'Mum.'

'Yes?'

'Do you miss Dad?'

Her mother looked up, hot iron stilled mid-air, her eyes suddenly darker, wet. 'What kind of question is that?' She slammed the iron down on the fabric, shoved it back and forth.

'I didn't —'

Her mother nodded. 'Yes, you did. You think you're the only one who loved him.' Her voice wavered.

Orla shook her head. 'I —'

Her mother set the iron hard on its heel again and straightened herself, fixed her daughter's gaze. Her hands gripped the edge of the ironing board. 'I had more than twenty years with him. More than twenty. You,' she waved her hand, 'all of you, should remember that.'

Orla saw her mother's flushed cheeks, the line of her mouth, her quivering chin. She cast around in the shocked white space of her head for words, better words, the right ones. But the silence stretched long and thin and, when it had become unbearable — tight and flat, when it covered everything Orla could see, from the horizon behind the faraway hills to the horizon over the sea, and when all the world's colour had drained and everything outside her was also white and shocked — she turned her head away, and her body followed and left the room.

~

In the shaded square of the sandpit, Orla and her sister lay on their backs, looking up. Between the lacework of leaves, the late January sky was shockingly blue. In some part of her head, Orla tried to count the days. Thirty days hath September.

Deebee said, 'When did I meet you?'

'What?' The numbers slipped out of her head.

'Were you a baby then?'

'No, you were.' All the rest have thirty-one.

'Where was I?'

'In Daddy's car.'

'What was I doing?'

'Nothing.'

'Like Whit?'

'She does things.' Excepting February — but it's not yet.

'She cries. Did I cry?'

'You were asleep.' So, that's.

'Was I nice?'

'I suppose.'

'Did you like me?'

'You were asleep.'

'And I woke up and then you liked me?'

'I suppose.' Thirty days hath. Leaves shifted spangles of sunlight.

'Am I a girl?'

Orla snorted. 'What?'

'Kids say I'm not.'

'Who?'

'Kids.'

'That's just stupid.'

'They say girls wear dresses and have long hair.'

'Well, that just goes to show how much they know.'

'You wear dresses. So does Mummy. And Cora and Mrs Thompson.'

'Wear a dress then.'

'And Kit. And Harry.'

'Wear one if you want to.'

'I don't.'

'Then why are you talking about it?'

Orla turned her head to look at her sister's face. Sun speckled Deebee's hair, clothes, skin; she was turning a button on her shirt, twisting it one way, then the other. Her hands like spiders.

'Do you have friends at your school?' Deebee asked.

Orla turned away, rolled onto her side. Light flicked into her eyes.

'Orly?'

'What.'

'Do you?'

'Yes.'

'Is your friend called Tiger?'

Orla pressed her eye with the heel of her hand. 'No-one's called that.'

'Mrs Thompson calls Johnny "Tiger".'

'That's just a nickname.' So, thirty plus ...

'What's a nitname?'

'*Nick*name. It's what people call you instead of your real name.'

'Like darling?'

'No,' Orla sighed. Like Deebee, she thought. She closed her eyes. The wind in the trees, the small calls of birds. Men who go to work and come back. Then don't.

'What's your friend's nitname?'

'*Nick*name. What friend?' Orla breathed.

'At school. Your friend. What's her *nick*name?'

Orla sat up, shook her head, turned to Deebee, watched her button twist. 'She doesn't have one.'

'Why?'

'Not everybody does.'

'Why?'

'Some people get them and some people don't.' She grabbed Deebee's hand. 'Can you stop doing that?'

Deebee looked up at her. 'Do you have one?'

She glanced away. 'Not really.'

'Do I?'

Orla dug her fingers deep into the sand by her feet. Beneath was colder. 'No.'

'Yes, I do.'

'Guess what my friend's nickname is.'

'What's my *nick*name, Orly?'

Orla clenched fistful of sand. 'Are you even listening to me?'

For a moment there was silence. Then Deebee said, 'Why don't you have a *nick*name?'

'Will you just try to guess?'

'What?'

'It's a flower.'

'My nickname is a flower?'

'No! The name of my friend!'

'What friend?'

'The friend you asked about!'

'Did she have to guess *my* nickname?'

Orla looked at Deebee's face, at her round, dark eyes. 'Okay, listen, sorry but the truth is,' Orla said, 'Daddy gave me a nickname but he didn't give you one.' She watched her words enter her sister and settle.

Deebee's face creased. 'That's not true.'

Orla looked away, shrugged. 'Sorry, but you wanted to know.'

'He did so give me a nickname!'

'No, he didn't. Really.' Orla lay back on the sand, closed her eyes. 'Deebee's not a nickname,' she said, quietly. 'It's a stupid name.'

Her sister's voice shook. 'My nickname is Tiger. That's what Daddy calls me.'

Orla laughed. 'What a coincidence. And when does he call you this? When he comes to pick you up from Mrs Thompson's?'

'You're a liar!' Deebee shouted, and brought her fist down hard on Orla's face.

She tried to sit up but Deebee was on her, pummelling. 'I hate you, and Daddy hates you, too!'

Orla pushed back blindly, turned away her softest parts — her belly, her face.

'He gave *me* a nickname,' Deebee yelled, hitting Orla's back and head. '*Me*, not you. Because he hates you! He hates you!'

Orla curled, her arms over her head, her curved back to her sister. The blows stopped as suddenly as they had begun; incoherent sounds in Deebee's throat.

Slowly Orla sat up, spitting out sand, brushing it gingerly from her eyes, rubbing it from her scalp. Her voice shook. 'Stop your stupid crying. It was just a joke.' But Deebee didn't stop. And the sound of it turned her stomach. Sand stung her eyes.

'It's not a joke; it's not funny,' Deebee replied, her voice small.

Orla stood. She couldn't bear to look at her.

'Don't tell Mummy,' Deebee said.

Orla brushed down her clothes. 'Why shouldn't I?'

Deebee stared up at her. 'You can have my red car.'

Orla crossed her arms. 'I don't want your stupid boys' toys.'

'You can have my telescope.'

Orla shook her head.

'Please, Orly!'

She looked down at her sister's wet eyes and quivering chin, then looked away, to the grey picket fence. Between the boards, narrow flashes of lawn, thick green, orderly and beautiful.

'Tell me a secret,' she said. 'Something you've never told anyone.' The morning light silvered the fence timber. She wanted to touch it.

'All right,' Deebee said, and Orla looked back to her sister, stared down at the top of her head, the white skin of her scalp shining at her crown, watched her stab her finger into the sand: stab stab stab.

Orla tapped her foot. 'Well?'

'I don't know any.'

'Now who's the liar. I've seen you.'

'I'm not a liar.'

'Oh yeah? Who do you talk to, then?'

Stab, stab stab.

'Who do you talk to,' Orla repeated, 'when there's no-one else there? Huh? I know. It's Daddy, isn't it? ' She gave a short laugh. 'You *pretend* you're talking to him, I mean. No wonder kids don't like you. You're such a loony.'

Deebee looked up, brow creased. 'But he *is* there, Orly.'

Orla bit her lip, tasted blood, turned her back. Her eyes prickled.

55

Desks in the year seven classroom were set in alphabetical rows; Orla's and Heather's desks were far apart. On the first day, Orla avoided Heather, looked about for someone new. Wandered silent and alone. On the second day there was still no-one. At recess, she stood behind Heather, watched her dig for something in her bag. 'Hi,' said Orla. But Heather didn't hear, so Orla leaned closer, spoke louder. 'Hi!'

Still Heather didn't turn. Orla stared at her two small pigtails, the pale blue ribbons on each side of her head, her crooked part, pink scalp. 'What's wrong?' she said.

Heather faced her, hands on hips. 'Did you have a nice holiday?'

She wasn't sure. 'Yes.'

'Why didn't you come to see me?'

Orla looked away. 'I couldn't.' She gazed at her hands, felt her cheeks burn. 'I had to look after my sister.'

'What — you couldn't come to see me even once.'

'Sorry, but I just told you. '

Heather's eyes narrowed. 'I don't believe you.'

Orla stared at her.

Heather's lip trembled. 'I don't believe you,' she repeated. 'You're not my friend.'

The words poured: 'And you're not my friend, either. You're a cheat. You changed the seven to an eight.'

Heather flushed. 'I did not! Liar!'

'Yes, you did! You're the liar!'

'Am not! I wish you were dead instead of your dad!'

Orla's body jolted. The world fled. She lurched forward, pushed. Hard. Heather staggered, and Orla launched at her, clawing. Then a voice, different, a man, a teacher, one strong hand on each of them, pulling them apart. 'What's going on here?'

Heather sobbed: 'She hit me.'

Orla saw the teacher's face turn to her. She opened her mouth. 'She said she wished it was me who had died instead of —' But she couldn't. She couldn't. She felt so ashamed. That she couldn't speak, that she had no friends, that her father was dead. She covered her face with her arms, the teacher made a sound in his throat, released his grip.

'Never mind,' he said, his hand on Orla's shoulder. 'Go wash your face.'

Never mind, never mind, she thought, never mind. She wanted to grab his shirt in her fists, pull him close enough that she felt his chest hard up against her, and say: 'Tell me how. How? How can I do that, that thing you say, that never mind?' But her body — sobbing, shaking — wouldn't let her.

56

She woke in the night. The steady sound of rain. Fell down the well of sleep, surfaced again. And it was louder, harder. By morning the world was sodden, the sky low, exhausted.

On her way to school early for choir, everything pale. Light grey and flat on puddles. Eaves dripped. Houses usually so solid in the summer, their blocks of shade and walls of bright, were watercolour paintings of themselves: soaked, mute. Verge trees drooped; even the disturbance of her body through the air, the tremor of her steps shook water from their leaves as she passed beneath them.

No kids in the street, the playground; none on the oval. Too early, too damp, too cold. Out in the middle where the grass grew long and thick and green, her shoes and socks grew wet; the leather squeaked. Too late to wish she had taken the other way, past the house of the ginger cat, the old church, the weedy vacant block, keeping to roads and footpaths. She hadn't thought it through, had imagined this way might be beautiful after rain towards the end of summer. But she was more than halfway now, the oval a great deep sea; no point turning back. Head down, she watched her legs, thought of the heater in winter at the front of her classroom — would the teacher bring it out of the cupboard today, would her shoes dry before the walk home? She glanced behind, saw where she had been, her trail flattened in the sparkling grass. For a moment she imagined she was the only girl on Earth. A giant girl. The green sea of grass parting for her with a swish. All around her, water quivered on the edge of its blades, flicked coldly onto her knees, her skirt, flashed in the sun, bright as Mrs Dodd's rings.

Perhaps she had been right to come this way after all. The world was bigger and lonelier here; it smelled all clean and new, and maybe this is what heaven is like, a place everyone can be alone to walk and think, no-one around to see what you do or hear what you say out loud or that you cry or sing to yourself. No-one but God, of course, who in the end must have noticed her, sent a man to kiss her hand, tell her she was beautiful, like a boyfriend, a lover — a lover, yes, that's the word, isn't it? The word she had heard Kit use? Had sent rain in summer and made the world quiet and empty, this space where she could walk and think, where one day she might hold someone's hand, might stand in the middle of the oval and kiss.

From somewhere in the distant eucalypts, a magpie — that run of notes. She sang the bird's trill to herself. And then it was quiet again and it was only the loudness of her body moving through. Her soft pulse, her breath, her wet shoes' squeak; the dull knock of her bag against her hip, its rustle against the fabric of her uniform. She sang, a little breathlessly: 'How much is that do-ggy in the win-dow,' a song Kit had taught her. Then, carefully, her choir part: 'I love a sun-burnt cou-oun-try,' so she would be good. She imagined Mrs Dodd's hands at the piano, the diamonds in the gold, the way they slipped around behind the knuckle as she played, bone rising white beneath her skin as she stretched for the chords. She had felt the music low, very low in her belly, had turned away, afraid then of where it might lead.

A memory of her father moved swiftly through her like a breeze, the scent of it caught somehow in the empty and full places of her heart. She thought about how it felt to sing, her own hand resting lightly on her belly where she needed to breathe. She remembered Nugget, her calm warm face. How she had flown, like the scarf, magically through the air one blue afternoon. Remembered a fragment of her dream: something glinting. That she had woken, gasping, heart crashing. And she would not think of Heather. Would not.

She frowned, began her part again. She knew that if she did it right there was no room for anything but the song.

And then there she was, approaching the road on the other side, her feet crunching a stony verge. She would cross the street, pass the bus stop, take a short road right that led uphill. From its crest she would see her school, would pause again before crossing that last road to make her way diagonally, beneath trees, across the playing fields, to choir. She slowed, looked left and right, began to cross.

Several men waited for a bus to town. As she approached, she gave them a glance. They were still and silent. A small herd of them waiting for the warmth of the sun. Some swivelled their faces to look at her, as horses do.

She looked back over her shoulder to the wide green sea she had crossed, as if she might have left someone there, someone still watching her, making sure she was all right, but there was just the green green green and, on the faraway shore, a squat toilet block, tiny swings and slides where she and Deebee had gone that day, after Deebee appeared at her bedroom window, and Orla lied that her head didn't hurt, the two of them slipping away. She looked ahead to the horse-men, thought again of Nugget patient at the hitching rail. She knew not all horses were like that. She looked down; her feet steady, treading softly now. As if she might spook them.

If they were horses she would have stopped, held out her hand and called — as she had called over a fence to a pair of geldings by the bus stop near her home in the hills. She would offer them her lunchtime apple. One of them would wander over, curious; she would bite the apple into pieces to sit on the flat of her palm, smile at their lips on her fingers.

The men were closer now, close enough, she felt, to hear her breathe. Because horses have sharp hearing; they know things humans don't. She felt all her air at the top of her chest, her shoulders moving up down up down, which was wrong, which was the wrong way to breathe altogether.

A seated man looked up from his newspaper. A standing man stared, took a drag of his cigarette. Smoke trailed from his nose and his fingers. No matter how she tried, she couldn't silence her step. Then she was beside them, could have stretched out her arm to touch. And then she was past them all but the one. There was always one standing outside; it's the hierarchy of horses. His back to her. The side of his face. Eyes closed. Face tilted up to catch the sun. Brown suit. Hands side by side, around the handle of a brown leather bag. His head swivelled on his neck. She looked down, saw his bag bump his knee. His brown leather shoes. She looked up. He was gazing at her. She took another step, faltered. Her eyes widened, her lips parted. His face opened, too, like sky. And all in a rush he swung away, turned his back to her.

The growl of the approaching bus. Newspapers, shoes, the jingle of change. No part of her moved. She watched his shoulders, the back of his head. Keeping his face turned away from her, he strolled to the end of the queue. As if she wasn't even there.

She looked from his shape to the bus, tiny at the bottom of the road. She glanced about: there were houses everywhere, streets and streets, all around the oval, each close against its neighbours, as far as she could see. There were people in the houses, waking, eating, dressing.

The brown-suited back, the shaggy hair. The other men in front of him, their shoes and jackets, newspapers tucked beneath their arms. The bus strained up the incline. She raised her arm. She lowered it. She thought she should point, she thought she should speak: 'That man. That man looked. Through my window.' She imagined the other men turning, following her accusing finger, to stare at the last man in the queue and then back at her. She imagined them frowning, looking at one another. The last man turning to them, his face a picture of shock, confusion. He would shrug as if he didn't have a clue.

The right house, the safe one. She would choose it; she would bang on the door: 'Help! Please! Call the police!' The father would open it, just like her dad, step onto the porch, say, 'Calm down, dear.' He'd listen, press his lips together, nod. He'd go back inside. She'd hear his voice, quiet: 'It's a girl, she's upset. You better talk to her.' She'd call after him, 'Daddy!'

The bus groaned, stopped; its doors squeaked open. She watched the men board quietly, one by one. She heard the murmur of their voices, the clack of the ticket machine. She stared into the back of the last man's head, into the width of his shoulders, the fabric of his jacket, its hem, she stared at his heels. She watched as he made his way down the aisle to a seat on the far side, his face perfectly averted. She thought: he gets up every morning; he goes to work. And then a man's voice: 'You right, love?' The bus driver, leaning forward in his seat to peer at her.

The doors jerked closed. Its engine groaned. She watched it move away. She should run, yell, wave her arms. She watched it grow smaller, smaller, turn, disappear. She stared after it. She stared for a long time. She gazed back across the oval. She gazed at all the houses. Their empty lawns, their quiet porches. Their closed-up safe front doors.

Mrs Dodd's mouth was fierce with smiling: 'Let's try that again.' But each time Orla reached for the note, her voice slipped down her throat.

The choir looked at her. Mrs Dodd sighed. 'Sounds like the collywobbles.' She placed her cool palm on Orla's forehead. 'Should you be home?' Orla shook her head, stared at the floor, her cheeks aflame.

At the door, Derek stopped her, his hand on her shoulder. 'You all right?'

She pulled away. She couldn't look at him. Even though he carried her bag, had a sweet face, sweet voice, small sweet hands. He wasn't her boyfriend. She glanced about, embarrassed: only Mrs Dodd by the piano, tidying her sheet music. They stepped through the door and onto the veranda.

'I heard about the fight,' Derek said.

Her mouth opened. She blinked. 'Fight?'

'With Heather.'

A shout of laughter; she knew it must be hers. 'Oh, yeah.' She looked down. 'How?'

'Everyone knows.'

She pressed the heels of her hands hard into her eyes. They sat side by side on the veranda's edge. Its boards still cool and damp from the rain. She gripped the edge of the boards, either side of her, and balanced there, looked at her feet hanging quietly off the end of her legs. Still no sun shone. She said it quickly. 'There's a man.'

'What do you mean?'

Her mouth opened. How to choose the right words, the right order? In her mind she saw her father emerging from the ocean, Mr McIntyre smiling, the man with the lovely eyes at Cora's table, Mr Woodland winding down his car window, the prowler with his radio. She shook her head. It was the prowler, wasn't it. She knew it. The prowler she had just seen. This morning. At the bus stop. In his brown suit.

So she took a deep breath and told him: the summer evening, the falling asleep, the Cat Stevens' song, the face, the face, the walk to school, the face, the way he had turned his back to her. 'That means he lives somewhere near there, doesn't it, if that's his closest stop.' She looked at Derek.

He was frowning at the ground. Everything smelled of the sweating earth. He said, 'That's weird.'

She was breathless with relief. 'I know.'

'He's never come to our house. Our windows are open all the time. Why would he go to your house and not to ours?'

Why? she thought. Ah. She thought she knew. Didn't he know, too? It was obvious. Yes. She balanced herself. She kept very still. She knew. She had always known. She thought. She thought Derek. That he might. And thought that she and he. Well, she was wrong. Wrong again, it seems, the way she always. Yes.

For a moment she was dizzy, as if dazzled, as if perched somewhere high up. Her stomach shuddered. Deep in the middle, in the pit of her. She turned her head carefully to look at him. Because she had to keep balance and she had to be sure. That he wasn't just. Wasn't laughing. That he really didn't know. And had no idea, either, why he didn't. And yes, there he was. And he was watching. His blue eyes cloudless. His sweet, puzzled face. Waiting. For her to. And all she wanted was. Not to have to. Not to have to say it. Not to have to make it real. Not to have to think about it anymore.

Suddenly she felt very tired, closed her eyes, leaned towards him. She couldn't. She just. She thought of her sister — her clothes, haircut, questions. What it is to be a girl.

Rested her cheek on his chest. Felt his hand on her back. His small, surprised breath. The loud thump of his heart: I am here, here.

Some people are here, she thought. And some people aren't. The dumb luck of it.

'We, we should …' he whispered.

Orla straightened and looked at him. 'What.'

'We should tell her.'

'What?'

'Your mum.'

She blinked. 'What?'

'You know. That you saw him.'

She looked away, over the playground. 'Oh,' she said. 'All right.'

~

She had no idea what 'after footy' meant. She stood under the verge tree and scanned the street. She sat on the edge of the porch, pushed her feet back and forth over the red path. The soles of her sandals made a scraping sound.

Henry came to the doorway behind her. 'What are you doing out here?'

Orla glanced over her shoulder. 'Just waiting.'

'What for?'

'A friend.'

'Oh. From school?'

'Yes.'

'Does she know the address?'

Orla turned away. Her face flushed. 'Um ... yes.'

'Well, couldn't you wait inside then?'

Orla shrugged. 'It's nice here.' She heard her mother make a sound, 'Hm,' heard her feet pad away, over the carpet.

Why hadn't she just asked him what time he meant? And why didn't she just say her friend is a boy? And why was it Derek who thought they should tell Henry? Why hadn't she thought of it? Everything was straightforward to him. Nothing was ever straightforward to her. Was he scared of anything? Didn't he have things he couldn't say?

She walked to the edge of the road again. No people, no cars. 'After footy' was something other kids would understand — kids like Heather with brothers and uncles and boy cousins, kids with dads who played kick-to-kick and coached their teams and drove them to games.

Once again under the verge tree, where three of them had waited for Henry months ago and talked about earthquakes, about why they couldn't go back inside, about aftershocks. Where other people's cars had parked. Where she had shredded blades of grass and tossed them into the air.

'Hi, Orla.' She spun around. Of course, he was smiling. There was dirt on his shorts and tiny bits of lawn in his hair. His feet were bare. He held a footy boot in each hand.

From the kitchen, Deebee's shout. 'Boyfriend! Boyfriend!' Orla breathed in sharply. Her throat constricted, her eyes widened; she fixed her gaze fix on the air in front of her.

Her mother's voice. 'What?'

Orla crossed the lounge room ahead of him. She didn't dare look back. She faced her mother, glanced at her expression, then out the kitchen window, then at the floor. 'Mum,' she gestured, 'this is Derek.'

She saw Derek hook both boots with the fingers of his left hand, and extend his right. Her mother blinked. 'Hello, Mrs Blest,' he said, as they shook hands. Henry looked him up and down. Orla looked at him again; she had to stop herself reaching out to brush the bits from him.

Deebee said, 'He's Orly's boyfriend.'

Orla elbowed her shoulder. 'Shut up,' she hissed.

'Don't be ridiculous.' She looked hard at Derek and then at Orla. 'They're much too young for that kind of thing.'

'Mu-um,' Orla whispered.

Henry took a deep breath and smiled at them. 'So,' she said. 'To what do we owe this pleasure?'

Orla's mouth moved but made no sound. Derek looked from her to Henry, said, 'Er,' he said, 'Orla wants to tell you something. Don't you.'

As Henry turned to Orla, her face was suddenly serious. 'Oh?'

The words tumbled. 'It's just about the prowler. I saw him. The other day. In the morning. On the way to school. At the bus stop. I was walking past and I recognised him. And he saw me. He saw me recognise him. I suppose the look on my face. And he turned his back on me. So I couldn't see his face again.'

'Oh. Oh. Yes,' Henry said. 'He, he did that —'

Orla frowned. 'What do you mean? When?'

'Nothing. It doesn't matter.'

Orla looked at Derek. 'But what are we going to do, Mum?' she said.

'Do?' Henry said. 'What do you mean, do?'

'He saw me. He knows I recognised him.'

Henry sighed loudly. 'How do you know it was him?'

'Mum! Did you hear me? I recognised his face!'

'His Satan face.'

Orla glanced at Derek. He was staring at her. 'He, he knows I recognised him, Mum.'

Henry nodded.

'Mum, I —. Do you think I'm —' Orla threw up her hands. 'Mum, listen. Cora saw him, too, remember?'

Henry nodded again. Orla looked back to Derek. He was still staring at her. She felt her eyes sting.

Derek said, 'I think Orla is worried, Mrs Blest, because the man knows where she lives.'

Henry turned to Orla. 'But did you see where he lives?'

Orla frowned. 'No …'

'He was at the bus stop,' Derek said.

'I'm talking to my daughter.'

'Mum,' Orla whispered. 'Can't we just…you know…tell the —'

'Is the man going to come?' Deebee said.

Orla looked down at her sister; Deebee's eyes were round and worried. Orla shook her head. 'No.' Because things like that don't really happen, do they. Because even the ones who should come don't. Even the ones we love. So.

Henry placed her hand on Deebee's head. 'Nooo, it's all right,' she said. She looked up. 'Derek, it's very nice to meet you.' She smiled. 'But, as you can see, this is upsetting everyone.'

~

He dropped his boots by the Chinese apple tree and got down on his hands and knees.

She laughed before she could stop herself. 'What are you doing?'

'Climb up,' he said.

She wanted to say she was good at climbing, could scramble up without anyone's help. But there he was, waiting, so she stepped carefully onto his back, felt him tense under her weight, and swung herself into the tree, wishing she were lighter. He followed her up, settled on a nearby bough. The fruits were purple and tender as flesh. When she bit them their insides were sweet and turning pink. She shifted her legs, glanced at him. He wasn't looking at her. Still, she hoped her hadn't seen up the legs of her shorts.

Deebee ran around the yard with a stick. She whacked the forty-four gallon drum. It boomed. She hit the Hills hoist. It pinged. She swiped at tufts of grass. She belted the trunks of trees. She looked up at them. 'I want some, too, Orly!'

Derek stretched his hand up towards Orla, passed several fruit to her. He looked at his palm then licked it. 'What did your mum mean?'

'About what?'

'Satan.'

She shrugged, said. 'Sometimes she's a bit weird.' She didn't look at him.

'So what are you gonna do now?'

She shrugged again. 'Dunno.' She didn't want to think about it. The sky was blue and she was sitting in a tree with a boy and thinking about it made her tired.

He reached for fruit above him. 'You know what your mum said.'

Orla wiped juice from her chin. 'What.' She opened her hand, let fruits fall to the earth; they bounced and rolled by Deebee's feet.

'About us being too young.'

'Mm.'

'What do you think?'

She shrugged again, smiled at him, her mouth full. 'I think,' she mumbled, 'she doesn't know what she's talking about.'

At the base of the tree, Deebee dug the stick into the soil. Dirt flew up. She gathered the bruised fruits Orla had dropped and inspected them, slipped the damaged ones deep inside Derek's boots.

57

One night after dinner, their mother emerged from her bedroom in her navy blue dress and pearls. Deebee grabbed her mother's skirt, her voice a whine. 'Where are you going?'

Henry crouched. 'It's all right. I just have to go out. Your sister will look after you.' She prised Deebee's fingers from her clothes.

Orla stared at her mother's face, at the pearls gleaming at her throat. 'When will you be back?'

'But where are you going, Mummy?' Deebee wailed.

'I won't be long.' She winked, reached into her bag. 'I bought chocolate.' She waved it at them, smiling.

Orla had never seen her mother wink before. She looked from the chocolate bar to Henry's face.

Deebee cried. 'I don't want you to go!'

'I know, but I have to.' Henry opened Orla's hand, placed the chocolate in it. Deebee followed her to the bathroom. Henry shut the door. Deebee leaned on it and wept.

Henry looked at her reflection. She had expected Deebee's reaction, but — did she imagine it? — surely Orla was too old to be frightened by this. She could have warned her but what difference did it make. What was two hours now if it meant the future. She hadn't started it; a door had opened, the way doors sometimes did, even at her age, and she would be a fool not to. The girls would thank her in the end. She wouldn't be late — he had promised that — and it wasn't as if the two of them weren't used to being alone. Orla had proved herself able to manage perfectly well. Henry smoothed powder over her face, coloured her lips, pushed her hair into place.

The bathroom door opened. Orla slipped in and closed the door behind her. She stared at her mother's face in the mirror. 'You look nice, Mum.'

Henry's reflection smiled.

Orla took a step closer. 'Do you really have to go?'

Henry turned to face her daughter. 'Look, darling.' She took Orla's hand. 'I'm going out with someone who might be able to help us. You want us to build the house, don't you? You want to stay with us. You want to go back to the hills.'

Orla nodded.

'Then just look after your sister for a little while.'

~

In the lounge room, Deebee was on the divan, her mouth full of chocolate. Henry wiped her sticky face.

A knock on the door, a shape in the glass. Orla's heart leapt; she couldn't help it. Deebee peered through the blinds. 'Someone's here!'

Henry smoothed her skirt, turned the lock. Deebee's voice grew shrill, incoherent. Orla moved close to her mother, stood behind her. Beyond her mother's shoulder, she caught a glimpse of a man in a white shirt, a dark tie.

'Come in,' Henry said. Deebee fell silent. Orla stared. Henry stepped back, gestured. 'These are my children.'

The man was large, swarthy, hair beginning to grey. He had big hands, a bunch of pink flowers in one fist. He plucked two, presented one to each of the girls, gave a little bow: 'How do you do.'

Orla smiled without teeth. He winked at her. 'They're beautiful,' he said, looking at each of them. 'Just like their mother.'

Orla watched Henry take the rest of the bouquet, saw her raise an eyebrow, give a smile. 'Why, thank you.' She watched her mother take this man's elbow, draw him into the room. 'This is my boss,' she said. 'Mr Konstantin.'

'Please, please,' he said, solemnly shaking Deebee's sticky hand. 'Call me Kon.' He took Orla's hand, looked her in the eye. 'Everyone does.'

Orla held his gaze as he smiled. 'You don't mind me taking your mother away for a little while, do you?' He had skin like orange peel.

Deebee said, 'I do mind.'

Orla watched the adults' laughing mouths, and laughed a bit, too, because sometimes it's hard not to.

Henry kissed the top of Deebee's head. 'Be good.' She caught Orla's eye. 'Just watch TV.' Orla nodded. They exchanged smiles.

Orla and Deebee watched the front door close, then looked at one another.

'Will she come back?' Deebee's voice was small. Her eyes trembled with tears.

'Of course she will.'

'But how do you know?'

'I — I just know.'

'Because you go to school?'

'What? No.'

'Because you're big?'

Orla put her hands on her hips. 'Look. I — yes, that's right. Because I'm big. You wanna watch TV?'

Deebee nodded gravely. 'I don't want the man to come.'

'What? What man?'

'The man.' She held Orla's gaze.

Orla frowned, looked at the closed door and back to her sister. 'What are you talking about?'

'You know. The man.'

Orla stared, thought why does Deebee always have to talk about things she doesn't understand? She doesn't know anything about anything, actually. When she said things like that, memory flickered in Orla's head like the start of a film. And it was hard to turn it off. The projector light went on and the reel turned. She saw the window again. She had been stupid. It had been open. But he could have brought a knife. Cut the flywire. Climbed in. He could have been quiet. Instead he brought a radio. He woke her with a song. 'I'm being followed ...' He must have wanted her to know he was there. How does that make sense. To know he was there, to see him, his face. She shivered. His face.

She shook the pictures from her head. Deebee was still gazing up at her. 'There's no-one else here,' said Orla. 'Just us.'

~

They turned on every light, checked window latches, screens, blinds. Inside cupboards and behind doors. Left the house incandescent. Orla sat on the divan with her legs tucked up, Deebee curled alongside, and watched the newsreader in his dark suit and tie, glancing up from his pages as he read to her about the launch of a rocket. The papers rustled softly in his hands.

Deebee said, 'Can we go outside and look at the stars?'

No, she thought, no. And then, the porch light's on, all the lights are; I would see if anyone.

'Orly? Did you hear me?'

'No.'

'Can we?'

'You can look through the blinds.'

'It doesn't work.'

The newsreader smiled broadly. Orla heard the rise and fall of his calm and even voice. He was talking about space.

'But please, Orly.'

'Just get your telescope.' Orla peered through the lounge room venetians. Deebee was right, of course; it was hopeless. She flicked off the porch light, pulled the cord hard. The blinds rattled up into the pelmet. She turned off the lights in the lounge room, dining room, kitchen, passageway. Light from the front bedrooms splayed yellow trapezoids on the lawn. She turned them off, too. And the laundry. She shut the bathroom and toilet doors to keep their light contained.

Deebee peered through her telescope. Behind them, a slice of light from their parents' room, the room right at the back, furthest from where people came and went, from the porch, the street. Orla turned around to stare at it: the house made strange, opposite angles and backward shadows. Their furniture lit up weirdly. Everything unfamiliar. Like Alice down that rabbit hole, she thought. The world as a pocket turned inside out.

Deebee whined. 'I can't see anything.'

Orla turned back to the window. She cupped her face with her hands, pressed her hands to the glass. Her eyes adjusted: verge tree; street; poplars; the low, white fence to the right; the neighbours' yards; yellow pools of streetlamps. Most of the sky was still behind the porch roof.

In their parents' room, Orla flicked off the light, flung back the curtains. 'There!'

Deebee raised her telescope to her eye like an explorer. Orla smiled. Its end tapped the glass as Deebee scanned the sky.

'Be careful.'

'I can't see the moon.'

Oral frowned. 'Oh. Well, that's because it's on the other side, in the east. This is the west. It'll be over here later.'

'But I want to see it.'

'Well,' she shrugged.

'But I want to see, Orly.'

'Deebee,' she said, exasperated. 'I can't move the moon for you.'

'Can we go outside, just for one minute?'

Orla looked away, down into the backyard. There were shadows so deep they could be holes. Sheoaks held the treehouse in place. The forty-four gallon drum kept perfectly still. The Hills hoist and paddle pool glowed faintly. There was no need to ask her sister why she had to see the moon, stars, rocket. She knew.

She knew how to prop open a door with a dining chair, too. Everyone knew about that. In case a sudden wind sprung up and slammed it. Leave the screen door shut for mozzies. The TV still on. Stand behind her on the verge. One cold foot on top of the other. No shoes. Because it's summer. And Mum's not here. And they won't be out here long. Hold still. Hold still. Stare at all the things you can see: the sleeping face of Mrs Thompson's house, and Cora's, close and quiet, curled-up. Stare harder into the darkest places, what's in there you can't quite. A sound behind, small squeak — bird, cat? — your breath or hers, the exclamation in her throat. Television music.

Deebee held the telescope to her eye, moonlight making the edges of it. Orla watched her turn her telescope face. And looked up, too. Some floating stars. The floating moon. Three-quarters full. Moon belly white as cut-out paper. The kind he used to type onto. All the cut away bits scraps of light falling over things in the dreaming world.

A gust. Shiver. The poplars rustled. Orla looked over her shoulder at the door held firm. Looked back. 'What can you see on the moon?' she asked.

'A face,' Deebee said.

'Well, everyone knows that,' Orla replied. And she thought, a smile, and why and why is he made that way? She said, 'Does he look happy? Do you think he's kind, that moon man up there?'

'Yes,' said Deebee.

'Can you see him?' Orla whispered.

'Yes.'

'That's enough,' Orla said eventually, 'I'm cold.'

She locked the front door after them, dropped the lounge room blinds, moved from room to room, flicked on the lights. Her hand on the laundry switch. The loud click of it. On the ceiling, the conical shade like a small white hat. The white shirt on its hanger. The white bright walls. Black floor shining. Ahead, the bathroom door. She thought she had closed it. She stood, looking. Hung her hands at her sides. Thought about the way air moved. Weather maps on TV. Isobars. She remembered she had closed it. But what did she really know about air.

Deebee called from the lounge room. 'Where are you, Orly?'

'Here,' she said.

'Orly!' Deebee's voice shrieked.

And she flew — how many steps between here and there? — her mind ahead of her, arriving at her sister's body, at Deebee standing on the charcoal grey in the middle of the room, with her fingers in her mouth, saying, 'Where did you go?'

Orla's body shook. Her voice trembled. 'If you ever, ever do that again.' She sat heavily on the edge of the divan, fixed Deebee with a glare.

Deebee stared, wide-eyed, swiped at her tears with her hand, said. 'I didn't know where you'd gone.' Swiped again. Watched Orla. On the TV someone screamed and screamed. Deebee turned. It was a woman with short blonde hair. She was looking at something through a window. Her fingers were stiff and spread out and she held her hands up to the sides of her face.

Orla wondered why she didn't just cover her eyes with them. The woman screamed again.

Orla said, 'Sit down. I can't see.'

Deebee sat on the divan. 'When is Mummy coming home?'

Orla broke up the remaining chocolate, held it bit by bit in front of her sister's mouth. Deebee opened like a baby bird. Orla smiled.

Later, on TV, three policemen argued in a room. Typewriters on their desks. One of them pressed some keys. The sound of it. To be watching Z-Cars. The program her father never missed. Being little in her bed, its theme music coming to her along the passageway, a long time ago. Curled up against her mother, Henry's voice gentle, her hand on Orla's hair.

Two of the policemen were driving somewhere, slowing, parking. They got out of the car and put on their hats. She looked at Deebee, asleep beside her now, and was glad she didn't have to see them knocking on someone's door. She stroked Deebee's hair, thought again about the bathroom. Who else had found the other, secret, way in, that big windowless wall. Who had stood against it, stretched their arm through it, reached in to open the bathroom door from the inside. She smiled a little because no-one, of course, how could it be. And the back door, all the windows, she knew, were closed.

In the distance a dog barked once. Again. No more. Her father had once told her: no pattern in a dog's bark means no danger. She listened. Behind the policemen's voices, behind the voice of the man who had answered their knocking. She listened to the east wind rising, a passing car, a floorboard's creak.

The breath of a movement and she turned and stood. The passageway was alive with light. She remembered how she had walked it, walked from her room that other night. And she could almost see herself, shocked from her sleep, see herself standing in shadow, looking out, looking into the lounge room, looking at her mother sitting just behind where Orla now stood, looking at her mother sitting on the other side of everything, that circle of lamplight around her head, her head in her hands. She remembered her mother's arms, how she had opened them, held them, and what choice did they.

She walked slowly along the passageway, past the memory of herself, to the bathroom door. It was still ajar and she almost laughed because what had she thought. She pushed it and it hit something, stopped, crept back towards her a little with a kind of tremble. She frowned. Thought what could be on its other side but the everyday space they left there. Shoes, perhaps. A mop.

She thought: night things are harder to understand. Her mother sitting on the other side of everything. Her mother's head in her hands. Rain falling through streetlight. Her father a statue. Her mother clicking the front door closed, clicking everything back into place.

Shoes or mop or Deebee's truck, what else, and she took a breath, gripped the edge of the door and looked around it because that's what and halfway round she had already seen jeans, belt, bottle-green shirt, the look on his face, but how could she stop, rewind, all the way back to that night when her mother had closed the door and kept them. When her father, turned to stone, would have let them go into the rain in their good shoes and coats.

Her hand squeezed the edge of the door hard and then let it go. The look on his face. Not the same as at the bus stop or at her bedroom window. He was so close. His mouth twitched. His finger moved to his lips to make shh.

Nowhere to hide. Every house light on. Bathroom light bounced off the bathroom ceiling, the tiles, the porcelain. And bounced off him. And how he shone. As if he'd been invited. As if it were a party.

She felt herself. Recoil. As if recoiling could. Fold. Her. Flat. As if flat she. Could. Push. Through. A wall or window. Slip safe into a drawer. Like a scarf. A piece of paper. Through gaps between pickets. Light between leaves. Between the wheels of a car. Like a glimpse of a dog. A shell held to an ear. Rain like sparks of light beneath streetlamp. The sun sparking on sea.

Inside her head the noise she made and made. Her arms and legs. His hand over her face. Pressing. Squeezing. Like being hit by a wave. Like being upended. No air, no air. The world awash. Blurred. Muffled. Which way up. His hand pushing her nose, her mouth, and she looked up, up, the bathroom light round bright, a sun, her arms and legs flailing and she deep, deep under no surface to break and nothing to breathe just his hand, his hand, and in her head the shape of her father walking ahead, up that hill and away, and her own voice shouting, shouting inside her head, calling him, 'Daddy!', calling him back, and she running after, running hard, 'Daddy!', her eyes big and wild, and Deebee's head out the car window and laughing, 'De-cab-it-at-ed!', all the air in the world rushing in, all the light in the world pouring down on face and limbs and her body felt heavy, tumbling, her mind turning over slow as a dream, and she felt her father's hand reach for her, he'd come back for her at last at last, come back as she always knew he would, and she gripped his hand as if her life depended, and he lifted, swung her up and high, and sat her on his shoulders, and she saw the way the sea stretched all the way ahead, the way the sun flashed so hard it hurt.

Deebee's eyes flicked open. The TV on, and all the lights. Bright walls and ceilings. The TV full of music and men tap dancing. She stood looking at the kitchen, at the bench, pale and flat as milk.

She stood looking at the front door open. Cool air poured in. Beyond the porch light, the world was just dark night. But it smelled like the bush, like where they used to live.

She stepped closer to the threshold.

Who had gone out the door and who had come home?

She shivered. 'Orly?' She rubbed her eyes, turned, walked back to the passageway into all that light.

Acknowledgements

This story has taken a decade to write and more decades of thought and feeling. It may appear and is often presented as being otherwise, but writing is a deeply embodied and socially connected experience, so there are many to thank.

This story's seed was sown while I was writing *The Edge of the World*. In a conversation over coffee, I listened to colleagues reminisce about Perth in the 1960s, and was struck by how very different from mine was their experience of growing up in that time and place. I was also researching intergenerational trauma and was lent a copy of Maxine Harris' *The Loss that is Forever: the Lifelong Impact of the Early Death of a Mother or Father*. My deep thanks to those responsible for these gifts.

Without the love and support of my partner, Mike Williams, and my sons, Julian and Brendan Polain, I suspect none of my books would exist. Whenever I see the distracted, electrified expression on their own faces as they stare into the middle distance, turning over a possibility emerging from their own research or towards an idea for their own art, I realise how I must also frequently look to them. That we are able to understand and celebrate this process in one another fills me with gratitude.

Friends have quietly, patiently listened, questioned and encouraged as I often stumbled about in the writing dark, trying to find a way forward. They have never made me feel too slow or too pedantic, and for all this I thank them —

in particular, Jan Teagle-Kapetas, Deborah Robertson, Morgan Yasbincek, Sari Smith, Gail Jones, Shevaun Cooley, Brendan Ritchie, Mal McKimmie, Kali Caramia, Nandi Chinna, Alexis Lateef, Vidya Rajan, Clinton Bell. Such joy to find like minds.

I am fortunate to have a job I love, and through which I'm able to talk about art, writing and books with colleagues and students every day. In so many ways, these conversations continually nurture and challenge my own writing. I think I am one of the luckiest people on Earth.

Special thanks must be given for the generosity and encouragement received from Jenny Darling and Robert Watkins. For a writer, nothing beats having an informed, dispassionate reader understand what you're trying to do. Working with them provided two gifts: a stronger manuscript because of their questions; and a clearer sense of the publishing landscape for literary fiction in Australia, and where my work fits in it.

Georgia Richter has been marvellous to work with. She got it from the outset, has read with excitement, thoroughness and empathy, yet has also been incisive; she has such a good ear and eye.

Finally, it's not clear to me how or why adults forget what it is like to be a child — don't we all carry our child selves within? — but believing that children don't have a complex interior life worthy of respect must serve something. So, my love and thanks to all the children I have known. Your presence alone makes the world so much better.

This novel was written with the assistance of a grant from The Australia Council, and with the support of Edith Cowan University, Perth. Thanks also to the Dorothea Mackellar Estate for permission to reproduce an adapted extract from Dorothea Mackellar's 'My Country'.

As a young man, Harvey Beam fled his hometown, confirming his suspicions you can successfully run away from your problems. But after forging a big-city career in talkback radio, Harvey is now experiencing a 'positional hiatus'. The words aren't coming out right, his mojo is fading and a celebrity host is eyeing his timeslot. Back in Shorton, Harvey's father appears at long last to be dying. It seems it's finally time for Harvey Beam to head home. In returning to a past that seems disturbingly unchanged, the last thing he expects is a chance encounter with a wonderful stranger …

'Like a talkback show, like Beam himself, this book is humorous all along the way. It has a jolly quality and sadness isn't lingered on. An impressive debut novel.' *Weekend Australian*

'The rehabilitation of Harvey, a deeply flawed character, is vulnerable, darkly comic, and assembled like a well-laid fire. Careful and precise.' *Foreword Magazine*

AND AT ALL GOOD BOOKSTORES

First published 2019 by
FREMANTLE PRESS
25 Quarry Street, Fremantle WA 6160
(PO Box 158, North Fremantle WA 6159)

www.fremantlepress.com.au

Printed by McPherson's Printing Group, Victoria, Australia.

A catalogue record for this
book is available from the
National Library of Australia

Driving into the sun, ISBN 9781925591996

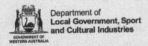

Fremantle Press is supported by the State Government through the Department of Local Government, Sport and Cultural Industries.

Publication of this title was assisted by the Commonwealth Government through the Australia Council, its arts funding and advisory body.